L

1695

Anthills
of the Savannah

Books by Chinua Achebe

The Sacrificial Egg and Other Stories
Things Fall Apart
No Longer at Ease
Chike and the River
A Man of the People
Arrow of God
Girls at War and Other Stories
Beware Soul Brother
Morning Yet on Creation Day
The Trouble with Nigeria
The Flute
The Drum

With John Iroaganachi

How the Leopard Got His Claws

With Others

Winds of Change: Modern Short Stories from Black Africa

With C. L. Innes (Eds)

African Short Stories

CHINUA ACHEBE

Anthills of the Savannah

ANCHOR PRESS
Doubleday
NEW YORK
1988

Library of Congress Cataloging-in-Publication Data

Achebe, Chinua.
  Anthills of the savannah.

  I. Title.
PR9387.9.A3A83   1987   823   87-18708

ISBN 0-385-01664-6

First published in Great Britain 1987 by William Heinemann Ltd.

Extract from "Africa" by David Diop is reprinted from *Modern Poetry from Africa* edited by Gerald Moore and Ulli Beier, published by Penguin, by permission of Présence Africaine.

Anthills
of the Savannah

1

First Witness
—Christopher Oriko

"YOU'RE WASTING everybody's time, Mr. Commissioner for Information. I will not go to Abazon. Finish! *Kabisa!* Any other business?"

"As Your Excellency wishes. But . . ."

"But me no buts, Mr. Oriko! The matter is closed, I said. How many times, for God's sake, am I expected to repeat it? Why do *you* find it so difficult to swallow my ruling. On anything?"

"I am sorry, Your Excellency. But I have no difficulty swallowing *and* digesting your rulings."

For a full minute or so the fury of his eyes lay on me. Briefly our eyes had been locked in combat. Then I had lowered mine to the shiny table-top in ceremonial capitulation. Long silence. But he was not appeased. Rather he was making the silence itself grow rapidly into its own kind of contest, like the eyewink duel of children. I conceded victory there as well. Without raising my eyes I said again: "I am very sorry, Your Excellency." A year ago I would never had said it again that second time—without doing grave violence to myself. Now I did it like a casual favour to him. It meant nothing at all to me—no inconvenience whatever—and yet everything to him.

I have thought of all this as a game that began innocently enough and then went suddenly strange and poisonous. But I may prove to be too sanguine even in that. For, if I am right, then looking back on the last two years it should be possible to point to a specific and decisive event and say: it was at such and such a point that everything went wrong and the rules were suspended. But I have not found such a moment or such a cause although I have sought hard and long for it. And so it begins to seem to me that this thing probably never was a game, that the present was there from the very beginning only I was too blind or too busy to notice. But the real question which I have often asked myself is why then do I go on with it now that I can see. I don't know. Simple inertia, maybe. Or perhaps sheer curiosity: to see where it will all . . . well, end. I am not thinking so much about him as about my colleagues, eleven intelligent, educated men who let this happen to them, who actually went out of their way to invite it, and who even at this hour have seen and learnt nothing, the cream of our society and the hope of the black race. I suppose it is for them that I am still at this silly observation post making farcical entries in the crazy log-book of this our ship of state. Disenchantment with them turned long ago into detached clinical interest.

I find their actions not merely bearable now but actually interesting, even exciting. Quite amazing! And to think that I personally was responsible for recommending nearly half of them for appointment!

And, of course, complete honesty demands that I mention one last factor in my continued stay, a fact of which I'm somewhat ashamed, namely that I couldn't be writing this if I didn't hang around to observe it all. And no one else would.

I could read in the silence of their minds, as we sat stiffly around the mahogany table, words like: *Well, this is going to be another of those days.* Meaning a bad day. Days are good or bad for us now according to how His Excellency gets out of bed in the morning. On a bad day, such as this one had suddenly become after many propitious auguries, there is nothing for it but to lie close to your hole, ready to scramble in. And particularly to keep your mouth shut, for nothing is safe, not even the flattery we have become such experts in disguising as debate.

On my right sat the Honourable Commissioner for Education. He is by far the most frightened of the lot. As soon as he had sniffed peril in the air he had begun to disappear into his hole, as some animals and insects do, backwards. Instinctively he had gathered his papers together and was in the very act of lifting the file-cover over them and dragging them into his hole after him when his entire body suddenly went rigid. Stronger alarms from deeper recesses of instinct may have alerted him to the similarity between his impending act and a slamming of the door in the face of His Excellency. A fantastic thing happened then. He drops the file-cover in such panic that everyone now turns to him and sees him perform the strangest act of all: the scattering again of his Council Papers in panic atonement and restitution for the sacrilege he has come so close to committing. Inadvertently. Then he glances round the table until his eyes meet His Excellency's and fall dead on the mahogany. The silence had not been broken since my second apology. I was quite certain that the poor fellow (never a strong one for originality) was getting ready to speak my very words, strictly in the same sequence. I swear it. He had drawn his upper arms tight to his sides as though to diminish his bulk; and clasped his hands before him like a supplicant.

But His Excellency speaks instead. And not even to him the latest offender but still to me. And he is almost friendly and conciliatory, the amazing man. In that instant the day changes. The fiery sun retires temporarily behind a cloud; we are reprieved and immediately celebrating. I can hear in advance the many compliments we· will pay him as soon as his back is turned: that the trouble with His Excellency is that he can never hurt a man and go to sleep over it.

That's one refinement, by the way, we've not yet lost: we do wait for his back to be turned. And some will add: That's a pity because what this country really needs is a ruthless dictator. At least for five good years. And we will all laugh in loud excess · because we know—bless our dear hearts—that we shall never be favoured with such an undeserved blessing as a ruthless dictator.

"Do you realize what you are asking me to do, Chris?" he said. I say nothing, make no motion, not even of the head. At these moments my head assumes the gravity of granite and though my thinking might remain perfectly clear and logical it seems to emanate from afar taking in these happenings through a telescope. I note for what it's worth that he has dropped the icy distancing of *Mister Commissioner* and *Mister Oriko*. But I no longer allow such niceties to distract me. He misread my quietude I think as either agreement or disagreement. It was neither. Pure, unadulterated disinterest.

"You are telling me to insult the intelligence of these people," he says, his tone mollified and rather superior. I shake my head then, slowly. "Yes, that's precisely what you are telling me to do," he says spiritedly, spurred to battle by my faint resurgent opposition. "These people believe in rainmakers and so let's go ahead and exploit their ignorance for cheap popularity. That's exactly what you are telling me to do, Chris. Well I can't do it. You all seem to forget that I am still a soldier, not a politician."

He is in mufti as he now tends to be more and more within the precincts of the Presidential Palace: a white *danshiki* tastefully embroidered in gold, and its matching trousers. By contrast many of my colleagues, especially the crew from the Universities, aspire to the military look. Professor Okong wears nothing but khaki safari suits complete with epaulettes. It is amazing how the intellectual envies the man of action.

I think His Excellency noticed the faint smile brought to my face by that reminder that he was still a soldier; he has such a knack for reading faces. I could see him hesitate ever so briefly between taking me up on that smile and ignoring it. What he ended up doing was neither of those but something really quite proficient. Fixing his gaze on me he yet managed at the same time to convey by his voice that I was excluded from what he was now saying; that his words were too precious to waste on professional dissidents.

"Soldiers are plain and blunt," he says defiantly. "When we turn affairs of state back to you and return to barracks that will be the time to resume your civilian tricks. Have a little patience."

At this point he is boldly interrupted by the Commissioner for Justice and Attorney-General and then by everybody else with an assortment of protests. Actually it is His Excellency's well-chosen words that signalled the brave interruption, for despite the vigour in his voice the words themselves had sounded the *All Clear* and told us it was all right now to commence our protestations. So we began to crawl out into the open again. In his precise manner the Attorney-General says: "Your Excellency, let us not flaunt the wishes of the people."

"Flout, you mean," I said.

"The people?" asked His Excellency, ignoring my piece of pedantry.

"Yes, Your Excellency," replied the Attorney-General boldly. "The people have spoken. Their desire is manifest. You are condemned to serve them for life." Loud applause and shouts of "Hear! Hear!" Many voices in contest for the floor.

"I am no lawyer," says His Excellency, his slightly raised tone breaking up a hand to hand tussle among the voices, "only a simple soldier. But a soldier must keep his word."

"But you, I beg pardon, I mean Your Excellency, cannot break a word you never even said. The nonsense about one hundred per cent was only the machination of a newspaper editor who in my judgement is a self-seeking saboteur."

"No obligation, Your Excellency, to keep faith with heretics," boomed the Reverend Professor Okong's voice.

"On point of order, Your Excellency." He glares at me now, and then nods to the Attorney-General, who had been interrupted by Okong and myself, to continue.

"Your Excellency, three provinces out of four is a majority anywhere." More applause.

"Your Excellency I wish to dissociate myself from the Attorney-General's reference to a saboteur and to appeal to my colleagues not to make such statements against public servants who are not present to defend themselves." I liked the look of terror on my colleagues' faces when I used the word *dissociate* and the relaxation that followed when they realized that I was not saying what they feared I was saying. Even His Excellency was thrown off his poise momentarily. But, unlike the rest, knowing that he has been teased does not amuse him or offer him relief; rather it fills him with anger. He swings his head sharply to his right where the Chief Secretary sits on the edge of his chair.

"Any other business?" The way he says it this time it no longer is an idle formula. It had the ring of a rebuke: something like *How many times do you want me to ask this question?*

This unexpected convergence of the crisis on his person threw the Chief Secretary into utter confusion and inelegance of speech.

"Oh no sir. Nothing at all, sir. Your Excellency." And then he looks across the table and our eyes meet. I don't like to take credit for this kind of thing but I think that the derisive smile on my face at that moment may have turned the bureaucrat right about. Perhaps he saw in my face a foreshadowing of peer taunts and ridicule lying in ambush for him beyond the massive doors of this citadel. He is very sensitive about accusations of boot-licking especially when they come from me because I think he has a lot of respect for me. And in a way I don't dislike him, either. He is after all, unlike the rest of us, a career civil servant who would have served a civilian president . . . or indeed the British raj as well as he now serves His present Excellency. But whatever it was that did it he now shows totally untypical spirit that for him almost borders on recklessness. He picks up his fallen words again: "But Your Excellency, if I may—erm—crave your indulgence—erm—Your Excellency's indulgence—and—erm—put in a word for the Honourable Commissioner."

"Which Honourable Commissioner? There are twelve of them, you know." This would have excited laughter at other times, but something totally new is happening now and we are all too amazed.

"Your Excellency I mean the Honourable Commissioner for Information." There is a long and baffled silence. Then His Excellency who, I should admit, is extremely good at such times says:

"He doesn't need a word from you. Remember, he owns all the words in this country—newspapers, radio and television stations . . ."

The peals of laughter that broke out engulfed everybody for minutes and put us all at ease again. Colleagues close enough were laughing and slapping my back. Others beamed their goodwill across.

"The Honourable Commissioner for Words," the Attorney-General manages through his laughter. "That's a good one. By God that's a good one." He is dabbing his eyes with a handkerchief still neatly folded.

"Opposed! It sounds too much like me," protested the Commissioner for Works.

"That's true," says the Attorney-General, pausing in his laughter to reflect. "Commissioner for Words and Commissioner for Works. There's a point there."

"Theologically speaking there is a fundamental distinction." This is Professor Okong in his deep pulpit voice.

"Ah, Professor done come-o," says the Commissioner for Education. We were all so merry. If the meeting ended now we would go home happy—the homely ones among us entitled to answer their wives with a smile should they ask what kind of day they'd had. But His Excellency wasn't done with us yet, alas!

"What were you going to say for the Commissioner of Information, anyway?"

"Your Excellency, it is—erm—about this visit to Abazon."

"In that case the meeting stands adjourned." He gets up abruptly. So abruptly that the noise we make scrambling to our feet would have befitted a knee-sore congregation rising rowdily from the prayers of a garrulous priest.

His Excellency sits down again and leans back calmly on his swivel chair in order to search under the table for the court shoes he always kicks off at the beginning of our meetings and which the Chief Secretary as always and quite unobtrusively arranges side by side with movements of his own feet to save His Excellency the trouble of prolonged searching at the end of the meeting. If His Excellency is aware of this little service he never acknowledges it, but takes it for granted like the attention of the invisible bell-boy who shines your shoes overnight in an expensive hotel. With consummate deliberation he looks down to the floor and slips in his right foot. He looks on the other side and slips in his left. And then discarding altogether the sprightliness of his first rising he now heaves himself slowly up by the leverage of his hands on the heavy arms of his chair. And the amazing thing is that this lumbering slowness and the former alacrity seem equally to become him.

We all stand stock-still. The only noise in the room comes from his own movements and the continuous whirring of the air-conditioners which have risen to attention in the silence of a deferential Cabinet waiting with bated breath on the Chief to become shod again and, in his good time, withdraw into the seclusion of his adjoining private enclosure.

Sometimes he would say *Good afternoon, gentlemen* on taking leave of us. Today, naturally, he said nothing. As he left his seat an orderly gathered up his papers quickly and followed him out. Another orderly, more stern-faced, opened the heavy doors of carved panels, stood aside and gave a long, hand-quivering salute.

"He is not in a good mood today," says the Chief Secretary, breaking the freeze. "We'll bring it up again next Thursday, Chris. Don't worry."

His Excellency is probably meant to overhear this and I believe he does. I could see a smile or the radiance of a smile from the back of his head like the faint memory of light at the edges of an eclipse.

In the final stages of His Excellency's retiring, the silence in the Council Chamber seemed to be undergoing a subtle change. Something indeterminate had entered it and was building up slowly within its ambience. At first I thought the air-conditioners had become just fractionally louder which would be perfectly consistent with the generating vagaries of the National Electric Power Authority. Then the Chief Secretary's observation and the flurry of conversation it started about His Excellency's changing moods kept us from noticing the sound for a while. The Attorney-General came over to my seat and clapped me on the shoulder.

"What's the matter with you, Chris? Why are you so tense these days? Relax, man, relax; the world isn't coming to an end, you know."

I was angrily but silently rebuffing his peace overtures when, as though on a signal, everyone in the room stopped talking. Then we all turned to the east window.

"A storm?" someone asks.

The low hibiscus hedge outside the window and its many brilliant red bells stood still and unruffled. Beyond the hedge the courtyard with its concrete slabs and neatly manicured bahama grass at the interstices showed no flying leaves or dust. Beyond the courtyard another stretch of the green and red hedge stood guard against the one-story east wing of the Presidential Palace. Over and beyond the roof the tops of palm-trees at the waterfront swayed with the same lazy ease they display to gentle ocean winds. It was no ordinary storm.

The Chief Secretary whose presence of mind is only inhibited by the presence of His Excellency moves over to the sill, unhooks a latch and pushes back a glass window. And the world surges into the alien climate of the Council Chamber on a violent wave of heat and the sounds of a chanting multitude. And His Excellency rushes back into the room at the same time leaving the huge doors swinging.

"What is going on?" he demands, frantically.

"I shall go and see, Your Excellency," says the Inspector-General of Police, picking up his peaked cap from the table, putting it on his head and then his baton under his arm and saluting at attention.

"Look at him! Just look at him," sneers His Excellency. "Gentlemen, this is my Chief of Police. He stands here gossiping while hoodlums storm the Presidential Palace. And he has no clue what is going on. Sit down! Inspector-General of Police!"

He turns to me. "Do you know anything about this?"

"I am sorry I don't, Your Excellency."

"Beautiful. Just beautiful. Now can anyone here tell me anything about that crowd screaming out there?" He looks at each of us in turn. No one stirs or opens his mouth. "That's what I mean when I say that I have no Executive Council. Can you see what I mean now, all of you? Take your seats, gentlemen, and stay there!" He rushes out again.

At the door he is saluted again by the orderly of the quivering hands. Perhaps it is the way the fellow closes those heavy doors now like a gaoler or perhaps some other subtle movement or gesture with the sub-machine-gun in his left hand that drew from the Attorney-General a deep forlorn groan: "Oh my God!" I put on a broad smile and flash it in his face. He backs away from me as from a violent lunatic.

Very few words are spoken in the next half hour. When the doors swing open again, an orderly announces: *Professor Okong Wanted by His Excellency!*

"I go to prepare a place for you, gentlemen . . . But rest assured I will keep the most comfortable cell for myself." He went out laughing. I too began to laugh quite ostentatiously. Then I said to my colleagues: "That is a man after my heart. A man who will not piss in his trousers at the first sound of danger." And I went to the furthest window and stood there alone gazing outwards.

Professor Reginald Okong, though a buffoon, is a fighter of sorts and totally self-made. Unfortunately he has no sense of political morality which is a double tragedy for a man who began his career as an American Baptist minister and later became Professor of Political Science at our university. Perhaps he has more respon-

sibility than any other single individual except myself for the remarkable metamorphosis of His Excellency. But, perhaps like me
he meant well, neither of us having been present before at the
birth and grooming of a baby monster.

As a bright pupil-teacher in lower primary school Reginald
Okong had attracted the attention of American Baptist missionar-
ies from Ohio who were engaged in belated but obdurate evange-
lism in his district. They saw a great future for him and ordained
him at the age of 26. In their *Guinness Book of Records* mentality
they often called him the youngest native American Baptist minister in the world. Native American? Good heavens no! Native
African. But, while they were conscientiously grooming Okong
slowly but surely into the future head of their local church in say
twenty or thirty years, the young Reverend, bright, ambitious and
in a great hurry was working secretly on schemes of his own, one
of which was to take him away altogether from the missionary
vineyard to the secular campuses of a southern Black college in the
United States of America itself to the dismay of his Ohio patrons
who did not stop at accusations of ingratitude but mounted a determined campaign with US Immigration aimed at getting him
deported. But he too was tough and overcame all his difficulties.
Augmenting his slender resources by preaching and wrestling he
graduated in record time by passing off his Grade Three Teachers'
Certificate as the equivalent of two years of Junior College. Four
years later he was back home with a Ph.D. in his bag, and went to
teach at the university.

I was editor of the *National Gazette* at the time and he approached me with a proposal for a weekend current affairs column. I was mildly enthusiastic and although I was aware of the
reservations some of his academic colleagues often expressed
about his scholarship I proceeded to build him up as a leading
African political scientist, as editors often do thinking they do it
for the sake of their paper but actually end up fostering a freak
baby. But I must say Okong was a perfect contributor in meeting
deadlines and that kind of thing. And his column, "String Along
with Reggie Okong," soon became very popular indeed. No one
pretended that he dispensed any spectacular insights, wisdom or
originality but his ability to turn a phrase in a way to delight our
ordinary readers was remarkable. He was full of cliché, but then a
cliché is not a cliché if you have never heard it before; and our

ordinary reader clearly had not and so was ready to greet each one with the same ecstasy it must have produced when it was first coined. For Cliché is but pauperized Ecstasy.

Think of the very first time someone got up and said: "We must not be lulled into a false sense of security." He must have got his audience humming. It was like that with Okong; he was a smash hit! My friend, Ikem Osodi, was always at me for running that column. He said Professor Okong deserved to be hanged and quartered for phrase-mongering and other counterfeit offences. But Ikem is a literary artist, and the *Gazette* was not there to satisfy the likes of him; not even now that he sits in the editorial chair! A fact he is yet to learn.

Naturally Okong never upset the politicians; he kept their constituency amused. I didn't mind, either. I had enough contributors like Ikem to do all the upsetting that was needed and a lot that wasn't. But on the very next day after the politicians were overthrown Okong metamorphosed into a brilliant analyst of their many excesses. I thought he had finally overreached himself changing his tune so abruptly; but not so my readers, judging by their ecstatic letters. Apparently he had scored another hit by describing the overthrow of the civilian regime as "a historic fall from grace to grass!" After that I doffed my cap to him. And when His Excellency asked me to suggest half-a-dozen names for his Cabinet Professor Okong was top of my list.

This calls for some explanation and justification. His Excellency came to power without any preparation for political leadership—a fact which he being a very intelligent person knew perfectly well and which, furthermore, should not have surprised anyone. Sandhurst after all did not set about training officers to take over Her Majesty's throne but rather in the high tradition of proud aloofness from politics and public affairs. Therefore when our civilian politicians finally got what they had coming to them and landed unloved and unmourned on the rubbish heap and the young Army Commander was invited by the even younger coup-makers to become His Excellency the Head of State he had pretty few ideas about what to do. And so, like an intelligent man, he called his friends together and said: "What shall I do?"

I had known him then for close on twenty-five years, from that day long ago when we first met as new boys of thirteen or fourteen at Lord Lugard College. And so I found myself advising "a whole

Head of State" who was, in addition, quite frankly terrified of his new job. This is something I have never been quite able to figure out: why the military armed to the teeth as they are can find unarmed civilians such a threat. For His Excellency, it was only a passing phase, though. He soon mastered his fear, although from time to time memories of it would seem to return to torment him. I can see no other explanation for his quite irrational and excessive fear of demonstrations, for example. Even pathetically peaceful, obsequious demonstrations.

In his first days of power his constant nightmare was of the people falling into disaffection and erupting into ugly demonstrations all over the place, and he drove himself crazy worrying how to prevent it. I had no clear idea myself. But I imagined that a person like Professor Okong without having any clearer ideas than either of us would be helpful in putting whatever came into our heads into popular diction and currency. And so he was number one on my list and His Excellency appointed him Commissioner for Home Affairs. He had his day and then went into partial eclipse. But I hardly think he is due for prison, yet.

2

His Excellency's deep anxiety had been swiftly assuaged by his young, brilliant and aggressive Director of the State Research Council (SRC). He proved once again in his Excellency's words as efficient as the Cabinet was incompetent. Every single action by this bright young man from the day of his appointment has given His Excellency good cause for self-congratulations for Major Johnson Ossai had been his own personal choice whom he had gone ahead to appoint in the face of strong opposition from more senior officers. And it had happened at the very tricky moment when His Excellency had decided to retire all military members of his cabinet and to replace them with civilians and, to cap it all, add President to all his titles. There were unconfirmed rumours of unrest, secret trials and executions in the barracks. But His Excellency rode the storm quite comfortably thanks to two key appointments he had personally made—the Army Chief of Staff and the Director of the State Research Council, the secret police.

So when Professor Okong was marched in by the fierce orderly he found His Excellency in a tough and self-confident mood.

"Good day, Your Excellency, Mr. President," intoned Professor Okong executing at the same time a ninety-degree bow.

No reply nor any kind of recognition of his presence. His Excellency continued writing on his drafting pad for a full minute more before looking up. Then he spoke abruptly as though to an intruder he wanted to be rid of quickly.

"Yes, I want you to go over to the Reception quadrangle and receive the delegation waiting there . . . Well, sit down!"

"Thank you, Your Excellency."

"I suppose I ought to begin by filling you in on who they are and what they are doing here, etc. Unless, of course, by some miracle you made the discovery yourself after I left you."

"No, sir. We didn't. I am sorry."

"Very well, then. I shall tell you. But before I do I want to remind you of that little discussion we all had after the Entebbe Raid. You remember? You all said then: What a disgrace to Africa. Do you remember?"

"I remember, Your Excellency."

"Very well. You were all full of indignation. Righteous indignation. But do you by any chance remember what I said? I said it could happen here. Right here."

"You did, sir, I remember that very well."

"You all said: Oh no, Your Excellency it can't happen here." The way he said it in mimicry of some half-witted idiot with a speech impediment, might have raised a laugh from a bigger audience or at a less grave moment.

"Yes, Your Excellency, we said so," admitted Professor Okong. "We are truly sorry." It wasn't yet very clear to him what point or connection was being made but what his answer should be was obvious and he repeated it: "Your Excellency we are indeed sorry."

"It doesn't matter. You know I've never really relied on you fellows for information on anything or anybody. You know that?"

"Yes, sir."

"I should be a fool to. You see if Entebbe happens here it's *me* the world will laugh at, isn't it?"

Professor Okong found the answer to that one somewhat tricky and so made a vague indeterminate sound deep in his throat.

"Yes, it is *me*. General Big Mouth, they will say, and print my picture on the cover of *Time* magazine with a big mouth and a small head. You understand? They won't talk about you, would they."

"Certainly not, Sir."

"No, because they don't know you. It's not your funeral but mine." Professor Okong was uneasy about the word funeral and began a protest but His Excellency shut him up by raising his left hand. "So I don't fool around. I take precautions. You und'stand?"

"Yes, sir. Once more, may I on behalf of my colleagues and myself give you—I mean Your Excellency—our undeserved—I mean unreserved—apology."

There was a long pause now like the silence of colleagues for a fallen comrade. His Excellency had been so moved that he needed the time to compose himself again. He took out a handkerchief and wiped his face and then his neck around the collar vigorously. Professor Okong stared on the tabletop with lowered eyes; like eyes at half-mast.

"The crowd that came in an hour or so ago," he said calmly and sadly, "has come from Abazon."

"Those people again!" said Okong in a flare-up of indignation. "The same people pestering you to visit them."

"It is a peaceful and loyal and goodwill delegation . . ."

"Oh I am so happy to hear that."

". . . that has come all the way from Abazon to declare their loyalty."

"Very good, sir. Very good! And I should say, about time too . . ." A sudden violent frown on His Excellency's face silenced the Professor's re-awakened garrulity.

"But I have been made to understand that they also may have a petition about the drought in their region. They want personally to invite me to pay them a visit and see their problems. Well you know—everybody knows—my attitude to petitions and demonstrations and those kinds of things."

"I do, sir. Every loyal citizen of this country knows your Excellency's attitude . . ."

"Sheer signs of indiscipline. Allow any of it, from whatever quarter, and you are as good as sunk."

"Exactly, Your Excellency."

"This is a loyal delegation though, as I've just told you and they have come a long way. But discipline is discipline. If I should agree to see them, what is there to stop the truckpushers of Gelegele Market marching up here tomorrow to see me. They are just as loyal. Or the very loyal marketwomen's organization trooping in to complain about the price of stockfish imported from Norway."

The Professor laughed loud but alone and stopped rather abruptly like a maniac.

"So I have a standing answer to all of them. No! *Kabisa.*"

"Excellent, Your Excellency." It may have passed through Professor Okong's mind fleetingly that the man who was now reading him a lecture had not so long ago been politically almost *in statu pupillari* to him. Or perhaps he no longer dared to remember.

"But we must remember that these are not your scheming intellectual types or a bunch of Labour Congress agitators but simple, honest-to-God peasants who, from all intelligence reports reaching me, sincerely regret their past actions and now want bygones to be bygones. So it would be unfair to go up to them and say: 'You can go away now, His Excellency the President is too busy to see you.' You get me?"

"Quite clearly, Your Excellency." Okong was beginning to get the hang of his summons here, and with it his confidence was returning.

"That's why I have sent for you. Find some nice words to say to them. Tell them we are tied up at this moment with very important matters of state. You know that kind of stuff . . ."

"Exactly, Your Excellency. That's my line."

"Tell them, if you like, that. I am on the telephone with the President of United States of America or the Queen of England. Peasants are impressed by that kind of thing, you know."

"Beauriful, Your Excellency, beauriful."

"Humour them, is what I'm saying. Gauge the temperature and pitch your message accordingly."

"I will, Your Excellency. Always at Your service."

"Now if indeed they have brought a petition, accept it on my behalf and tell them they can rest assured that their complaints or rather problems—their problems, not complaints, will receive His Excellency's personal attention. Before you go, ask the Commissioner for Information to send a reporter across; and the Chief of Protocol to detail one of the State House photographers to take your picture shaking hands with the leader of the delegation. But for God's sake, Professor, I want you to look at the man you are shaking hands with instead of the camera . . ."

Professor Okong broke into another peal of laughter.

"I don't find it funny, people shaking hands like this . . . while their neck is turned away at right angles, like that girl in *The Exorcist,* and grinning into the camera."

"Your Excellency is not only our leader but also our Teacher. We are always ready to learn. We are like children washing only their bellies, as our elders say when they pray."

"But whatever you do, make sure that nothing about petitions gets into the papers. I don't want to see any talk of complaints and petitions in the press. This is a goodwill visit pure and simple."

"Exactly. A reconciliation overture from Your Excellency's erstwhile rebellious subjects."

"No no no! I don't want to rub that in. Let's leave well alone."

"But Your Excellency, you are too generous. Too generous by half! Why does every bad thing in this country start in Abazon Province? The Rebellion was there. They were the only ones whose Leaders of Thought failed to return a clear mandate to Your Excellency. I don't want to be seen as a tribalist but Mr. Ikem Osodi is causing all this trouble because he is a typical Abazonian. I am sorry to be personal, Your Excellency, but we must face facts. If you ask me, Your Excellency, God does not sleep. How do we know that that drought they are suffering over there may not be God's judgement for all the troubles they have caused in this country. And now they have the audacity to write Your Excellency to visit their Province and before you can even reply to their invitation they *carry their nonsense come your house.* I think Your Excellency that you are being too generous. Too generous by half, I am sorry to say."

"I appreciate your strong feeling, Professor, but I must do these things my way. Leave well alone."

"As you please, Your Excellency. I shall do exactly as Your Excellency commands. To the last letter. I don't think Your Excellency has said anything about television coverage."

"No no no no! I am glad you raised it. No television. Undue publicity. And before you know it everybody will be staging goodwill rallies all over the place so as to appear on television. You know what our people are. No television. Oh no!"

"Your Excellency is absolutely right. I never thought of that. It is surprising how Your Excellency thinks about everything."

"You know why, Professor. Because it is my funeral, that's why. When it is your funeral you jolly well must think of everything. Especially with the calibre of Cabinet I have."

"Your Excellency, may I seize this opportunity to formally apologize on my behalf and on behalf of my cabinet colleagues for our, shall I say, lack of vigilance. I say that in all humility and in the spirit of collective responsibility which makes each and everyone of us guilty when one of us is guilty. One finger gets soiled with grease and spreads it to the other four . . . Your Excellency may be aware that I have never wished to interfere in the portfolios of my cabinet colleagues. It is not because I am blind to all the hanky-panky that is going on. It is because I have always believed in the old adage to paddle my own canoe. But today's incident has shown that a man must not swallow his cough because he fears to disturb others . . ."

"I don't quite get you, Professor. Please cut out the proverbs, if you don't mind."

"Well, Your Excellency, I have been debating within myself what my path of duty should be. Whether to alert you, I mean Your Excellency, on your relationship with the Honourable Commissioner for Information and also the Editor of the *Gazette*."

"Relationship, how do you mean? Can't you speak more plainly?" The level of irritation in his voice was now pretty high.

"Well, Your Excellency, I am sorry to be personal. But I must be frank. I believe that if care is not taken those two friends of yours can be capable of fomenting disaffection which will make the Rebellion look like child's play. And if my sixth sense is anything to go by they may be causing a lot of havoc already."

"That's fine, Mr. Okong. I deal with facts not gossip. Now run along and deal with that crowd and report back to me as soon as it's over. No rush though. After they've had their say and you have replied I want you to stay with them and act as host on my behalf. I have arranged for them to be entertained to drinks and small chop. You are to mingle with them and make them feel at home. They are not students of Political Science but I am sure you will manage. The State Research Council is in charge of the entertainment but you are the visible host. Is that clear? Make them feel they are here on my invitation."

"Very well, Your Excellency."

Poor Professor Okong's last words were drowned by His Excellency's loud impatient buzzer and such was his confusion as he withdrew from the audience that he just narrowly escaped crashing full tilt against the heavy swing-door bringing in the orderly. Outside the door he stood for a while trying to regain full control of his legs which were suddenly heavy like limbs of mahogany. He felt he needed to find a chair somewhere and sit down for a while. But there was no chair in sight, only the vast expanse of grey-carpeted corridor. In any case he really had no time to stand and stare. He had an urgent national assignment to perform. He began to move again although three-quarters of his mind stayed on the crushing manner of his dismissal and particularly on the fact that His Excellency had called him mister. He stopped walking again. "I am in disgrace," he said aloud. "God, I am in disgrace. What did I do wrong?"

"You still de here?" barked the orderly from behind him, and Professor Okong sprang into life once more. He felt somewhat light in the head. Perhaps the Chief of Protocol down the corridor would have some brandy in his cabinet. He could do with a shot.

Meanwhile the hard-faced orderly who overtook him on the corridor a while ago had turned into the Council Chamber, dismissed the detained Cabinet on his Excellency's latest orders and summoned the Attorney-General to his presence.

WHAT EXACTLY did the fellow mean, His Excellency wondered. I handled him pretty well, though. I certainly won't stand for my commissioners sneaking up to me with vague accusations against their colleagues. It's not cricket! No sense of loyalty, no *esprit de corps,* nothing! And he calls himself a university professor. No wonder they say he now heads a handclapping, spiritualist congregation on campus. Disgraceful. Soft to the core, that's what they all are. Professor! My semi-literate uncle was right all the way when he said that we asked the white man to pack and go but did not think he would take with him all the utensils he brought when he came. Professor! The white man put all that back in his box when he took his leave. But come to think of it whatever put it into our head when we arrived on this seat that we needed these half-baked professors to tell us anything. What do they know? Give me good military training and discipline any day!

"Come in, Attorney-General . . . Sit down. I sent for you to ask you a direct, simple question. I realize that you are a lawyer but I am extremely busy and I want plain speaking and to the point. Right? I have received intelligence from various sources indicating that the Commissioner for Information is perhaps not as loyal to me as he might be. Now as you are well aware this is a very serious and very sensitive and very delicate matter and I am asking you in the strictest confidence. Nothing about this must get outside these four walls." He indicated the four walls two at a time like an airline hostess pointing out exits in emergency drill before take-off. The Attorney-General nodded four or five times in quick succession.

"Fine. What would you make of such intelligence?"

The Attorney-General was perched on the edge of his chair, his left elbow on the table, his neck craning forward to catch his Excellency's words which he had chosen to speak with unusual softness as if deliberately to put his hearer at a disadvantage; or on full alert on pain of missing a life and death password. As he watched his victim straining to catch the vital message he felt again that glow of quiet jubilation that had become a frequent companion especially when as now he was disposing with consummate ease of some of those troublesome people he had thought so formidable in his apprentice days in power. It takes a lion to tame a leopard, say our people. How right they are!

As he savoured this wonderful sense of achievement gained in so short a time spreading over and soaking into the core of his thinking and his being like fresh-red tasty palm-oil melting and diffusing itself over piping hot roast yam he withdrew his voice still further into his throat and, for good measure, threw his head back on his huge, black, leather chair so that he seemed to address his words at the high, indifferent ceiling rather than the solicitous listener across the table.

Suddenly suspicious like a quarry sniffing death in the air but uncertain in what quarter it might lurk the Attorney-General decided to stall. For a whole minute almost, he stood on one spot, making no move, offering no reply.

"Well?" His Excellency was stung into loudness by the other's delay and silence. He was also now sitting bolt upright. "Did you hear what I said or should I repeat?"

"No need to repeat, Your Excellency. I heard you perfectly.

You see, Your Excellency, your humble servant is a lawyer. My profession enjoins me to trust only hard evidence and to distrust personal feeling and mere suspicion."

"Attorney-General, I sent for you not to read me a lecture but to answer my question. You may be the Attorney but don't forget I am the General."

The Attorney-General exploded into peals of laughter, uncontrollable and beer-bellied. Through it he repeated again and again whenever he could: "That's a good one, Your Excellency, that's a good one!" His Excellency, no doubt pleased with the dramatic result his wit had produced but not deigning to show it, merely fixed a pair of immobile but somewhat indulgent eyes on his Attorney-General, patiently waiting for his mirth to run its course. Finally it began to as he took the neatly-folded silk handkerchief out of his breast-pocket and dabbed his eyes daintily like a fat clown.

"You will now answer my question?" said His Excellency in a slightly amused tone.

"I am sorry, Your Excellency. Don't blame me; blame Your Excellency's inimitable sense of humour . . . To speak the truth, Your Excellency, I have no evidence of disloyalty on the part of my honourable colleague." He paused for effect. But nothing showed on His Excellency's face. "But lawyers are also human. I have a personal feeling which may not stand up in court, I agree, but I hold it very strongly and if Chris were here I would say it to his face. I don't think Chris is one hundred percent behind you."

"Why do you think you have that feeling?"

"Why do I have it? well let's put it this way. I have watched my colleague in question closely in the last year or so and my impression is that he does not show any joy, any enthusiasm in matters concerning this government in general and Your Excellency in particular. I was saying precisely that to him only a few minutes ago. 'Why do you go about with this tight face all the time?' I said. 'Cheer up my friend.' But he can't cheer up. Why? The reason is not far to seek. Two of you were after all class-mates at Lord Lugard College. He looks back to those days and sees you as the boy next door. He cannot understand how this same boy with whom he played all the boyish pranks, how he can today become this nation's Man of Destiny. You know, Your Excellency it was the same trouble Jesus had to face with his people. Those who knew him and knew his background were saying: 'Is it not the same fellow who was born in a goat shed because his father had no money to pay for a chalet?' . . .''

He was going on and on, but His Excellency's mind was now divided between what he was saying and the echoes of old President Ngongo's advice: "Your greatest risk is your boyhood friends, those who grew up with you in your village. Keep them at arm's length and you will live long." The wise old tortoise!

A new respect for his Attorney-General was now reflected on the mirror of his face where the shrewd lawyer saw and caught its beams in both hands. This giant iroko, he thought to himself, is not scaled every day, so I must get all the firewood it can yield me now while I am atop.

"As for those like me, Your Excellency, poor dullards who went to bush grammar schools, we know our place, we know those better than ourselves when we see them. We have no problem worshipping a man like you. Honestly I don't. You went to Lord Lugard College where half of your teachers were Englishmen. Do you know, the nearest white men I saw in my school were an Indian and two Pakistanis. Do you know, Your Excellency, that I was never taught by a real white man until I went to read law at Exeter in my old age as it were. I was thirty-one. You can't imagine, Your Excellency how bush people like me were. During my first year in Britain I saw Welsh Rarebit on the menu one fine day and I rubbed my hands together and my mouth began to water because I thought I was going to eat real bush-meat from the forests of Wales!''

His Excellency was now definitely amused and smiling. The Attorney-General was dazzled by his own performance and success. Who would have believed His Excellency would listen this long to a man talking about himself and even smile at his jokes?

"I say this, Your Excellency, to show that a man of my background has no problem whatsoever worshipping a man like you. And in all fairness to my colleague—and I want to be scrupulously fair to him—he does have a problem; he wants to know why you and not him should be His Excellency. I don't mean he has said so in so many words to me but it is in his mind. I am not a mind reader but I am sure it is there, Your Excellency . . .''

"Thank you. You have no evidence, only a rather interesting theory. I appreciate it. You know I don't as a rule go about snooping for this kind of information, or setting my commissioners to spy on each other. I can assure you there is a very special reason, reason of state, why I put that question to you. And I appreciate your candid answer. In a way I am relieved and very happy that there is no evidence whatsoever. Now, you must forget we ever talked about it. As I said before, not a word about this to any living soul, you und'stand?"

"Perfectly, Your Excellency. You can count on my absolute discretion."

"Discretion? No, Mr. Attorney-General, you mean your absolute silence. If a word of this ever gets around, it's either from me or from you. Is that clear?"

"Absolutely, Your Excellency."

"Good day."

3

CHRIS CALLED IKEM on the telephone and asked him to send a photographer to the Reception Room of the Presidential Palace to cover a goodwill delegation from Abazon.

"That's a new one. A goodwill delegation from Abazon! A most likely story! What shall we hear next?"

"And for God's sake let me see the copy before it goes in."

"And why, if one may have the temerity to put such a question to the Honourable Commissioner?"

"You've just said it. Because I am the Honourable Commissioner for Information. That's why."

"Well that's not good enough, Mr. Commissioner for Information. Not good enough for *me*. You seem to be forgetting something, namely that it is *my* name and address which is printed at the bottom of page sixteen of the *Gazette* and not that of any fucking, excuse my language, any fucking Commissioner. It's me who'll be locked up by Major Samsonite if the need arises, not you. It's my funeral . . ."

"Quite irrelevant, Ikem. You ought to know that. We have gone over this matter a million times now if we've gone over it once; and I'm getting quite sick and tired of repeating it. I am doing so now for the last time, the very last time. Chapter Fourteen section six of the Newspaper Amendment Decree gives the Honourable Commissioner general and specific powers over what is printed in the *Gazette*. You know that well. I will now invoke the letter of that law and send you my instruction in writing. Expect it in the next half-hour. It is clear that's how you want it, so I will oblige."

He hung up and called in his new secretary. As she pulled up her chair and turned to a clean page of her dictation pad the telephone came alive and she made to answer it. But the Commissioner got to it before her and placed his hand on it, and while it continued to ring he said to her: "I am not in, no matter who it is." Then he took his hand off and she picked up the receiver.

It was Ikem and he was shouting. Chris could hear his strangled disembodied voice quite clearly because the secretary held the handset a little way from her ear to save her ear-drum.

"He is not on seat, sir."

"Don't lie to me! He bloody well must be on seat because he just now hung up on me."

"Well, sir, this is not the only telephone in the city, is it? He could have called you from his home or from the Presidential Palace or anywhere."

Chris was smiling a mirthless smile. An angry man is always a stupid man. Make a thorough fool of him, my dear girl, he thought. Ikem's concessionary silence was long and heavy. Then without another word he clanged the phone down so heavily that the girl jumped.

"Full marks, dear girl," said Chris without a smile now. "And my apologies for the behaviour of my graceless friends."

"Who was it?"

"Didn't you know? That was the Editor of the *Gazette*."

Her flag of victory seemed all of a sudden to lose its wind. Her face fell; Chris noticed it, the look of awe.

The sun in April is an enemy though the weatherman on television reciting mechanically the words of his foreign mentors tells you it will be fine all over the country. Fine! We have been slowly steamed into well-done mutton since February and all the oafs on our public payroll tell us we are doing just fine! No, my dear countrymen. This is Brigadier Misfortune of the Wilting 202 Brigade telling you you are *not* fine. No my dear countrymen, you will not be fine until you can overthrow the wild Sun of April. Later tonight, fellow countrymen, you will hear the full text from General Mouth himself—I am only a mouthpiece—you will hear the words direct from him after the national anthem shall have been played backwards. Until then, beloved countrymen, roast in peace.

The half kilometre to the Presidential Palace had already taken an hour and fifteen minutes in the closing-time heat and traffic, and he was not half-way there yet. The irresistible temptation of Abazon had brought him to this pass. As he inched forward and stopped and inched again and jammed his foot on the brakes he remembered: in heavy traffic the car to watch is the one ahead of the one behind you. Stupid cleverness, barren smartness that defeats ordinary, solid, sensible people. Like Elewa. She could never even begin to unravel that traffic conundrum.

He looked far ahead just before the next big bend in the road and saw another welcome twitch of motion working its way down the line towards him. He awaited it eagerly but when it got to him he saw it amounted to no more than a miserable metre's progress. So he decided it was not worth the trouble of a gearshift. Save it up and add it to the next incremental move and you will have a nice ride of two metres. Besides, irritating the clutch unnecessarily can lead to . . . The car behind him blared its horn so loud that he fairly jumped on his seat and out of his heat-haze reverie; he looked and saw through his rearview mirror a man in great anger, his perspiring head thrust out of his yellow taxi-cab, gesticulating wildly to him to move on. Other cars and drivers were joining now in the blaring and shouting protest. He decided to ignore them all and protect the precious little space ahead of him, even if the heavens should fall! The noise increased tenfold now and began to infect some of the cars ahead which could not possibly know what the matter was but were quite gratuitously joining the horn-blowers behind. He stuck to his guns. Rather than yield he would occupy his mind by observing the surroundings . . . The traffic going in the opposite direction on his left was luckier, as usual, than the one he found himself trapped in. But he gauged that even if, for the sake of moving at all, one should decide to turn around and join these people speeding away from one's destination the problem of space in which to turn would kill the proposition on the spot . . . There was nothing else of much interest on that side so he turned to his right and saw for the first time a street decoration of old and dirty flags and bunting lining the route. Some Ministry of Information decorators must have been at work here today putting up these filthy rags saved up and stowed away in mouse-ridden cartons in a Ministry store after last year's May Day celebrations.

It was at this point that he caught with the tail of his eye just in time the driver behind him manoeuvring his taxi out of the line; it was now virtually level with him, albeit on the grass kerb. He cranked his ignition which, mercifully, responded to the first attempt, shifted gear and moved forward to obliterate the prize space into which his antagonist had virtually wedged himself obliquely. From then on a war of nerves ensued between the two men whenever the forward traffic yielded an inch. In all known such encounters in the past between taxi and private drivers the taxi always won, its decisive weapon the certainty that the owner-driver will sooner concede his place than risk a dent on his smooth, precious carapace. But today, for the first time in the traffic history of this land, a taxi driver had met more than his match. This crazy owner-driver adversary failed altogether to live by the norms of his kind. One look at the condition of his car might have forewarned the other; but he either did not look or looked but failed to see.

"What shall I tell Mama-John?" a middle-aged civil servant was fabled to have wept when a taxi drew an ugly gash along the entire length of the shining side of his new Volvo. Well, Ikem had no wife to fear at home and no child called John, James or any other name. So the contest was more than equal. Grimly oblivious of the car beside him riding with its two legs in the bush, Ikem pursued the red brake-lights ahead like a randy he-goat sniffing the bottom of his mate.

After fifteen minutes of dangerously close brushes the contender-driver conceded victory with a heavy curse, pulled back and returned again to second place behind the victor thanks to the cooperation of the bronze medallist who halted for him to resume his original position.

Ikem heaved a very deep sigh and then, gallant in victory, pronounced it the work of the sun. We are parboiled as farmers do their rice to ease the shelling. Thereafter we take only five minutes to cook.

That night he composed his Hymn to the Sun:

Great Carrier of Sacrifice to the Almighty: Single Eye of God! Why have you brought this on us? What hideous abomination forbidden and forbidden and forbidden again seven times have we committed or else condoned, what error that no reparation can hope to erase?

Look, our forlorn prayers, our offerings of conciliation lie scattered about your floor where you cast them disdainfully away; and every dawn you pile up your long basket of day with the tools and emblems of death.

Wide-eyed, insomniac, you go out at cock-crow spitting malediction at a beaten, recumbent world. Your crimson torches fire the furnaces of heaven and the roaring holocaust of your vengeance fills the skies.

Undying Eye of God! You will not relent, we know it, from compassion for us. Relent then for your own sake; for that bulging eye of madness that may be blinded by soaring motes of an incinerated world. Single Eye of God, will you put yourself out merely that men may stumble in your darkness. Remember: Single Eye, one-wall-neighbour-to-Blindness, remember!

What has man become to you, Eye of God, that you should hurt yourself on his account? Has he grown to such god-like stature in your sight? Homeward-bound from your great hunt, the carcass of an elephant on your great head, do you now dally on the way to pick up a grasshopper between your toes?

Great Messenger of the Creator! Take care that the ashes of the world rising daily from this pyre may not prove enough when they descend again to silt up the canals of birth in the season of renewal.

The birds that sang the morning in had melted away even before the last butterfly fell roasted to the ground. And when songbirds disappeared, morning herself went into the seclusion of a widow's penance in soot and ashes, her ornaments and fineries taken from her—velvets of soft elusive light and necklaces of pure sound lying coil upon coil down to her resplendent breasts: corals and blue chalcedonies, jaspers and agates veined like rainbows. So the songbirds left no void, no empty hour when they fled because the hour itself had died before them. Morning no longer existed.

The trees had become hydra-headed bronze statues so ancient that only blunt residual features remained on their faces, like anthills surviving to tell the new grass of the savannah about last year's brush fires.

Household animals were all dead. First the pigs fried in their own fat; and then the sheep and goats and cattle choked by their swollen tongues. Stray dogs in the market-place in a running battle with vultures devoured the corpse of the madman they found at last coiled up one morning in the stall over which he had assumed unbroken tenancy and from where he had sallied forth every morning to mount the highest rung of the log steps at the centre of the square and taunt the absent villagers. Where is everybody? You have not forgotten your own market day? Come! Bring your long baskets of yams and your round baskets of cocoyams. Where are the fish women and the palm-oil women, where the high headloads of pottery? Come, today may be your lucky day, the day you may find a blind man to trade against. You have nothing to sell? Who said so? Come! I will buy your mother's cunt.

The dogs growled as they tore him apart and snapped at the vultures who struck back fearlessly with their beaks. After that last noisy meal the vultures pushed in their wicked, bashed-in heads and departed for another country.

In the end even the clouds were subdued though they had held out longest. Their bedraggled bands rushed their last pathetic resources from place to place in a brave but confused effort to halt the monumental formations of the Sun's incendiary hosts. For this affront the Sun wreaked a terrible vengeance on them cremating their remains to their last plumes and scattering the ashes to the four winds. Except that the winds had themselves fled long ago. So the clouds' desecrated motes hung suspended in a mist across the whole face of the sky, and gave the Sun's light glancing off their back the merciless tint of bronze. Their dishonoured shades sometimes would stir in futile insurrection at the spirit-hour of noon starting a sudden furious whirling of ash and dust, only to be quickly subdued again.

In last desperate acts the Earth would now ignite herself and send up a shield of billowing black smoke over her head. It was pitiful and misguided for the heat of the brush fires merely added to the fire of the Sun. And soon, anyhow, there was no fodder left to burn.

No one could say why the Great Carrier of Sacrifice to the Almighty was doing this to the world, except that it had happened before, long, long ago in legend. The earth broke the hoes of the grave-diggers and bent the iron tip of their spears. Then the people knew the time had come to desert their land, abandoning their unburied dead and even the dying, and compounding thereby whatever abominations had first unleashed the catastrophe. They travelled by starlight and lay under the shade of their mats by day until the sands became too hot to lie upon. Even legend is reticent about their plight recounting only that every night when the journey began again many failed to rise from under their mats and that those who did stagger up cast furtive glances at the silent shelters and set their stony faces to the south. And by way of comment the voice of legend adds that a man who deserts his town and shrine-house, who turns his face resolutely away from a mat shelter in the wilderness where his mother lies and cannot rise again or his wife or child, must carry death in his eyes. Such was the man and such his remnant fellows who one night set upon the sleeping inhabitants of the tiny village of Ose and wiped them out and drank the brown water in their wells and took their land and renamed it Abazon.

And now the times had come round again out of storyland. Perhaps not as bad as the first times, yet. But they could easily end worse. Why? Because today no one can rise and march south by starlight abandoning crippled kindred in the wild savannah and arrive stealthily at a tiny village and fall upon its inhabitants and slay them and take their land and say: I did it because death stared through my eye.

So they send instead a deputation of elders to the government who hold the yam today, and hold the knife, to seek help of them.

4

Second Witness
—Ikem Osodi

"LOOK HERE, Elewa, I don't like people being difficult for no reason at all. I explained this whole thing to you from the very beginning. Didn't I?"

"You explain what? I beg you, no make me vex . . . Imagine! Hmm! But woman done chop sand for dis world-o . . . Imagine! But na we de causam; na we own fault. If I no kuku bring my stupid nyàrsh come dump for your bedroom you for de kick me about like I be football? I no blame you. At all!"

"I don't know what you are talking about."

"How you go know? You no fit know."

There is a car coming into the driveway and I go back to the window to see. No, it's only one of the people in the flats, but I stay at the window all the same and watch the car creep towards the common garage building on the right. One of the brake lights shows a naked white bulb in a broken red casing. So it was Mr. So

Therefore, the notorious Posts and Telegraphs man in the next flat. He crawled through the third door. Perhaps he will beat his beautiful wife tonight; he hasn't done it now in months. Do you miss it then? Confess, you disgusting brute, that indeed you do! Well, why not? There is an extraordinary surrealistic quality about the whole thing that is almost satisfyingly cathartic. I start hearing it in my dream and then pass into a state of half-waking, and stay there for the rest of the act because he always chooses that hour when sleep is at its most seductive—the hour favoured also by the most discriminating armed robbers. And in the morning I find myself wondering how much of it had happened and how much I had dreamt up on my own. I ran into them once the very next morning on the short walk to the garage and they were so outrageously friendly and relaxed! She especially. I was dumbfounded. Later I hear how a concerned neighbour once called the police station—this was before I came to live here—and reported that a man was battering his wife and the Desk Sergeant asked sleepily: "So Therefore?" So, behind his back, we call him Mr. "So Therefore." I can never remember his real name.

Elewa is still equitably cursing her woman's lot and me. I shall say nothing more, just sit here on this window-sill and keep a lookout for the taxi which is taking much too long to appear. I wonder why. At this time of night you can generally get them to come within the hour.

"Imagine . . . To put a girl for taxi at midnight to go and jam with arm robbers in the road."

"You know very well, Elewa, that there are no more armed robbers in Bassa."

"The woman dem massacre for motor Park last week na you killam."

"Nobody will kill you, Elewa."

"Nobody will kill you Elewa. Why you no drive me home yourself if say you know arm robbers done finish for Bassa. Make you go siddon."

"I can't take you home because my battery is down. I have told you that twenty times already."

"Your battery is down. Why your battery no down for afternoon when you come pick me."

"Because you can manage a weak battery in the daytime but not at night, Elewa."

"Take your mouth comot my name, ojare. Tomorrow make you take your nonsense battery come pick me again. Nonsense!"

She is turning really aggressive. If I didn't know my Elewa I would be really worried. But she will call me first thing in the morning; perhaps during my nine o'clock editorial conference. The first time we parted in this kind of mood I was convinced I had lost her for good. That was the night I first tried to explain my reason for not letting her sleep in my flat. I should not have bothered with reasons at all if she hadn't kept saying I had another girl coming, that was why. "Your compliment to my stamina notwithstanding," I said totally and deliberately over her head, "the reason is really quite simple. I no want make you join all the loose women for Bassa who no de sleep for house." She stared at me with her mouth wide open, quite speechless. Thinking to press home my point and advantage I said something like: "I wouldn't want a sister of mine to do that, you see." She fired back then: "Anoder time you wan' poke make you go call dat sister of yours, you hear?"

When we parted I thought we were through. But next morning in the middle of my editorial conference my stenographer came in from the outer office and asked me to take a call.

"Who is that?" I asked angrily.

"A certain girl," he said, in his stupid officialese.

"Tell her to call again whoever it is. Oh, never mind I'll take it. Excuse me gentlemen."

It was Elewa asking if I would take her to the beach in the afternoon to buy fresh fish from fishermen coming ashore before the "thick madams" of the fish market had a chance to gobble up everything. "I go cook you nice pepper soup, today," she said.

In the end the taxi does appear and I grab my torchlight and take her down our unswept and unlit stairs. Whenever I go up or down those stairs I remember the goat owned in common that dies of hunger. The driver opens the rear door from his seat. No interior light comes on. I flash my light where it ought to have been and see a few tangled wires. To reassure Elewa I make a show of studying the driver's face in the light of my torch. The driver protests:

"I beg make you no flash light for my eye. Wayting?"

"I want to be able to recognize you in the morning."

"For sake of what?"

"For nothing. Just in case." I move to the front of the car and flash the light at the registration number.

"Na him make I no de gree come for dis una bigman quarter. Na so so wahala."

"Do you know it is an offence to operate a vehicle without interior lights according to the Criminal Code chapter forty-eight section sixteen subsection one hundred and six?"

"Na today—even na jus' now as I de come here de light quench out."

His lie is as good as mine but I have an advantage: I know he is lying; he doesn't know I am, and he is scared.

"OK. Tomorrow morning, first thing, make you go for mechanic fixam proper."

"OK, oga."

I seal our mutual understanding with a twenty kobo tip and then turn to Elewa who has withdrawn totally into herself and the far corner of the back seat. "You'll be alright, love."

"Driver, kick moto make we de go, I beg you."

I will keep trying till I find a reason that clicks with her.

I have never seen the sense in *sleeping* with people. A man should wake up in his own bed. A woman likewise. Whatever they choose to do prior to sleeping is no reason to deny them that right. I simply detest the very notion of waking up and finding beside you somebody naked and unappetizing. It is unfair to you but especially to her. So I have never bargained with my right to repossess my apartment and my freedom fully. To shower and retire to my bed, alone is, it seems to me, such a simple, straightforward and reasonable expectation. But many women take it as a personal affront, which I find very odd indeed. They are their own worst enemy, women are.

Elewa thinks it proves I don't love her well enough. It proves the exact opposite. I am extremely fond of the girl, more than anybody I can remember in years. And her lovemaking is just sensational. No gimmicks. I suppose I shall never discover where in that little body of hers she finds the power to lift you up bodily on her trunk while she is slowly curving upwards like a suspension bridge, her head and feet alone driven like steel piles into the riverbed. And then—mixed metaphors, unmixed blessings—shake you like a miner panning for gold! When we agree about sleeping separately we will have great times together. She is really a fine, fine girl.

Who was it invented the hot shower? It's the kind of thing one ought to know and never does. We clutter up our brains with all kinds of useless knowledge and we don't know the genius who invented the shower or the paper stapler . . . Let us now praise famous men and our fathers that begat us. Except that our fathers were not very famous in the invention line. But what does it matter? The French taught their little African piccaninnies to recite: *our forefathers, the Gauls* . . . It didn't stop Senghor from becoming a fine African poet . . . A true descendant of the Mandingauls!

I must get to work. That's the other thing about sleeping together. It prevents work. And if we are to improve on our fathers' performance in the invention business we must learn the sweet uses of hard work. I couldn't write tomorrow's editorials with Elewa's hands cradling my damp crotch.

Chris keeps lecturing me on the futility of my crusading editorials. They achieve nothing. They antagonize everybody. They are essays in overkill. They're counter-productive. Poor Chris. By now he probably believes the crap too. Amazing what even one month in office can do to a man's mind. I think that one of these days I shall set him down in front of a blackboard and chalk up for him the many bull's-eyes of my crusading editorials. The line I have taken with him so far is perhaps too subtle: *But supposing my crusading editorials were indeed futile would I not be obliged to keep on writing them?* To think that Chris no longer seems to understand such logic! Perhaps I have been too reluctant to face up to changes in my friends. Perhaps I should learn to deal with him along his own lines and jog his short memory with the many successes my militant editorials have had. Except, there is a big danger in doing it.

Those who mismanage our affairs would silence our criticism by pretending they have facts not available to the rest of us. And I know it is fatal to engage them on their own ground. Our best weapon against them is not to marshal facts, of which they are truly managers, but passion. Passion is our hope and strength, a very present help in trouble. When I took over the *National Gazette* from Chris I had no strong views one way or another about capital punishment. I even had no particular abhorrence about staging it publicly. If I had to vote I would probably vote against it by instinct but without much excitement. But all that was changed for me in the course of one afternoon. I became a passionate crusader. Chris said I was a romantic; that I had no solid contact with the ordinary people of Kangan; that the ordinary people of Kangan believed firmly in an eye for an eye and that from all accounts they enjoyed the spectacle that so turned my stomach.

From all accounts! From one account, mine, Chris never went to the show. I did. And by God he is right about the enjoyment! But, thank God again, also totally wrong.

By two o'clock there was no standing room on the beach, neither on the hot white sand nor the black granite boulders of the great breakwater wall stretching out to sea. On ordinary days only suicidal maniacs climbed those giant rocks that halted the galloping waves as the fierce horsemen at the durbar are stilled by an imaginary line before the royal pavilion. But this was no ordinary day. It was a day on which ordinarily sane people went berserk. The crowd on the perilous sea-wall had a fair sprinkling of women. And even children.

The camera crew from the national Television perched on their mobile tower were much admired by the crowd. As they swivelled their machine from one side of the amphitheatre to another taking in all that colour in the brilliant sun—the yellow and red and white and blue—especially the blue—of Kangan indigo dyes, the people smiled and made faces and waved to the camera.

The only room not taken yet was on the raised platform with numbered seats for VIPs and at the four stakes backed by their own little sea-wall of sandbags. The sun's heat honed with salt and vapour came down so brutally on the forehead that we all made visors with our hands to save our eyes. Those who had had the foresight to bring along umbrellas could not open them without obstructing others. A mild scuffle began right in front of me and ended only when the offending umbrella was folded up again.

"I beg una-o," said its peace-loving owner, "make I de use my thing for walking-stick."

"E better so. No be for see umbrella we de roast for sun since we waka come here dis morning."

I began to wonder at one point if I hadn't made a foolish gesture in refusing the ticket for one of those nicely spaced-out, numbered seats, that now seemed so desirably cool. Hardly anybody was sitting on them yet. Isn't the great thing about a VIP that his share of good things is always there waiting for him in abundance even while he relaxes in the coolness of home, and the poor man is out there in the sun pushing and shoving and roasting for his miserable crumbs? Look at all those empty padded seats! How does the poor man retain his calm in the face of such provocation? From what bottomless wells of patience does he draw? His great good humour must explain it. This sense of humour turned sometimes against himself, must be what saves him from total dejection. He had learnt to squeeze every drop of enjoyment he can out of his stony luck. And the fool who oppresses him will make a particular point of that enjoyment: *You see, they are not in the least like ourselves. They don't need and can't use the luxuries that you and I must have. They have the animal capacity to endure the pain of, shall we say, domestication.* The very words the white master had said in his time about the black race as a whole. Now we say them about the poor.

But even the poor man can forget what his humour is about and become altogether too humorous in his suffering. That afternoon he was punished most dreadfully at the beach and he laughed to his pink gums and I listened painfully for the slightest clink of the concealed weapon in the voluminous folds of that laughter. And I didn't hear it. So Chris is right. But how I wish, for the sake of all the years I have known and loved him, that the day never came when he should be that kind of right. But that's by the way.

I had never expected that Authority should excel in matters of taste. But the ritual obscenities it perpetrated that afternoon took me quite by surprise—from the pasting of a bull's eye on the chest of the victim to the antics of that sneaky wolf of a priest in sheep's clothing whispering God knows what blasphemies into the doomed man's ear, to the doctor with his stethoscope rushing with emergency strides to the broken, porous body and listening intently to the bull's eye and then nodding sagely and scientifically that all was finished. Call him tomorrow to minister to genuine human distress and see how slow he can be! And how expensive! Authority and its servants far exceeded my expectations that day on the beach.

But it wasn't Authority that worried me really; it never does. It wasn't those officious footlings, either. It wasn't even the four who were mangled. It was the thousands who laughed so blatantly at their own humiliation and murder.

As the four men were led out of the Black Maria the shout that
went up was not like any sound I had ever heard or hoped to hear
again. It was an ovation. But an ovation to whom for Christ's sake?

The four men were as different as the four days in the sky. One
had totally lost the power of his legs and was helped to the stakes
between two policemen, his trouser front entirely wet. The second
was crying pathetically and looking back over his shoulders all the
time. Was it to avoid looking ahead to those hefty joists sunk into
concrete or was there a deliverer who had given his word in a
dream or vision to be there at the eleventh hour? The third had
dry eyes and a steady walk. He was shouting something so loud
and desperate that the nerves and vessels of his neck seemed ready
to burst. Though he had just stepped out of a car he was sweating
like a hand-truck pusher at Gelegele Market. The fourth was a
prince among criminals. The police said he had eluded them for
two years, had three murders to his name and a fourth pointed in
his direction. He wore a spotless white lace *danshiki* embroidered
with gold thread, and natty blue terylene trousers. His appearance, his erect, disdainful walk hurled defiance at the vast mockery
and abuse of the crowd and incensed it to greater vehemence. He
saved his breath for the psychological moment when the crowd's
delirious yelling was suddenly stilled by its desire to catch the
command of the officer to the firing squad. In that brief silence, in
a loud and steady voice he proclaimed: "I shall be born again!"
Twice he said it, or if thrice, the third was lost in a new explosion
of jeers and lewd jokes and laughter so loud that it was clearly in
compensation for the terrible truth of that silence in which we had
stood cowed as though heaven had thundered: Be still and know
that I am God. The lady in front of me said:

"Na goat go born you nex time, noto woman."

My tenuous links with that crowd seemed to snap totally at that
point. I knew then that if its own mother was at that moment held
up by her legs and torn down the middle like a piece of old rag
that crowd would have yelled with eye-watering laughter. I still
ask myself how anyone could laugh at the proclamation of such a
terrible curse or fail to be menaced by the prospect of its fulfil-
ment. For it was clear to me that the robber's words spoken with
such power of calmness into the multitude's hysteria just minutes
before his white lace reddened with blood and his hooded head
withered instantly and drooped to his chest were greater than he,

were indeed words of prophecy. If the vision vouchsafed to his last moments was to be faulted in any particular it would be this: that it placed his reincarnation in the future when it was already a clearly accomplished fact. Was he not standing right then, full grown, in other stolen lace and terylene, in every corner of that disoriented crowd? And he and all his innumerable doubles, were they not mere emulators of others who daily stole more from us than mere lace and terylene? Leaders who openly looted our treasury, whose effrontery soiled our national soul.

The only happy memory of that afternoon was the lady in front of me who vomited copiously on the back of the man with the umbrella and had to clean the mess with her damask headtie. I like to believe that there were others like her in every section of that crowd, picking up their filthy mess with their rich cloths. Certainly there were many who fainted although my news reporters put it all to the blazing sun. They also reported, by the way, a very busy day for pick-pockets, minor reincarnations of the princely robber.

The next day I wrote my first crusading editorial calling on the President to promulgate forthwith a decree abrogating the law that permitted that outrageous and revolting performance. I wrote the editorial with so much passion that I found myself ending it with a one verse hymn to be sung to the tune "Lord Thy Word Abideth."

> The worst threat from men of hell
> May not be their actions cruel
> Far worse that we learn their way
> And behave more fierce than they.

A bad hymn, as most hymns tend to be. But people sang it up and down the street of Bassa. Chris was critical of my tone and of my tactlessness in appearing to command His Excellency. But when the said Excellency proceeded to do exactly what I had demanded Chris had to come up with a new tune. My editorial suddenly had nothing whatever to do with the new decree. His Excellency had quite independently come to the conclusion that he could earn a few credits by reversing all the unpopular acts of the civilian regime. And the Public Executions Amendment Decree was only one of them. And this was the same Chris who had just rebuked me for not knowing that public executions were such a popular sport.

In the one year or more since those particular events I have successfully resisted Chris's notion of editorial restraint. But for how much longer?

"I CALLED YOUR OFFICE three or four times," he says as soon as I enter. He is not looking at me but at the sheaf of typed papers he is bouncing up and down on the table between his palms to line them up.

"I take it you are asking me to explain why I was not on seat."

"Oh don't be silly, Ikem. I'm only telling you . . ."

"Well, sir. I had to go to GTC to hire a battery and have them place mine on twenty-four hour charge. I am sorry about that."

"I was calling you about this morning's editorial." He is still not looking at me but the irritation on his face and in his voice is clearly mounting despite the quietness. I don't seem to be able to arouse anger in him these days; only irritation.

"What about it?"

"What about it! You know, Ikem I have given up trying to understand what you are up to. Really, I have."

"Good! At last!"

"How can you go about creating stupid problems for yourself and for everybody else."

"Come on now! Speak for yourself, Chris. I am quite able to take care of myself. As for my editorials, as long as I remain editor of the *Gazette* I shall not seek anybody's permission for what I write. I've told you that many times before. If you don't like it you know what to do, Chris, don't you? You hired me, didn't you?"

"Firing could be the least of your problems just now let me tell you. You had better have some pretty good explanations ready for H.E. The only reason I called you is that he is likely to ask me first and I want to tell you now that I am sick and tired of getting up every Thursday to defend you."

"Defend me? Good heavens! Who ever asked you to defend me? From what, anyway. Sounds to me like busy work, Chris."

"Well, never mind. I shan't do it any more. From now on you can go right ahead and stew in your own water."

"Thank you, sir. If there is nothing else, may I leave now?"

"You certainly may!"

"That was short and sweet," says his little painted doll of a secretary in the outer office. At a loss I simply glare at her and then slam her door after me. But a few steps down the corridor what I should have said comes, too late, to me. Something like: I've heard that you like it long and painful. I stopped; weighed it; changed my mind and continued walking.

That young lady has a reputation for never putting Chris on the telephone until the secretary at the other end has put on the boss. Apparently she considers it a serious breach of protocol for the Honourable Commissioner to say hello to an assistant. I wonder why everything in this country turns so readily to routines of ritual contest. The heavyweight champion must not show his face but wait in his locker until the challenger has cooled his heels in the ring. I must say the whole charade is so unlike Chris that it must be done without his knowledge. But when will he learn that power is like marrying across the Niger; you soon find yourself paddling by night.

IT SEEMS CHRIS has tortured himself for nothing. A week has gone by and no despatch-rider has delivered a query to me in the loud type-face of palace Remingtons. No green army jeep or blue police jeep has pulled up outside the *Gazette* or in front of the flats. Chris is totally shamefaced. Naturally. Who can blame him? I'll have to go over to his place this evening and see if I can make him feel better.

Worshipping a dictator is such a pain in the ass. It wouldn't be so bad if it was merely a matter of dancing upside down on your head. With practice anyone could learn to do that. The real problem is having no way of knowing from one day to another, from one minute to the next, just what is up and what is down. It seems that when Chris was last at the palace the Big Shot had said quite categorically that he would pay a visit to Abazon. Chris came away and began dutifully to relay the news to everyone including myself. But in the meantime the Big Shot has had a brief snooze and on waking up has begun to see the world differently. "I must not go and visit my loyal subjects of Abazon," he now says. And all plans are immediately cancelled. Which is fine, except that nobody remembers to tell the Honourable Commissioner who has charge for disseminating such vital information throughout the four provinces of the empire. So poor Chris is left totally in the lurch.

Nobody told *me* either. But the great difference between me and Chris is that I never did expect to be told. I happened to feel a certain way in the matter and like a free agent, sat up at night after Elewa had gone away in the taxi and composed my thoughts. I keep telling Chris that life is simpler that way. Much simpler. Stop looking back over your shoulder, I tell him. There ain't no deliverer running just a little behind schedule. March to the stake like a man and take the bullet in your chest. Much simpler.

But the real irony of the situation is that my own method is more successful even on Chris's own terms. How many times now have I managed to read the Big Shot's mind better than all the courtiers? Who knows, I may soon be suspected of witchcraft or of having a secret hot-line to the palace! For it does not stand to reason that from my hermit's hut in the forest I should divine the thoughts of the Emperor better than the mesmerized toadies in daily attendance. But it is quite simple really. The Emperor may be a fool but he isn't a monster. Not yet, anyhow; although he will certainly become one by the time Chris and company have done with him. But right now he is still OK, thank God. That's why I believe that basically he does want to do the right thing. Some of my friends don't agree with me on this, I know. Even Chris doesn't. But I am sure I am right; I am sure that Sam can still be saved if we put our minds to it. His problem is that with so many petty interests salaaming around him all day, like that shyster of an Attorney-General, he has no chance of knowing what is right. And that's what Chris and I ought to be doing—letting him glimpse a little light now and again through chinks in his solid wall of court jesters; we who have known him longer than the rest should not be competing with them. I have shown what light I can with a number of controversial editorials. With Chris I could do much more. If Sam were stronger or brighter he probably wouldn't need our offices; but then he probably wouldn't have become His Excellency in the first place. Only half-wits can stumble into such enormities.

Chris has a very good theory, I think, on the military vocation. According to this theory military life attracts two different kinds of men: the truly strong who are very rare, and the rest who would be strong. The first group make magnificent soldiers and remain good people hardly ever showing let alone flaunting their strength. The rest are there for the swank. The truth of this came to me on two separate occasions afterwards, both of them interestingly enough at the Gelegele Market. A tottering pugnacious drunkard was provoking a fight with a towering stranger carrying a small portmanteau and obviously on his way to the Motor Park. I think the drunk was claiming the box or even the man's clothes as his own. Everyone in the market, it seemed, knew the drunk because many of the witnesses to the scene gave the same advice to the strong man with the box. "If you don't handle that fool quite firmly, my friend, he will pester you to death," they said. But the stranger appeared more eager to slip past his tormentor than follow the crowd's advice. Which annoyed many of the people in the end. They didn't see why anybody should let a drunken idiot walk all over him in this outrageous way unless there was something indeed wrong with him. Perhaps he didn't own the clothes he wore. At that point a newcomer into the watching crowd recognized the stranger as last night's new champion wrestler of Kangan. "No wonder," said someone in a simple matter-of-fact voice and the rest of the people seemed to understand too. I was really amazed at their perceptiveness.

The other incident was at the Motor Park itself. I was sitting in my car reading and waiting for a friend who was having her hair plaited down at the hairdressers' shed. All around the parked cars young sellers of second-hand clothes displayed their articles on wooden clothes-horses. From time to time there would be a sharp stampede at some secret signal for the approach of a policeman or the Market Master, for none of these boisterous hawkers apparently had any right whatsoever to display their goods at that section of the market reserved for cars. It took no more than one second of unbelievable motion and all those hundreds of wooden frames bedecked with the heavy castoffs of distant affluent and consumer cultures of cold climates would simply melt away in the bright noonday sun. Usually the alarm would prove to be false and they would reappear as promptly and miraculously as they had vanished, with much laughter and joking, and take up their illegal positions again. I never pass up a chance of just sitting in my car, reading or pretending to read, surrounded by the vitality and thrill of these dramatic people. Of course the whole of Gelegele Market is one thousand live theatres going at once. The hair-plaiting shed, for example, where Joy was now having her hair done, seated on a mat on the floor her head held between the knees of the artist into whose nimble hand she fed lengths of black thread, did not lack its own entertainment. But I would pick my vivacious youngsters of the used clothes, any day.

It was a great shock to me then when that army car drove up furiously, went into reverse before it had had time to stop going forward and backed at high speed into a young man and his clothes who just barely managed to scramble out of the car's vicious path. A cry went up all round. The driver climbed out, pressed down the lock button and slammed the door. The young trader found his voice then and asked, timidly:

"Oga, you want kill me?"

"If I kill you I kill dog," said the soldier with a vehemence I found totally astounding. Quite mechanically I opened my door and came out. I believe I was about to tell the fellow that there was no need for him to have said that. But I am glad I didn't in the end, because there are things which an observer can only see if he resists the temptation to jump into the fray and become an actor himself. So I watched the ass walk away with the exaggerated swagger of the coward, and went back into my car. But I was truly seething with anger. My young friends were stunned into total silence. But then the one who had had the brush with the car suddenly laughed and asked:

"Does he mean that after killing me he will go and kill a dog?"

And the others joined in the laughter.

"No, he means that to kill you is like to kill a dog."

"So therefore you na dog . . . Na dog born you."

But the victim stuck to his far more imaginative interpretation. "No," he said again. "If I kill you I kill dog means that after he kill me he will go home and kill his dog."

Within ten minutes the life of the group was so well restored by this new make-believe that when the offensive soldier returned to his car to drive away his victim of half an hour ago said to him:

"Go well, oga." To which he said nothing though it diminished him further still, if such a thing could be conceived. And then I was truly glad that I had not interfered with that impeccable scenario.

TO SAY THAT SAM was never very bright is not to suggest that he was a dunce at any time in the past or that he is one now. His major flaw was that all he ever wanted was to do what was expected of him especially by the English whom he admired sometimes to the point of foolishness. When our headmaster, John Williams, told him that the Army was the career for gentlemen he immediately abandoned thoughts of becoming a doctor and became a soldier. I am sure the only reason he didn't marry the English girl MM found for him in Surrey was the shattering example of Chris and his American wife Louise whom he married, if you please, not in New York which might have made a certain sense but in London. I suppose it is not impossible for two strangers to fabricate an affinity of sorts from being exiled to the same desert island even from opposite ends of the earth. Unfortunately Chris and Louise didn't make it once in bed, or anywhere else, throughout their six months cohabitation.

John Williams, our teacher, whose favourite phrase was "good and proper, pressed down and flowing over," in describing punishment, probably made the best choice for Sam after all. He grew so naturally into the part, more easily, I think, than he would have slipped into the role of doctor although I am sure his bedside manner would have been impeccable. But after Sandhurst he was a catalogue model of an officer. *His* favourite expression after he came home was: *it's not done,* spoken in his perfect accent.

I went to see Sam the morning after I heard news of his promotion to Captain. It was Sunday and the time about ten o'clock. I found him in his morning coat lounging in a sofa with Sunday papers scattered around him on the floor, a half-smoked pipe on a side-table and from his hi-fi Mozart's *Eine Kleine Nachtmusik* on a 45 r.p.m. record playing at 33 1/3 . That was Sam's problem. Not very bright but not wicked. And completely tone-deaf. Nothing is more entertaining than Sam trying to whistle a tune.

There is something else about Sam which makes him enormously easy to take: his sense of theatre. He is basically an actor and half of the things we are inclined to hold against him are no more than scenes from his repertory to which he may have no sense of moral commitment whatsoever. He was fascinated by the customs of the English, especially their well-to-do classes and enjoyed playing at their foibles. When he told me about his elegant pipe which he had spent a whole morning choosing in a Mayfair shop I could see that he was not taking himself seriously at all. And therefore I had no reason to do so.

Of course one may well question the appropriateness of these attitudes in a Head of State. But quite frankly, I am not troubled by that. In fact the sort of intellectual playfulness displayed by Sam must be less dangerous than the joyless passion for power of many African tyrants. As long as he gets good advice and does not fall too deeply under the influence of such Rasputins as Reginald Okong we may yet avoid the very worst.

Perhaps I am altogether too sanguine but his response to the doctors' crisis gave me great hope and encouragement. He saw right away—just as I did and Chris refused to—that it wasn't Mad Medico's insane graffiti that brought all those worthy people so viciously about his throat. Far from it. His crime was rather that he had dared to get one of their number disgraced. Publicly they admitted that Dr. Ofe may have behaved unethically. But did that give a layman, especially one who was also a foreigner, the right to instigate relatives of a dead patient and even give them his own money to sue the very hospital in which he works? Their answer to their own rhetorical question was, of course, an emphatic no. Mine was an equally strong yes and so, thank God, was His Excellency's. In fairness to Chris he did not disagree with us on the Ofe affair but took the legalistic line that the doctors' complaint about Mad Medico's notices must be seen in isolation and entirely on its own merit. That shyster of an Attorney-General must have given free lessons to Chris.

Admittedly Mad Medico made a complete fool of himself putting up those atrocious jokes. He was both irresponsible in his action and careless of his safety. After his brush with the doctors he should have known that he had made enemies who would deploy themselves in various ambushes for his head. He obliged them far beyond the call of duty by offering it on a platter of gold.

When I launched my editorial crusade on his behalf I had no reason to belittle his gross abuse of good taste. But I had to place beside it the image of that wretched man lying in unspeakable agony for four days and nights in the surgical ward while his distracted relations ran from hospital to a distant village and back again trying in vain to raise the twenty-five manilla that Dr. Ofe must have before he would operate. All witnesses spoke of the man's screams which filled the Men's Ward and could be heard as far away as the Emergency Room at the Hospital Gate. They spoke of the nurses unable to shut him up and leaving the ward for hours on end to get a little peace somewhere else. Three nurses spoke of their efforts to call Dr. Ofe on the telephone and his threats of disciplinary action against them if they continued disturbing him at home and of his instructions to give the man yet another shot of morphia. And the doctor who finally performed the operation after Mad Medico began to interfere in the matter spoke at the inquiry of all those lengths of black intestine, four feet or perhaps eight, I don't now recall, which he had to take out and how everything was already much too late.

That was the story I had to place beside Mad Medico's folly in deciding whether I should sit back and let him be hounded out of the country. It seemed to me perfectly clear that whatever foolishness Mad Medico should get into now it would be morally intolerable to allow Dr. Ofe's friends to triumph however vicariously over him. Fortunately His Excellency saw it my way too. Chris says I am sentimental. Well, let me be.

Perhaps I am so indulgent about Sam's imitation of the English because I believe that a budding dictator might choose models far worse than the English gentleman of leisure. It does not seem to me that the English can do much harm to anybody today. After a long career of subduing savages in distant lands they discovered the most dangerous savage of all just across the English Channel and took him on and brought him to heel. But the effort proved too great and the cost too high, and although they acquitted themselves with honour they made sure that they would not be called upon to do it again. And so they anointed the hero of their dazzling feat the greatest Englishman who ever lived, dumped him at the polls and voted Clement Attlee in. Whatever fear the ghost of British imperial vocation may still hold over the world's little people was finally removed when a renegade Englishman and his little band of thugs seized Her Majesty's colony in Rhodesia and held it for thirteen years. No, the English have, for all practical purposes, ceased to menace the world. The real danger today is from that fat, adolescent and delinquent millionaire, America, and from all those virulent, misshapen freaks like Amin and Bokassa sired on Africa by Europe. Particularly those ones.

I think that much of the change which has come over Sam started after his first OAU meeting. Chris and I and a few other friends called at the Palace to see him as we used to do quite often in those days. I noticed right away that it was not the same Sam who had left Bassa only a week before. Everybody remarked on the change later—Chris, Mad Medico and the others. He spoke like an excited schoolboy about his heroes; about the old emperor who never smiled nor changed his expression no matter what was going on around him.

"Perhaps he doesn't hear very well," said Mad Medico.

"Nonsense," said His Excellency. "His hearing is perfect. I had breakfast with him on the fifth morning. He heard everything I said and has the most lively mind and the most absolutely delightful sense of humour."

"So he wears his mask-face only for the gathering-in of the tribes," I said.

"I wish I could look like him," said His Excellency wistfully, his thoughts obviously far away. If somebody else had reported that exchange to me, especially the sentence *I wish I could look like him* I would not have believed it. A young man wishing he could look like an octogenarian!

But the leader Sam spoke most about was President Ngongo—I beg your pardon—President-for-Life Ngongo, who called Sam his dear boy and invited him over to his suite for cocktails on the second day. I have little doubt that Sam learnt the habit of saying *Kabisa* from old Ngongo. Within a week it spread to members of the Cabinet and down to the Bassa cocktail set. From there it made its way more or less rapidly into the general community. The other day the office driver who drove me to GTC said: "Charging battery na pure waste of money; once battery begin de give trouble you suppose to buy new one. *Kabisa.*"

It is unlikely that Sam came away with nothing but *Kabisa* in his travelling bag. I may be wrong but I felt that our welcome at the palace became distinctly cooler from that time. The end of the socializing is not important in itself but its timing must be. I set it down to Sam's seeing for the first time the possibilities for his drama in the role of an African Head of State and deciding that he must withdraw into seclusion to prepare his own face and perfect his act.

5

"SAME HERE," says Ikem.

"Shit!" replies Mad Medico. "You don't have to follow your fucking leader in this house, you know. Come on, have Scotch or Campari or anything—even water—just to show him."

"Too late," says Ikem. "We were enslaved originally by Gordon's Dry Gin. All gestures of resistance are now too late and too empty. Gin it shall be forever and ever, Amen." Jovial words, but there is not the slightest sign of gaiety in the voice or face.

"I wonder where you got the idea that Ikem follows my lead. Once again, you are the last to know. He'd sooner be found dead. I thought everyone, even you, knew that."

"Following a leader who follows his leader would be quite a circus," said Ikem with unabated grimness.

Mad Medico pours out two long gins made longer still by ice cubes he has transferred with his fingers from a plastic bowl. He pours a little tonic water into each and I ask him to add more to mine. Then he throws into each glass a slip of lemon from another bowl giving it a little squeeze between thumb and forefinger before letting it drop, and stirs. Twice or thrice in the preparation he has licked his fingers or wiped them on the seat of his blue shorts. I can see that Ikem's new girl, Elewa, is at first horrified and then fascinated. She is seeing Mad Medico at close quarters for the first time though she has obviously heard much about him. Everyone has. Perhaps she is seeing any white man at close quarters for the first time, for that matter.

Mad Medico's proper name is John Kent but nobody here calls him by that any more. He enjoys his bizarre title; his familiar friends always abbreviate it to MM. He is of course neither a doctor nor quite exactly mad. Ikem once described him as an aborted poet which I think is as close as anyone has got to explaining the phenomenon that is John Kent. And the two of them, poet and aborted poet, get on very well together. MM got on very well too with His Excellency, as everybody knows. It was their friendship which brought him here in the first place, made him hospital administrator and saved him a year ago from sudden deportation.

Elewa's fascination grows as she explores with wide amazed eyes Mad Medico's strange home. I find her freshness quite appealing. Now she nudges Beatrice and points at the legend inscribed in the central wall of the bar above the array of bottles in a semi-literate hand and Beatrice obligingly chuckles with her although she has seen it at least a dozen times. Mad Medico notices the young lady's fascination and explains that he owes the inspiration for that poem to his steward, Sunday.

ALL DE BEER
DEM DRINK FOR HERE
DE MAKE ME FEAR

If indeed the inspiration was Sunday's it only goes to prove that birds of the same feather flock together. For Mad Medico has a strange mania for graffiti which was the cause of all the *wahalla* that would have cost him his job and residence in the country about a year ago had his Excellency and Ikem not gone to his rescue, their one and only joint effort to date. The doctors were ready to cut him up alive and I still can't say that I blame them entirely. Ikem insists that some of them used the occasion to unload themselves of other grievances but I still think the inscriptions were inexcusable and in deplorable taste. *Blessed are the poor in heart for they shall see God* cannot anywhere in the world pass as a suitable joke to be nailed up in the ward for heart patients, never mind that one stupid defender of MM's said the patients were either too ill or too illiterate and so no one could have been hurt! The thing was in abominable taste. His other inscription outside the men's venereal diseases ward: a huge arrow sitting between two tangential balls and pointing like a crazy road sign towards the entrance and the words TO THE TWIN CITIES OF SODOM AND GONORRHEA was, if such a thing could be conceived, worse.

"How is my wonder boy?" asks MM. "I never get a chance to see him these days. I suppose rescuing a bungling old fool from deportation must take its toll on the hardiest of friendships. Oh well. How's he?"

"He is flourishing," I said. "Last Friday afternoon he placed the entire cabinet on one hour's detention."

"He did? How boring," said Mad Medico. "You know something, Dick, the most awful thing about power is not that it corrupts absolutely but that it makes people so utterly boring, so predictable and . . . just plain uninteresting." He spoke more to his guest from England than to us. "I told you this boy was such a charmer when I first met him. I'd never seen anyone so human, so cultured." Dick nods disinterestedly. He has scarcely said a dozen words all afternoon. He drinks gin and lime as though it were Alka Seltzer. But in contrast to his dark mood his complexion is bright, almost girlish, unlike Mad Medico's excessively coarse tan. It was Mad Medico himself who first drew our attention to this when he introduced Dick to us. "A white man in the tropics," he had said, "needs occasionally to see someone fresh from his tribe to remind him that his colour is perhaps not as wrong, and patchy as it may seem."

Dick is now speaking in his lugubrious way. He is sitting on the far end of the three-sided bar across from me. Ikem and the two girls are between us on the forward and longer section of the counter facing Mad Medico, our bartender in the pit. Dick is saying that Acton's corruption was probably intended to encompass dehumourization if such a word exists.

"It doesn't but certainly should," says Mad Medico offhandedly. "What did you do?" he asks me.

"What?"

"You said you were all detained."

"Oh, that. No, we didn't do anything. That was the trouble. A delegation arrived at the Presidential Palace from Abazon—you know the drought place—and none of us knew they were coming. Naughty, isn't it? So His Excellency gets mad at us."

"That's beautiful," says Mad Medico, and then turning to Dick he plays the knowing Old Coaster to a ruddy newcomer: "Abazon is in the north-west and has had no rain for a year. So the poor devils up there send a delegation to ask His Excellency to give them rain." He then turns to me for confirmation. "That's about the size of it?"

"More or less," replies Ikem before I can say anything.

"That's marvellous," says Dick brightening up. "A kind of native Henderson. Absolutely fascinating. And what did he do?"

"He locks these fellows up—not the delegation, mind you, but his own cabinet . . . That must have been the original meaning of cabinet. People you put away in a wooden locker, ha ha ha! You had such a winner and you didn't put it in your rag the very next morning, Ikem. I'm surprised at you."

"NTBB" replies Ikem. "Not To Be Broadcast," he adds dispelling the puzzlement in a few faces. The girls and Mad Medico laugh. Dick still looks puzzled.

"I don't see the connection," he says.

"Between what?"

"The delegation from this desert place and the cabinet."

I am going to explain again but Mad Medico has a better explanation and drowns me out.

"That's a Britisher for you, Chris. He is looking for connections. There aren't any, young man. This is negritude country, not Devonshire."

"Oh, I wouldn't go quite that far," I say. "We are no more illogical in these parts than any other people, yourselves included." There is perhaps more shrillness in my voice than is required.

"Come! Come!" says Dick in a most offensively patronizing tone. "John is only joking."

"You see what I mean," says Mad Medico before I can claim to be joking too. "No sense of humour left. None whatsoever. They are all so stiff and damned patriotic, so quick to take offence. You can't make a joke here if you are white. You should have heard the names they called me because I was so naive as to try to cheer up some dreary wards in their blasted hospital. Imperialist! White racist! Red Neck! The best though was Negrophobist. Do you know that one? I didn't. Negrophobist. Apparently the opposite of nigger-lover."

"Let's face it, MM," (I am now really irritated) "would you have put up those jokes of yours in an English hospital?"

"Of course I wouldn't. Never said I would. But the English are not supposed to have a sense of humour to begin with. And this is not England, is it? Look outside. What do you see? Sunshine! Life! Vitality. It says to you: Come out and play. Make love! Live! And these dusky imitators of *petit bourgeois* Europe corrupted at Sandhurst and London School of Economics expect me to come here and walk about in a bowler hat and rolled umbrella like a fucking banker on Cheapside. Christ!"

We all laugh and applaud the brief oration. Except Dick. He is watching intently as Mad Medico perspiring refreshes his glass with campari and soda, drops in two ice cubes and licks his fingers.

Dick, it turns out, is the founding editor of a new poetry magazine in Soho called *Reject.* Prompted by Mad Medico he tells the story, at first reluctantly and in instalments of one sentence or two a piece.

"How did it begin? I am sure Ikem will be interested to hear."

"Oh, simply by placing advertisements in well-known literary journals calling for manuscripts rejected by other poetry magazines. Simple."

"That was three years ago?"

"Well, almost four."

"And it caught on?"

"Our success was immediate and total."

From now something like animation begins to enter his voice. The expression on his face changes too. At first it looks like a sneer but is presumably his own way of pride. He is now more open-handed with information. "In under two years we exploded the pretensions of the poetry establishment and their stuffy party organs. It was the most significant development in British poetry since the war."

The group gradually splits in two: Ikem and the editor at one end of the bar with Elewa sticking to them, understanding little; and Mad Medico joining Beatrice and me.

"I am sorry to tell you this," MM says to Beatrice, "but you waited five years too late to meet Chris. He and Sam were much nicer people then."

"Who wasn't? But five years ago BB was below the legal age and would have been of limited interest to me."

"I beg your pardon," she says.

"Really, they were such fun then, he and Sam," says MM almost to himself. He stirs the tiny iceberg floating in his Scotch with his index finger. A touch of genuine wistfulness has come into his voice. And his eyes.

"You know, MM," I say, "you are the only person in this country—perhaps in the whole wide world who calls him Sam still."

"Yes and I'll be damned if I should ever join your ridiculous *Excellency* charade. I would sooner be deported!"

"*Sam* is even more ridiculous, you know. It's a name that no longer fits the object. But then you have never been a good judge of what fits or doesn't . . . which is your great attraction."

"Thank you," he says with an embarrassed, boyish smile. At such moments the mischievous lad living inside him peers through his eyes. Beatrice who has said very little up to now asks pointedly: "Tell me, would you walk up to your Queen and say, 'Hi, Elizabeth'?"

"To hell, I wouldn't. But why are all you fellows so bent on turning this sunshine paradise into bleak Little England? Sam is no bloody queen. I tell you he was such a nice fellow in those days. He had a wholesome kind of innocence about him. He was . . . what shall I say? He was morally and intellectually intact—a kind of virgin, if you get my meaning. Not in its prudish sense, of course. He was more assured, knew a lot more than his fellow English officers and damn well spoke better English, I tell you. And yet he could still be pleasantly surprised by things . . . I found that so healthy and so attractive . . . You know I found him a girl once . . ."

"Who?" asks Elewa shifting sideways on her bar-stool to join our group and bringing Ikem and his poetry friend in tow—the last ostensibly unwilling.

"His Very Excellency, your ladyship," says Mad Medico bowing. "I found him this girl after he left the Camberley hospital."

"I had no idea you had a procuring past," says Dick with a solemnity that seems surprising even for him.

"Well, you might call it that," says Mad Medico. "You must

look at it this way, though. A nice young fellow comes all the way from the warmth of Africa to the inhospitable climate of an English hospital—no pun intended, by the way. And he is recovering miserably from double pneumonia. The least I could do was fix him up with a warm friendly girl to cheer him up. Nothing serious. A reasonable magistrate would let me off, I'm sure."

"But woman done suffer for dis world-o," says Elewa.

"A modern Desdemona, I see. Did she cheer him up?" asks Beatrice totally ignoring Elewa's more basic solidarity call.

"Did she indeed! He couldn't get her out of his system for years. He called me up the next morning. 'Uncle John,' he said, 'you wicked old soul.' And the way he laughed and seemed happy with the world after that! I shouldn't be in the least surprised if he also called long distance to Chris at the London School of Economics . . . Did he?"

"Well, almost. That was a famous story. He didn't wait too long to tell me, I can tell you."

"What did he tell you?" From Beatrice.

"NTBB."

"NT what?"

"BB. You've just been told, BB. That's what my friends at the radio station write in bold yellow letters across the face of records too dirty to play on the air."

"It means Not To Be Broadcast," explains Ikem again. "Chris might have added though that it doesn't now apply to dirty records alone. Anything *inconvenient* to those in government is NTBB."

"Quite right. I should have added that. My primary duty as Commissioner, you see, is to decide what is inconvenient and inform Ikem who promptly rejects the information . . . But going back to the more interesting subject, I confess I broke the code later and divulged the secret to BB."

"To me?" asked Beatrice, wide-eyed. "My own Beatrice?"

"Yes," said Chris. "I told you, didn't I, of the girl with the . . . how shall I call it . . . the invigorating tongue."

"Oh! It's the same girl? Oh my God!" She and Chris burst into a laugh which left everyone in the cold as it were.

"You two seem to know something that even the procurer here doesn't appear to have heard," said MM, "but never mind."

The poetry editor has been trying for some time to recapture his lost little audience disrupted by Elewa's defection at the prospects of low talk. He makes one last bold bid and takes the entire company. The expression on his face has been quite funny for some time too. Actually he has an extremely expressive face if by expressive one means a constant procession of shadowy grimaces all of them indeterminate. You cannot look at him and say: now he is sad, or he is enjoying himself now. You always have to wait and figure it out and still you are not entirely sure. And then all of a sudden you are angry with yourself for letting your mind engage with so much trouble on something so inconsequential. He is that kind of infuriating person. His expression now is a puritanic scowl without the moral gravity of a puritan.

"We were so successful," he is saying, as though unaware that his story was ever interrupted, "that it became difficult to be sure that all the stuff that came in was *bona fide* Reject. We did insist on the rejection slip accompanying every manuscript but anybody can make up a rejection slip. You know what I mean. Most magazines are pretty sloppy about their slips . . . Like some girls, you know. Present company of course excepted . . . They don't print them at the Royal Mint . . . So there was really no way we could be absolutely certain that what we were getting was always genuine Reject. But as I was telling you . . ." It seems that having got everyone again to listen to him his one desire now is to show his indifference to the rest of us by pretending to talk still to Ikem alone. Some people have nerve. ". . . our biggest problem was our success. We were soon printing no more than a fraction, a tiny fraction, of the manuscripts that came in. For a while I even toyed with the idea of a companion magazine to be called *Reject Two* or *Double Reject* which, I can tell you, would have been just as successful as *Reject*. But in the end I had to decide against it. Spreading yourself too thin, you know."

"Fascinating," says Ikem. "When Chris fires me here perhaps I could hop across and run *Double Reject* for you. I'm totally taken with the idea."

"You're the editor of the local . . ."

"Rag called the *National Gazette*," says Mad Medico. "Ikem is a fine journalist . . . But shit! Who am I to be awarding him marks? Anyway, his brilliant editorials did as much as anything else to save me from the just consequences of my indiscretion. But what I want to say really is that he is an even finer poet, in my opinion one of the finest in the entire English language."

"Yes, John told me what a fine poet you are. I'm ashamed to say I haven't yet read anything of yours but I certainly will now."

"Take your time," says Ikem. "And remember MM is not a disinterested witness. I did him a good turn."

"And I didn't tell you either," said MM, "that girl there sitting meekly and called Beatrice took a walloping honours degree in English from London University. She is better at it than either of us, I can assure you."

"That doesn't surprise me in the least. I understand that the best English these days is written either by Africans or Indians. And that the Japanese and the Chinese may not be too far behind," said Dick with somewhat dubious enthusiasm.

PERHAPS MM had a point when he said Beatrice waited too long to meet me. Sometimes I wonder myself whether our relationship is not too sedate, whether we are not too much like a couple of tired swimmers resting at the railing. An early scene returns to my memory, a scene from two years ago and more, stored away in incredible detail and freshness yet, as I think of it, suffused also with ethereality.

I offered to take Beatrice to the Restaurant Cathay and she said no. Chez Antoine? Still no. They were her two favourite places— not too large, no glaring lights and good food. What would she like to do then?

"Can I come home with you?"

"But of course," was all I could find to say right away. I was still not sure that I had heard right. She divined the puzzlement in my mind and offered something like an explanation. "We've both had a long day. All I want to do now is sit still somewhere and listen to records."

"Wonderful!" Of course she had been to my place quite a few times before but the initiative had never come from her. It was not coyness but she had a style and above all a pace that I decided from the very beginning to respect. After the few whirlwind affairs I had had in my time including a full-fledged marriage in London for six months I was actually ready and grateful for BB's conservative style. Sometimes when I thought of her what came most readily to my mind was not roses or music but a good and tastefully produced book, easy on the eye. No pretentious distractions. Absolutely sound. Although I realized the folly of it I could not help comparing BB and my ex-wife. Louise was so bent on proving she had a mind of her own she proved instead totally frigid in bed despite weekly visits to the psychiatrist. There was another type—at the opposite pole—the aspirant sex symbol, flaunting her flesh before you. I'd met her too. Her style usually worked for a while and then out of nowhere a coldness descended into your soul and you wanted only to tell her to cut out the moans and all that ardent crap and get to it fast. Beatrice is a perfect embodiment of my ideal woman, beautiful without being glamorous. Peaceful but very strong. Very, very strong. I love her and will go at whatever pace she dictates. But sometimes I just wonder if I am not reading her signs wrong; if as MM says, without fully intending it, I have become too wizened by experience; if I have lost the touch, so to say.

Neither of us was really hungry. So we decided on a bottle of wine and some fried shrimps. My cook, Sylvanus, was always upset if a guest came and he was not allowed to display the full extent of his culinary arts. Even as we ate his exquisite shrimps he kept at us.

"Make I fix madame small sometin," he pleaded. We begged him not to worry and he went away but soon returned to hover around the door of the kitchen. He could not understand how two grown people could eat nothing but "crayfish" for dinner.

"Or sometaim you wan go for hotel?" he said. And when Sylvanus said that you had to swear that his cooking was better than that of any chef, French, Italian or whatever on the west coast of Africa.

"No Sylvanus," said Beatrice trying to mollify him, "we no de go anywhere. We jus wan sidon for house. Make you take evening off. If at all oga wan anything I fit getam for am." I knew at once and she soon realized she had committed a blunder. Sylvanus did not exactly storm out but his resentment was very clear on his face and in the tone of his goodnights.

"Do you know why I wanted us to come here and stay by ourselves?"

"Well, yes and no."

"OK, let's have the yes first."

"You don't want to be seen too often with me in public." It sounded premeditated but wasn't. Beatrice didn't reply at once;

she seemed to be weighing the point as if to say: there may be something there. Then she shook her head gently a few times and said simply: "It was a year today that you first asked me to dinner here."

I was completely overwhelmed with feelings I had been skirting for months. I drew her to me on the sofa and kissed her—a little too roughly perhaps. I thought of making apologies for my own forgetfulness. With any other girl I would have proceeded to do so at once. But with her I couldn't pretend. I am not the anniversary kind and it would be utterly deceitful to say it just escaped my mind. I kissed her again and said instead: "You are a great girl." We were silent for quite a while.

"How long has Ikem known that Joy girl?" I asked.

"I can't tell you. I had only seen her a couple of times before this afternoon."

"She seems so young. And so illiterate. What can he possibly be saying to her?" I asked.

"Ikem doesn't say much to any girl. He doesn't think they have enough brains."

"Good for him, the great revolutionary."

"Well, you know, I am exaggerating a little. But really women don't feature too much in his schemes except as, well, comforters. I think that's about the only chink in his revolutionary armour . . . Do you notice how much he resents you now?" she asked in a sudden change of tack. "I don't think you are even aware of it. It bothers me because it wasn't there before. I can see plenty of trouble ahead for the two of you."

"Oh, you exaggerate. But you are right about the resentment. And I think it is quite natural. Especially since the coup and Sam's elevation and ·to a lesser degree mine. Literally Sam is now my boss and I am Ikem's boss."

"Do you mean Ikem is jealous of you two?"

"Yes, why not? But I resent him just as much. Perhaps more, for his freedom."

"I don't understand you people."

"Very simple really. It goes back, you see, to our first days at Lord Lugard College. Ikem was the brightest in the class—first position every term for six years. Can you beat that? Sam was the social paragon . . . He was the all-rounder—good student, captain of the Cricket Team, Victor Ludorum in athletics and, in our last year, School Captain. And girls worshipped at his feet from every Girls' School in the province. But strangely enough there was a kind of spiritual purity about Sam in those days despite his great weakness for girls. Maybe not purity but he seemed so perfect and so unreal, in a way."

"Too much success."

"Perhaps. Too much success. He never failed once in anything. Had the magic touch. And that's always deadly in the long run. He is paying the bills now, I think. And if we are not lucky we shall all pay dearly. How I wish he had gone to Medical School which had been his first ambition. But he fell instead under the spell of our English headmaster who fought the Italians in Abyssinia in 1941 and had a sword from an Ethiopian prince to prove it. So Sam enrolled in the first school cadet corps in the country and was on his way to Sandhurst."

"I asked you about Ikem not His Excellency," says BB, a mischievous twinkle in her eyes and snuggling closer to me.

"It's your fault. You are such a good listener."

"And you haven't said anything about yourself," she adds, ignoring my backhanded compliment.

"We are all connected. You cannot tell the story of any of us without implicating the others. Ikem may resent me but he probably resents Sam even more and Sam resents both of us most vehemently. We are too close together, I think. Lord Lugard College trained her boys to be lonely leaders in separate remote places, not cooped up together in one crummy family business."

"OK, Ikem was the intellectual, Sam the socialite, what about you?"

"I have always been in the middle. Neither as bright as Ikem and not such a social success as Sam. I have always been the lucky one, in a way. There was a song we sang as children, do you know it? *The one in front spots evil spirits, the one at the rear has twisted hands, the one in the middle is the child of luck.* Did you sing it? I was the child of luck."

"Can I tell you something? You promise not to be angry? Promise? Well, you fellows, all three of you, are incredibly conceited. The story of this country, as far as you are concerned, is the story of the three of you . . . But please go on."

"Actually you are quite right. That's what I've just said myself. We tend sometimes to forget that our story is only one of twenty

million stories—one tiny synoptic account. But that's the only one
I know and you are such a sweet listener as I said."

"A sweetener? A sweetener has its reasons . . . By the way do
you keep a detailed diary of what is happening day to day? I think
you should. But please go on."

"I do keep a journal. But, no let's change the subject. Tell me
something for a change."

"Today is your day . . . Why should His Excellency resent the
two of you? He has all the success." I sense she merely wants me
to keep talking. About anything. She finds my voice soothing,
perhaps. At the same time she has such a quick mind and such a
knack for asking inconvenient questions, like a precocious child.

"Why should he resent us? Why indeed? He has all the success.
From school to Sandhurst; the first African Second Lieutenant in
the Army; ADC to the Governor-General; Royal Equerry during
the Queen's visit; Officer Commanding at Independence; Colonel
at the time of the coup; General and His Excellency, the Head of
State, after. Why indeed should he resent any mortal? Now that
you ask I confess I don't know. He wasn't like that right away. In
fact he kept very close to us in the first six months or so. And then
. . . But let's talk about better things on the golden anniversary
of our first date."

She shot up from my chest where she was lying and gave my
face a quick scrutiny. "I hope you are not being sarcastic," she
said. I affect great solemnity, pull her back and kiss her mildly. She
offered up her lips again; we were both trembling.

"Hadn't I better be going?"

"Why? I thought you were staying."

"Why?"

"Because I want you to."

"Is that a good reason?"

"Yes."

"I have a better one."

"For going or staying?"

"For going."

"What is it?"

"Because I don't want to . . ." We laughed and I tried to kiss
her but she covered my mouth with the palm of her hand . . .
"Wait! I haven't finished yet . . ." And she sang the rest: *"but
twelve o'clock done knack and my mama go vex with me."* Then she re-

arranged her countenance from the angelic model demanded by her song and offered to stay . . . on one condition, she said.

"What is it? Don't tell me, I know."

"What is it?"

"That I don't make love to you."

She shook her head. "Maybe I should add that now that you mention it. Have another guess."

"That we first talk about ourselves."

"Who wants to hear any more about you? You will end up talking about other people, anyway."

"I give up."

"Promise me that you will go in now and switch off that air-conditioner in your bedroom." I burst into uncontrollable laughter. BB, feigning great seriousness, informed me that she nearly froze to death just walking through to the bathroom a short while ago. Incredible girl, BB; her demands were never such as to break a man's back!

Not for her the lover as tiger that some women crave, a bloody spoor strewn with shredded garments. The day I first made love to her, months after we began to go together, I wrote down in my diary: *Her passion begins like the mild ripples of some tropical river approaching the turbulence of a waterfall in slow, peaceful, immense orbits.* Pompous? No. Immense.

"You were telling me about the white girl and your big friend," she said abruptly, switching on the bed lamp I had just turned off and holding back my hand reaching again for the rope-switch. Before I could answer she said: "Why did you call her a miracle worker?" I had said I would go at BB's pace but I'd be damned if I would spend the rest of the night talking about Sam and Gwen who had already come up for mention at lunch with Ikem and his new girl, Joy. So I went straight to the point.

"In the morning after a very exhausting night this girl, Gwen, wakes him up and wants to begin again. I remember how Sam put it: *My brother, there was absolutely nothing left in the pipeline.* So Gwen swings herself around and picks up his limp wetin-call with her mouth. And from nowhere and like magic life surges back into it. Sam had never seen that kind of thing before."

BB didn't respond immediately except to get a little closer to me. Then she asked: "You mean people actually do that?"

"All the time."

"Disgusting," she said.

"Well, I don't know."

"You sound as if you wouldn't mind yourself. Or perhaps you have done it already."

"No, I haven't. It's the girl who does it."

"All right Mr. Smart. Has any girl done it for you?"

"Let's not make it personal."

"OK. I won't pry any more. But I think it is disgusting, don't you? And they didn't even shower first, did they?"

"I wasn't there, you know; but I don't suppose they did. She woke him up as I understand it and went straight to work."

"With all that stuff on it!"

"Dry and caked, yes."

"Disgusting. I won't do that. Not for anybody."

"Don't worry, love. I won't ever ask you."

"What if it happens inside her mouth?"

"What? I see. But isn't that the whole point?"

"Na Beatrice you de ask? Na me de tell de tori, no be you?"

"Well that's the whole point, I am told. To give it to her right in the mouth."

"You're joking!"

"I swear."

"Chris, are you sure you haven't done it?"

"No. It's the girl who does it."

"Oh shut up; you know what I mean. And don't you start anything because I won't wash it in my mouth."

"We'll shower first."

"You are joking. Oh Chris! Please."

6

Beatrice

WHEN I PICKED UP the telephone and a completely unfamiliar voice said, "Can I speak to Miss Beatrice Okoh," my heart fluttered violently in panic fear. I don't know why but the thing that came into my mind right away was: Oh God, there's been an accident involving Chris, and someone is calling from the Casualty Ward of the Teaching Hospital. Why my mind should have gone to an accident I've no idea but the feeling was so strong that it blocked other lines of thought. So when the caller said, "Hold on for His Excellency," my answer was a confused and near-hysterical: "His what? Who are you?" It was only when the confident, resonant drawl asked if he was such an unwelcome caller that I realized what I had heard before and stammered an incoherent string of apologies. Even so, while he spoke, my thoughts kept leap-frogging over themselves and it was not until quite some time after he rang off that I had regained enough composure to begin to sort out the details of what he had said. He was inviting me to a small private dinner. On Saturday. Something important and personal he wanted to talk to me about. A car would be sent to pick me up from my flat at six-thirty. Dress absolutely informal, or even casual. See you then. And he rang off. Just like that!

In the early days of his coming to power I had gone fairly often to the Palace with Chris and sometimes Chris and Ikem. But then things had changed quite dramatically after about one year and now apart from viewing him virtually every night on television news I had not actually set eyes on him nor had any kind of direct contact for well over a year. So the telephone call and the invitation were baffling to me and totally unexpected.

Of course Chris had kept me posted on the steady deterioration in their relationship. Would the important and personal discussion be about that? Was I going to find myself listening to awkward recrimination between two friends who'd known each other since I was in nappies . . . Well, not exactly but almost. That might account for the very early time of six-thirty. It was only then it occurred to me that I was simply assuming that I would be going to the Palace as in the old days with Chris but that nothing of the sort had been said in the invitation. So I rushed to the telephone and called Chris's house without luck and then his office where he was at work as usual long after everybody else had gone home, eaten their lunch and even had their siesta, and told him the news. No, he hadn't been asked but he would rather not talk on the telephone. He would pass by my place on his way home shortly. That was on a Thursday evening.

My doorbell rang at exactly six-twenty-five. I was at the dressing-table and soon could hear Agatha, as prompt on the Sabbath as on any other day to open the front door to callers, in lively conversation with a male voice. When she had had whoever it was as long to herself as she thought necessary she came to the door of the bedroom to inform me that one soja-man from President house de for door; he say na President sendam make he come bring madam.

"Tellam make he siddon," I said, "I de nearly ready."

Soon the two voices were floating in to me again as I put on the finishing touches. When I got to the living-room a couple of minutes later Agatha was just disappearing through the kitchen door. The soldier who was still on his feet saluted as I entered and I began at once to apologize for my maid's manners in not offering him a seat.

"No be like dat madam," he said gallantly. "Your girl polite well well. She tell me make I siddon, she even ask wetin I wan drink. So no be her fault at all madam. Na me one refuse for siddon. You know this soja work na stand-stand work e be."

"OK. You are taking me to the Palace? I am ready."

"Ah madam. No be Palace we de go. Na for Palace dem tell you?"

"What? Na where we de go?"

"You mean to say dem no tell you? Wonderful! Na for President Guest House for Abichi Lake na there dem say make I take you. And dat must correct because why? the President been de there since yesterday. He no dey for Palace at all."

The strange feelings I had been nursing since Thursday afternoon now threatened to explode in violent froths of anger as this latest ingredient of insult was dropped with such casualness into the brew. God! Who did this fellow think he was? First he orders me to dinner and rings off before I have had time to express my profound gratitude. Then he doesn't think it is necessary to warn me that I have a forty-mile journey to make for the privilege! What in heaven's name was going on in this country?

My first act of rebellion which was to bring a wan smile to my face five minutes later for its sheer futility was to refuse my escort's offer to sit in the owner's corner of the black Mercedes standing in my driveway. As he rushed ahead of me and opened and held the door I simply said sorry, walked over to the other side and let myself in. The chauffeur turned sharply round on his seat perhaps to get a good look at today's eccentric cargo. When I said good evening to him on top of all that, he seemed dazed to begin with and then his bafflement gave way to a wide happy grin which pleased me very much for it confirmed that I had successfully compounded my rebellion—first to spurn a seat of honour and then to greet a mere driver first. That was when I smiled at myself and my puny, empty revolts, the rebellion of a mouse in a cage.

And I recalled Chris's advice to me to stay cool no matter what. My complaint that the fellow had not even bothered to ask if I was free nor wait for me to accept had merely brought an indulgent smile to Chris's face. "Look, BB," he said. "In any country and any language in the world an invitation by the Head of State is a virtual command even when he does not pick up the phone personally to issue it. So my dear girl you will go and you may do some good. Sam is not such a fool you know. He knows things are now pretty hopeless and may see in you a last hope to extricate himself. You may be able to help."

"How?"

"My dear, I don't know. But let's keep all options open. It's never too late."

Chris is damn too reasonable. That's all I can say. All options? I knew of one at least I would not keep open.

We got to Abichi village and then the lake at about seven-thirty. Although I had been to the Presidential Retreat twice before it was both in daytime. Going up to it now with the great shimmering expanse of the artificial lake waters stretching eastwards into the advancing darkness on your left and the brightly lit avenue taking you slowly skywards in gigantic circles round and up the hill, on top of which the Presidential Retreat perches like a lighthouse, was a movingly beautiful experience even to a mood as frayed and soured as mine that evening. The rumoured twenty million spent on its refurbishment by the present administration since the overthrow of the civilians who had built it at a cost of forty-five million may still be considered irresponsibly extravagant in our circumstances but . . . But what? Careful now, before you find yourself slowly and secretly leaning towards Chris's reasonableness!

As a matter of fact he and Ikem had had one of their fierce arguments in my presence over the vast sums spent on the refurbishment of the Retreat. Money, incidentally, which had not been passed through the normal Ministry of Finance procedures. On that occasion I had been totally on the side of Ikem.

"Retreat from what? From whom?" I recall him demanding with characteristic heat. "From the people and their basic needs of water which is free from Guinea worm, of simple shelter and food. That's what you are retreating from. You retreat up the hill and commune with your cronies and forget the very people who legitimize your authority."

"Don't put it on me," cried Chris. And then he side-stepped the issue completely to produce one of those beautiful historical vignettes his incredibly wide reading and fluency makes him so good at. "Nations," he said, "were fostered as much by structures as by laws and revolutions. These structures where they exist now are the pride of their nations. But everyone forgets that they were not erected by democratically-elected Prime Ministers but very frequently by rather unattractive, bloodthirsty medieval tyrants. The cathedrals of Europe, the Taj Mahal of India, the pyramids of Egypt and the stone towers of Zimbabwe were all raised on the backs of serfs, starving peasants and slaves. Our present rulers in Africa are in every sense late-flowering medieval monarchs, even the Marxists among them. Do you remember Mazrui calling Nkrumah a Stalinist Czar? Perhaps our leaders have to be that way. Perhaps they may even need to be that way."

"Bloody reformist," said Ikem, infuriated and impressed for though he may be a great writer yet when it comes to speaking off the cuff he is no match for Chris.

A pleasant-faced army major searched my handbag at the entrance and another officer took me up a wide and red-carpeted flight of stairs. At the landing a huge open door led into an enormous and opulent room where guests were already settled in. As soon as I had appeared at the door His Excellency had rushed out to meet me, planted a kiss on my forehead and led me by the hand into the room. The guests sat in scattered groups of twos and threes on chairs, settees and pouffes drinking and dipping into bowls of assorted finger-food laid out on stools and on the floor.

"Who don't we know?" asked the host and without waiting for an answer added: "Let's start with the ladies." Meanwhile the men had all struggled to their feet to stand guard, as it were.

"Come and meet Miss Cranford of the American United Press. Lou is in Bassa to see if all the bad news they hear about us in America is true." The dark-haired girl who would have fitted my stereotype of an Italian beauty if I hadn't been told she was American was smiling and playing her hand like a pair of cymbals to get them free of salted peanuts in preparation for a hand-shake which when it came would have given her Americanness away for its over-eager firmness. Meanwhile His Excellency was literally reciting my CV. "Lou, this is one of the most brilliant daughters of this country, Beatrice Okoh. She is a Senior Assistant Secretary in the Ministry of Finance—the only person in the service, male or female, with a first-class honours in English. And not from a local university but from Queen Mary College, University of London. Our Beatrice beat the English to their game. We're very proud of her."

"Wow," said Lou. "That's terrific. How did you do it Beatrice?"

The rest was routine. There were I think eight men and seven women including myself.

Of the men I knew only one reasonably well—Joe Ibe, the Commissioner for Works. When His Excellency got to him and said: "But of course you know Beatrice," he had replied: "Me? I am sorry sir, I have never seen her before," which must be about the most predictable and tired of Bassa witticisms and yet it always produced some laughter most of it on this occasion from the humorist himself who immediately added as if to bring everything down again to the literal level of those not bright enough for high humour: "Long time no see, Beatrice. How's my friend Chris?" To which I replied with my own feeble effort at joke-making: "But I should ask you. You see him more often than I do. He is always at one or other of your meetings."

"That's what he tells you?" And that really cracked everybody up.

"Joe is right, you know," said His Excellency with a wink. "If I were you I would do spot checks now and again."

As soon as the introductions were over the American journalist came rushing to me to say she hoped that besides getting acquainted this evening we would be able to sit down somewhere in the next seven days over a meal or something and talk about things in general. Especially the woman's angle, you know. To which I replied rather sharply that I couldn't see what a reporter who could stroll in any time and get it all direct from the horse's mouth could want to hear from the likes of me. Involuntarily perhaps her eyes narrowed into a fighting squint for the briefest moment and then just as swiftly changed tactics back to friendliness.

"I won't leave the country now without talking to you," she said. "Not after all the things I've just heard. It's a promise!" And she moved off and left me in peace for the moment.

I knew I had been unduly shrill in our brief exchange. But I seemed not to be fully in control of my responses. Something tougher than good breeding had edged it aside in a scuffle deep inside me and was imparting to my casual words the sharp urgency of incantation. I assumed to begin with that I was still over-reacting to the abnormal circumstances of my invitation to the party and remembered Chris's advice to remain calm. To his shade I promised now to try harder.

So these were the new power-brokers around His Excellency! I was seeing the controversial Director of SRC at close quarters for the first time and did not, as I might have expected, like him in the least. He is youngish and good-looking, and strong in a vaguely disagreeable way. Perhaps it was those enormous hands of his like a wrestler's which struck you at once as being oversize even for a man as big as he. I think he feels awkward about them and is constantly shifting them around from beside to behind him and then inside his pockets which of course draws more attention to them. He speaks only when spoken to and then in an absurdly soft voice. And to finish him off finally as far as I was concerned he was so excessively obsequious to His Excellency during the dinner. Was he a guest like the rest of us or some kind of superior steward? He would leave a guest in midsentence and go after the serving crew because a glass somewhere was three-quarters empty.

The Chief of Army Staff was more popularly known, more self-assured and a more agreeable person altogether.

The ladies were the most surprising. They were all over-dressed or perhaps nobody had told them about the informality of the occasion; and none of them had very much to say. These couldn't be some of the wild and fashionable set that rumour claimed dominated His Excellency's current party life. Perhaps this drab group was chosen on pathetically incompetent advice to impress the American girl. Wasn't it conceivable that some daft fellow on the President's staff seeing so many raving American and American-trained preachers on sponsored religious programmes nightly on television might actually believe that a show of Presidential decorum would be desirable!

The food was simple and tasty. Shrimp cocktail; *jollof* rice with plantain and fried chicken; and fresh fruit salad or cheese and English crackers for dessert. The wines were excellent but totally wasted on the company, only His Excellency, the American girl and myself showing the slightest interest. The Bassa men stuck as usual to the beer they had been drinking all day; one of the ladies had double gins and lime and the other two a shandy of stout and Seven Up which one of them—Irene, I think her name was—apostrophized as *Black Is Beautiful.*

His Excellency was a perfect host. From the head of the oval-shaped table he dispensed conviviality and put every one at their ease. Had there been just a little less eagerness on the part of the guests to agree with everything he said and laugh excessively

whenever they thought he was making a joke the evening might
have been quite remarkable really. He had placed me on his right
and the American girl on his left so that we faced each other across
a thin end of the oval. On my right was the reticent Major Ossai
and across the table from him the Commissioner for Works. The
Chief of Army Staff controlled the far end of the table like a second-class chief attentive, whenever required to do so, to the para-
mount chief but sometimes out on his own quietly filling the gin-
and-lime girl with giggles.

The host's efforts to get the American girl and me talking together failed dismally. I simply couldn't muster anything you
could call enthusiasm to sustain an exchange even with the Head
of State chipping in to fan the failing flames. The other, after my
initial rebuff was no more than merely polite. Whenever I was not
talking to the host I would turn to the gentleman on my right and
engage him seemingly in deep exchanges. And he was ideal for
my purpose having no greater will for social courtesies than a
standby generator has to produce electricity when the mains are
performing satisfactorily.

The American girl drank three large glasses of Moselle in addition to the dry sherry she had had as a starter with the shrimp
cocktail and whatever else she had tucked away in the lounge
before dinner, all of which was clearly proving too much for her.
She became increasingly voluble and less restrained as the evening
wore on although she still seemed in full control of her faculties as
far as giving me the widest possible berth was concerned. Which
of course suited me very well. I could listen and watch without
appearing to do so and without the strain of exchanging politeness
for provocation.

Her manner with His Excellency was becoming outrageously
familiar and domineering. She would occasionally leave him hanging on a word she had just spoken while she turned to fling another at Major Ossai whom she now addressed only as Johnson.
And wonder of wonders she even referred to the Chief of Staff,
General Lango, as Ahmed on one occasion. And for these effron-
teries she got nothing but grins of satisfaction from the gentlemen
in question. Unbelievable!

But we hadn't seen noth'n yet. Without any kind of preamble
she began reading His Excellency and his subjects a lecture on the
need for the country to maintain its present (quite unpopular,

needless to say) levels of foreign debt servicing currently running at slightly more than fifty-one percent of total national export earnings. Why? As a *quid pro quo* for increased American aid in surplus grains for our drought provinces!

"Have you been reading editorials in the *National Gazette* lately?" I asked in utter dumbfoundment.

"Yes, Johnson kindly showed me some comments earlier in the week. The editor who I hear is a Marxist of sorts appears to imagine he can eat his cake as well as have it, as we all tend to do this side of democracy. Admiring Castro may be fine if you don't have to live in Cuba or even Angola. But the strange fact is that Dr. Castro, no matter what he says, has never defaulted in his obligations to the international banking community. He says to others, 'Don't pay,' while making sure he doesn't fall behind himself in his repayments. What we must remember is that banks are not houses of charity. They're there to lend money at a fair and reasonable profit. If you deny them their margin of profit by borrowing and not paying back they will soon have to shut down their operations and we shall all go back to saving our money in grandmother's piggy-bags."

"Or inside old mattresses," added His Excellency whose deferential attitude to this piece of impertinence had given me a greater shock than anything I could think of in recent times. Deference and a countenance of martyred justification. He seemed to be saying to the girl, "Go on; tell them. I have gone hoarse shouting the very same message to no avail." And *them* in the context was *me*.

What I did when the dancing started may need a little background. We left the dinner-table and reconvened in the greater ease of the lounge for coffee and liqueur during which His Excellency and Lou were ensconced in deep and intense conversation on a sofa.

Then suddenly I heard my name. "Beatrice, come and sit here by me," he ordered patting the sofa on the other side of him. "African Chiefs are always polygamists." Naturally this was greeted with an explosion of laughter. He seemed a little tipsy to me. "Polygamy is for Africa what monotony is for Europe," he pronounced into the still raging flames of laughter stoking them recklessly to the peril of the rafters. I think the girl beside him had chipped in "And America!" but I can't bet on it, such was the uproar.

Before his voice had impinged on my thoughts I had temporarily withdrawn into them while physically appearing to attend to the Commissioner of Works struggling overconscientiously with an almost casual comment from General Lango that our highways break up even as they are being laid unlike highways he had seen in Europe and America and even Kenya. The Commissioner who had obviously been long enough in contact with professionals to have picked up a smattering of their language was explaining to a now inattentive general something about the weight of heavy lorries not being the real problem but rather their axle weight or something to that effect.

At that point a renewed sense of questioning had assailed me and I had withdrawn to attend to it. Why am I here? Why was I sent for? Obviously the reason that had first offered itself that it might have to do with mediating between two old friends (even in the absence of one of them) could hardly stand a chance now. Why was I there then? To meet this American girl and arrange to give her the woman's angle. That was it! I had been dragged here to wait upon this cheeky girl from Arizona or somewhere. Fine. We shall see!

And then came the master's voice summoning me to have my turn in the bedchamber of African polygamy!

The first time it happened I was a student in England. My boyfriend had taken me to an end-of-year dance at St. Pancras Town Hall. It was crowded and we eventually had to share a table with someone my boyfriend knew who was already seated with a white girl. After a couple of dances I whispered into Guy's ear that we should exchange partners out of politeness. After two dances with the white girl Guy went completely berserk. He would withdraw with her to the farthest corner of the huge dance-hall and stay there at the end of one dance waiting for the band to strike up another number. The white girl's boyfriend danced a couple of numbers with me and vanished altogether. So I found myself dancing with strangers who had come to the party with no girls of their own. I became *kabu kaboo*, for the first time in my life.

When Guy and the girl finally showed up again at our table during a longish interval and he promptly took off to buy drinks, the girl said to me in her heavy Cockney as she peered into her handbag mirror to mend her rouge: "Your boys like us, ain' they?

My girlfriend saiz it's the Desdemona complex. Nice word Des-de-mona. Italian I think. Ever hear it?"

So I was locked in combat again with Desdemona, this time itinerant and, worse still, not over some useless black trash in England but the sacred symbol of my nation's pride, such as it was. Corny? So be it!

So I threw myself between this enemy and him. I literally *threw* myself at him like a loyal batman covering his endangered commander with his own body and receiving the mortal bullet in his place.

I did it shamelessly. I cheapened myself. God! I did it to your glory like the dancer in a Hindu temple. Like Esther, oh yes like Esther for my long-suffering people.

And was I glad the king was slowly but surely responding! Was I glad! The big snake, the royal python of a gigantic erection began to stir in the shrubbery of my shrine as we danced closer and closer to soothing airs, soothing our ancient bruises together in the dimmed lights. Fully aroused he clung desperately to me. And I took him then boldly by the hand and led him to the balcony railings to the breathtaking view of the dark lake from the pinnacle of the hill. And there told him my story of Desdemona. Something possessed me as I told it.

"If I went to America today, to Washington DC, would I, could I, walk into a White House private dinner and take the American President hostage. And his Defence Chief and his Director of CIA?"

"Oh don't be such a racist, Beatrice. I am surprised at you. A girl of your education!"

And he stormed away and left me standing alone on the balcony. I stood there staring at the dark lake and my tears flowed in torrents. I was aware of people from the room coming stealthily to the door of the balcony to have a peep. I did not see them; I was merely aware of their coming and retreating again into their dimmed lights and music. Then I heard bold footsteps on the terrazzo floor of the balcony and Major Ossai's voice behind me: "There is a car waiting downstairs to take you home."

7

FOR WEEKS AND MONTHS after I had definitely taken on the challenge of bringing together as many broken pieces of this tragic history as I could lay my hands on I still could not find a way to begin. Anything I tried to put down sounded wrong—either too abrupt, too indelicate or too obvious—to my middle ear.

So I kept circling round and round. Until last Saturday; after my weekly ordeal at the market. Hot and grimy from hours of haggling in the sun and now home and fighting for breath after the steep climb with the grocery up the dizzying circular staircase to the kitchen table I dumped the bags and wraps there in transit as it were to get a cold drink, and never went back. Quite extraordinary. Normally I am very particular about the meat especially which I must wash and boil right away or wash with a dash of Milton solution and put in the freezer. But, after gulping down half of the tall glass of lemonade, I carried the rest under a strange propulsion to the spare bedroom which I had turned into a kind of study and began scribbling and went on right into the night. I was vaguely aware of Agatha's voice saying good evening at the door at some point but took no special interest in it.

The single idea or power or whatever that flashed through my mind that afternoon as soon as I got out of the traffic into the open stretch between the Secretariat Buildings and the GRA had seized me by the forelock! But although it got me seated it neglected to dictate the words to me because on Monday I had to begin all over again having thrown away all that labour of Saturday and Sunday. But the elation was undiminished. I had started. The discarded pages and the nearly spoilt meat seemed like a necessary ritual or a sacrifice to whoever had to be appeased for this audacity of rushing in where sensible angels would fear to tread, or rather for pulling up one of those spears thrust into the ground by the men in the hour of their defeat and left there in the circle of their last dance together.

My housegirl, Agatha, goes to one of these new rapturous churches with which Bassa is infested nowadays. Her sect is called YESMI, acronym for Yahwe Evangelical Sabbath Mission Inc., and apparently forbids her from as much as striking a match on Saturdays to light a stove. She leaves the house before I am out of bed and stays away all day. Around five she returns looking like a wilted cocoyam leaf and eats bread and cold stew or any odd scrap of food she can lay her hands on or even plain *garri* soaked in iced water with eight lumps of sugar and a whole tin of milk. I discovered, though, that if I struck the match and lit the stove and warmed up the food she would not be prohibited from eating it. But I made it clear to her from the start that I wasn't ready yet to wash and wipe the feet of my paid help. It is quite enough that I have to do the weekly grocery at the Gelegele market while she is clapping hands and rolling eyes and hips at some hairy-chested prophet in white robes and shower cap.

But something had happened not so long ago to change our lives and, on this particular Saturday, Agatha must have been so overcome by the sheer power of something else quite extraordinary happening in the house that she set the law of the Sabbath aside and put away the meat, already a little high, and the wilting vegetables. Or perhaps, being no stranger herself to possession, she could recognize it quite quickly in another!

My name is Beatrice, but most of my friends call me either B or BB. And my enemies—that's one lesson I've learnt from the still unbelievable violences we went through—that even little people like me could also rate enemies. I had naively assumed that enemies were the privilege of the great. But no. Here was I keeping quite a few hands busy fashioning barbed and poisoned aliases for me as readily as they were renaming the heroes fallen, as our half-literate journalists say, from grace to grass.

It was quite a revelation, and quite frankly it bothered me for a while, especially the crude insinuations of what our men sniggeringly call bottom-power. But then I said to myself, what do I care really, why should I ask the world to interrupt its business for no other reason than to find out what one insignificant female did or did not do in a calamity that consumed so many and so much? A little matter of personal pride for me perhaps but so what?

Still there is one account of me it seems I will never get used to, which can still bring tears to my eyes. Ambitious. Me ambitious! How? And it is this truly unjust presentation that's forcing me to expose my life on these pages to see if perhaps there are aspects of me I had successfully concealed even from myself. Pretentious journalists hoping to catch the attention of the new military rulers created an image of me as "the latter-day Madame Pompadour" who manipulated generals and patronized writers.

Throughout my life I have never sought attention; not even as a child. I can see, looking back at my earliest memories, a little girl completely wrapped up in her own little world—a world contained, like Russian dolls, inside the close-fitting world of our mission-house, itself enclosed snugly within the world of the Anglican Church compound. It was a remarkable place. Apart from the church building itself there were the two school buildings, the parsonage, the catechist's house, the long-house in which the school teachers had, according to their rank, a shared room, a full room or even two rooms. Male teachers, that is. The female teachers lived in the smallest building of all, a three-room thatched house set, for protection I suppose, between the pastor and the catechist. In the farthest corner of the compound was the churchyard, a little overgrown, where one of my sisters, Emily, lay buried.

World inside a world inside a world, without end. *Uwa-t'uwa* in our language. As a child how I thrilled to that strange sound with its capacity for infinite replication till it becomes the moan of the rain in the ear as it opened and closed, opened and closed. Uwa t'uwa t'uwa t'uwa; Uwa t'uwa.

Uwa-t'uwa was a building-block of my many solitary games. I could make and mould all kinds of thoughts with it. I could even rock it from side to side like my wooden baby with the chipped ear.

My friendship with the strange words began no doubt quite early when I first recognized it and welcomed it at the end of my father's family prayers to begin or end the day—prayers so long that I would float in and out of sleep and sometimes keel over and fall on my side. *Uwa-t'uwa* was always the end of the ordeal and we all, would shout: *Amen! Good-morning, sah! good morning mah!* or good night for evening prayers.

One evening, some devil seized hold of me as the words *uwa t'uwa* were pronounced and jolted me into wakefulness. Without any premeditation whatsoever I promptly raised a childish hymn of thanksgiving: uwa-t'uwa! uwa-t'uwa! uwa-t'uwa! uwa-t'uwa! t'uwa t'uwa! uwa t'uwa!

My sisters' giggles fuelled my reckless chant.

My father sprang to his feet with Amen barely out of his mouth, reached for the cane he always had handy and gave us all a good thrashing. As we cried ourselves to sleep on our separate mats that night my sisters saw fit to promise through their snivelling to deal with me in the morning.

He was a very stern man, my father—as distant from us children as from our poor mother. As I grew older I got to know that his whip was famous not only in our house and in the schoolhouse next door but throughout the diocese. One day the local chief paid him a visit and as they say in the long outer room we called the piazza eating kolanut with alligator pepper and I was hanging around as I was fond of doing when there was company, the chief was full of praise for my father for the good training he was giving the children of the village through his whip. My father, with a wistful look I had never seen on his face before, was telling the chief of a certain headmaster in 1940 who was praised by some white inspectors who came from England to look at schools in their colonies and found his school the most quiet in West Africa. "Das right!" said the chief in English.

I remember the incident well because we were doing the map of West Africa in our geography class at the time. So I left my father

and his friend and went to my raffia schoolbag and pulled out my
West African Atlas and was greatly impressed by the size of the
territory over which the 1940 headmaster was champion.

There were times I suspected that he may have flogged our poor
mother, though I must say in recognition of the awesomeness of
the very thought that I never actually saw it happen. None of my
sisters had seen it either, or if they had they preferred not to tell
me, for they never took me much into confidence. Looking back
on it I am sometimes amazed at the near-conspiracy in which they
circled me most of the time. I had this strong suspicion nevertheless, which I could neither confirm nor deny because on those
occasions my father always took the precaution to lock the door of
their room. She would come out afterwards (having unlocked the
door, or perhaps he did) wiping her eyes with one corner of her
wrapper, too proud or too adult to cry aloud like us. It didn't
happen too often, though. But it always made me want to become
a sorceress that could say *"Die!"* to my father and he would die as
in the folk-tale. And then, when he had learnt his lesson, I would
bring him back to life and he would never touch his whip again.

And then one day as my mother came out wiping her eyes I
rushed to her and hugged her legs but instead of pressing me to
herself as I had expected she pushed me away so violently that I hit
my head against the wooden mortar. After that I didn't feel any
more like telling my father to die. I couldn't have been more than
seven or eight at the time but I know I had this strong feeling then
—extraordinary, powerful and adult—that my father and my
mother had their own world, my three sisters had theirs and I was
alone in mine. And it didn't bother me at all then, my aloneness,
nor has it done so since.

I didn't realize until much later that my mother bore me a huge
grudge because I was a girl—her fifth in a row though one had
died—and that when I was born she had so desperately prayed for
a boy to give my father. This knowledge came to me by slow
stages which I won't go into now. But I must mention that in
addition to Beatrice they had given me another name at my baptism, Nwanyibuife—A female is also something. Can you beat
that? Even as a child I disliked the name most intensely without
being aware of its real meaning. It merely struck me at that point
that I knew of nobody else with the name; it seemed fudged!
Somehow I disliked it considerably less in its abridged form,

Buife. Perhaps it was the *nwanyi,* the female half of it that I particularly resented. My father was so insistent on it. "Sit like a female!" or "Female soldier" which he called me as he lifted me off the ground with his left hand and gave me three stinging smacks on the bottom with his right the day I fell off the cashew tree.

But I didn't set out to write my autobiography and I don't want to do so. Who am I that I should inflict my story on the world? All I'm trying to say really is that as far as I can remember I have always been on my own and never asked to be noticed by anybody. Never! And I don't recall embarking ever on anything that would require me to call on others. Which meant that I never embarked on anything beyond my own puny powers. Which meant finally that I couldn't be ambitious.

I am very, very sensitive about this—I don't mind admitting it.

That I got involved in the lives of the high and mighty was purely accidental and was not due to any scheming on my part. In the first place, they all became high and mighty after I met them; not before.

Chris was not a Commissioner when I met him but a mere editor of the *National Gazette.* That was way back in civilian days. And if I say that Chris did all the chasing I am not boasting or anything. That was simply how it was. And I wasn't being coy either. It was a matter of experience having taught me in my little lonely world that I had to be wary. Some people even say I am suspicious by nature. Perhaps I am. Being a girl of maybe somewhat above average looks, a good education, a good job you learn quickly enough that you can't open up to every sweet tongue that comes singing at your doorstep. Nothing very original really. Every girl knows that from her mother's breast although thereafter some may choose to be dazzled into forgetfulness for one reason or another. Or else they panic and get stampeded by the thought that time is passing them by. That's when you hear all kinds of nonsense talk from girls: Better to marry a rascal than grow a moustache in your father's compound; better an unhappy marriage than an unhappy spinsterhood; better marry Mr. Wrong in this world than wait for Mr. Right in heaven; all marriage is *how-for-do;* all men are the same; and a whole baggage of other foolishnesses like that.

I was determined from the very beginning to put my career first and, if need be, last. That every woman wants a man to complete her is a piece of male chauvinist bullshit I had completely rejected before I knew there was anything like Women's Lib. You often hear our people say: But that's something you picked up in England. Absolute rubbish! There was enough male chauvinism in my father's house to last me seven reincarnations!

So when Chris came along I was not about to fly into his arms for the asking, although I decidedly liked him. And strangely enough he himself gave me a very good reason for caution. He was so handsome and so considerate, so unlike all the brash fellows the place was crawling with in the heady prosperity of the oil boom that I decided he simply had to be phony!

Unreasonable? Perhaps yes. But I can't be blamed for the state of the world. Haven't our people said that a totally reasonable wife is always pregnant? Scepticism is a girl's number six. You can't blame her; she didn't make her world so tough.

One of my girlfriends—a more sensible and attractive person you never saw—except that she committed the crime to be twenty-six and still unmarried; she was taken by her fiancé to meet his people in some backwater village of his when an aunt or something of his made a proverb fully and deliberately to her hearing that if *ogili* was such a valuable condiment no one would leave it lying around for rats to stumble upon and dig into! Well, you can trust Comfort! The insult didn't bother her half as much as her young man's silence. So she too kept silent until they got back to the city and inside her flat. Then she told him she had always suspected he was something of a rat. I can hear Comfort saying that and throwing him out of the flat! Now she is happily married to a northerner and has two kids.

My experience with Chris was, of course, entirely different. He seemed to understand everything about me without asking a single question. In those first days he would very often startle me with insights about little things like colours or food or behaviour I liked or didn't like and I would ask: But how did you know? And he would smile and say: I am a journalist, remember; it's my business to find out. Just the way he said it would melt any woman.

Emotionally then I had no reservations whatsoever about Chris from the word go. But intellectually I had to call into full play my sense of danger. In a way I felt like two people living inside one skin, not two hostile tenants but two rather friendly people, two people different enough to be interesting to each other without being incompatible.

I recall clearly that the very first time we met the thought that flashed through my mind was to be envious of his wife. And yet it was weeks before I could bring myself to probe delicately about her, not directly through Chris but surreptitiously via a third party, Ikem. But such was the carefully balanced contrariness induced in me by Chris that the news of his wife's nonexistence, though it admittedly gave me a measure of relief, did not bring total satisfaction. There was a small residue of disappointment at the bottom of the cool draught, so to say. Was it the disappointment of the gambler or the born fighter cheated out of the intoxication of contest and chancy victory? Or did the affair lose some of its attraction for me because deep inside I was not unlike the dreadful, cynical aunt in the village who believed that nothing so good could wait this long for me to stumble upon? What an awful thought!

Even when I found myself begin to pick and choose what dress or what make-up to wear whenever I thought I might run into him I simply dismissed it as a little harmless excitement I was entitled to indulge in as long as I remembered to keep a sharp look-out.

It was in a supermarket one Saturday morning, I think, that Ikem gave me an opening to ask about Chris's wife. I don't remember the exact details now but I think it was a vague invitation to go with him, his girlfriend and Chris to some friend of their's birthday party. I said no for one reason or the other but also managed to ask as offhandedly as I could where Chris's wife was anyway; or was he one of those who will pack their wife conveniently away to her mother and the village midwife as soon as she misses her period?

"BB!" he screamed in mock outrage, his large eyes beaming with wicked pleasure. "Looking at your demure lips . . ."

"I know, I know. You couldn't tell, could you? Like looking at a king's mouth you couldn't tell, could you?"

"Or looking at a lady's gait, you couldn't tell, could you?"

"Enough!" I said in my own counterfeit outrage, my index finger against my lips. "All I asked you was where your friend packs his wife."

"There is no wife, my dear. So you can rest easy."

"Me! Wetin concern me there."

"Plenty plenty. I been see am long time, my dear."

"See what? I beg commot for road," and I made to push my trolley past him to the cashier but he grabbed my arm and pulled me back and proceeded to give me in loud whispers accompanied by conspiratorial backward glances a long and completely absurd account of all the actions and reactions he had meticulously observed between Chris and me in the last few months which could only have one meaning—his friend, Chris, done catch!

"You de craze well, well . . . I beg make you commot for road."

That was the year I got back from England. I had known Ikem for years—right from my London University days. How he did it I can't tell but he became instantly like a brother to me. He had completed his studies two or three years earlier and was just knocking about London doing odd jobs for publishers, reading his poetry at the Africa Centre and such places and writing for Third World journals, before his friends at home finally persuaded him to return and join them in nation-building. "Such crap!" he would say later in remembrance.

When he finally left for home I was just getting into my degree year at Queen's College and we had become very close indeed. There was a short period when the relationship veered and teetered on the brink of romance but we got it back to safety and I went on with Guy, my regular boyfriend and he with his breathless succession of girlfriends.

I have sat and talked and argued with Ikem on more things serious and unserious than I can remember doing with any other living soul. Naturally I think he is a fantastic writer and it has given me such wonderful encouragement to have him praise the odd short story and poem I have scribbled from time to time. I don't even mind too much that his way of praising my style was to call it muscular on one occasion and masculine on another! When I pointed this out to him jokingly as a sure sign of his chauvinism he was at first startled and then he smiled one of those total smiles of his that revealed the innocent child behind the mask of beard and learned fierceness.

In the last couple of years we have argued a lot about what I have called the chink in his armoury of brilliant and original ideas. I tell him he has no clear role for women in his political thinking; and he doesn't seem to be able to understand it. Or didn't until near the end.

"How can you say that BB?" he would cry, almost in despair.

And I understand the meaning of his despair too. For here's a man, who has written a full-length novel and a play on the Women's War of 1929 which stopped the British administration cold in its tracks, being accused of giving no clear political role to women. But the way I see it is that giving women today the same role which traditional society gave them of intervening only when everything else has failed is not enough, you know, like the women in the Sembene film who pick up the spears abandoned by their defeated menfolk. It is not enough that women should be the court of last resort because the last resort is a damn sight too far and too late!

That was about the only serious reservation I had about Ikem's political position. I have to admit that, although he tended to be somewhat cavalier with his girlfriends and has even been called unprincipled by no less a friend than Chris, he did in fact have the most profound respect for three kinds of women: peasants, market women and intellectual women.

He could be considerate to a fault and I have known him to go to great lengths of personal inconvenience to help a lady in distress. I still have goose-flesh just thinking of one bitterly cold winter night he got himself stranded on the last train in London and nearly caught his death on my account.

I had been foolish enough to telephone him after I had suffered one of the most humiliating evenings of my life in the hands of my boyfriend, Guy, at a Nigerian Christmas dance at the St. Pancras Town Hall. I wasn't really asking Ikem to set out for my place at that hour but just needed to talk to someone like him, someone different from that noisy, ragtag crowd of illiterate and insensitive young men our country was exporting as plentifully at the time as its crude oil. But apparently I sounded so out of my mind on the telephone that Ikem donned his wool cap and muffler and his coat and headed into the snow and caught the last train in a South London station well after midnight. When he finally made it to my door, after an extended adventure on night buses, it was half-past three in the morning. I felt so bad I didn't need any further comfort for myself. I was ready to start cooking whatever meal would make him warm. Rice? Semolina? Plantain? He shook his head, his lips too frozen to speak. In the end all I could persuade him to take was a cup of coffee without cream or sugar; and he doffed his coat, slumped on the bed-sitter and went to sleep instantly. I stripped my bed of the last blanket and piled it on him.

Of all the absurd things people have found to say about us lately the most ridiculous was to portray Ikem as one of my trio of lovers. Damn it, the fellow was a brother to me!

In the last year I didn't see too much of him—a couple of times at Mad Medico's, a few times at parties and one or two visits to my house. He was never a great one for home visits but every one he made left a lasting impression.

The final one was in August. I remember it was August because he walked into my flat out of a huge and unseasonal tropical storm. The doorbell screeched in the kitchen followed by loud, panic bangs on the front door. I sprang up not to answer it but to bar the way to my maid, Agatha, who had dashed out of the kitchen like a rabbit smoked out of its hole and was making for the front door. No matter how I tried to explain it with details of multiple rape and murder, Agatha remained blissfully impervious to the peril of armed robbers surrounding us. She simply says yesmah and nosemah to everything you tell her and goes right ahead doing whatever she was doing before.

"Go back to the kitchen!" I thundered at her and with the same voice turned to the presence outside my door. I had been feeling somewhat more protected lately since I had all doors and windows in the flat reinforced with iron grills so that even if the fellow outside did manage to knock down the outer wooden door he would still have to face the iron, all of which gave you some time to plan your escape. Even so I stood well away from the front door with one eye on the kitchen exit and the fire-escape beyond it.

"Who is that?" I shouted. Whoever it was didn't seem to hear and continued ringing the alarm and banging on the door. Well, I wasn't going to budge either and continued screaming who? This went on literally for minutes and I was getting scared when he either heard me or else it occurred to him independently to use his voice instead of his fists. And I caught it in one of those brief spells when a storm pauses to take a deep breath. I unchained the iron grill and unlocked the door.

"It wasn't raining in my place," he shouted sheepishly as he came in. "I ran full tilt into it just there around the Secretariat. It was literally like barging into a pillar of rain, you know. You could stand there with the forward foot wet and the other dry."

"Come on in. We'll go hoarse shouting out here."

He left his dripping umbrella with my potted plants on the land-

ing and followed me into the parlour. Once inside, with door and
window-louvres tightly shut, the noise of the rain receded dramatically to a distant background leaving us in muffled cosiness.

"When we were children," Ikem said as he threw himself into
the sofa and began to remove his wet shoes and tuck his socks
inside them, "August used to be a dry month. August Break we
called it. The geography textbooks explained it, the farmer in the
village expected it. The August Break never failed in those days."

"Really?"

"What's happened to the days of my youth, BB?"

"Wasted, squandered, Ikem. Lost for ever, I'm afraid."

"I hoped you would not say that. Not today. Oh, well."

"What's wrong with today. Your birthday or something?"

"I have no birthdays. There was no registration of births and
deaths in my village when I was born. Signed Notary Public." I
laughed and he joined me . . . "I wasn't one of your spoilt maternity births. I arrived on banana leaves behind the thatched
house, not on white bed sheets . . . Those are lovely flowers,
what are they?"

"I have never known you to notice flowers or women's clothes
and rubbish like that before. What's the matter."

"I'm sorry, BB, that's a lovely dress. And lovely flowers, what
are they?"

"Agatha is roasting corn and *ube.* Would you like some. Or with
coconut if you prefer . . ."

"I prefer both *ube* and coconut."

"Glutton!"

"That's right! Terminal stage when it attacks your grammar!
You still haven't told me what these flowers are. I may not have
noticed flowers before but I do now. It's never too late, is it?"

"No. It's called hydrangea."

As I went into the kitchen to open the store for Agatha to get a
coconut out I kept asking myself what Ikem might be up to. Was it
Chris? Had their relationship, dangerously bumpy in recent
months, taken a nose-dive now for the crash? Ikem always avoided
complaining about Chris to me. Was he going to break his own
scrupulous practice for once? When I returned to the parlour he
had lifted the vase of flowers to his nose and was sniffing it.

I ate my corn with *ube* and he his with *ube* and coconut in alter-
nate mouthfuls. Outside, the storm raged the way I like my storms

—far away, its violent thunder and lightning distanced and muted
as in a movie. I would have felt completely comfortable if Ikem
had not been behaving a little strangely. Let's hope it's the storm, I
prayed. Tropical storms can do so many different things to different creatures. That I have known from childhood. My older sister
Alice always ran around the yard, if our father happened to be out,
singing a childish rain song:

> ogwogwo mmili
> takumei ayolo!

Finally exhausted she would come indoors shivering, eyes red and
popping out, teeth clattering away and make for the kitchen fire.
As for me whom she nicknamed salt, or less kindly Miss Goat, on
account of my distaste for getting wet, my preference was to roll
myself in a mat on the floor and inside my dark, cylindrical capsule
play my silent game of modulating the storm's song by pressing
my palms against my ears and taking them off, rhythmically. There
was for me no greater luxury in those days than to sleep through
nightrain on a Friday knowing there was neither school nor church
in the morning to worry about.

"When you were little," I asked Ikem, "what did you do when
it rained like this?"

"But I told you it never rained at all in August. We had a month
of dry weather called the August Break."

"OK! In July then, or September."

"When I was really little I used to take off my scanty clothes and
run into it."

"Singing *ogwogwo mmili takumei ayolo?*"

"Did you sing to the rain too?" He fairly jumped with excitement.

"No, but my older sister did."

"Oh . . . what did *you* do?"

"I listened. The rain sang to me."

"Lucky girl! What did it say, the rain?"

"Uwa t'uwa t'uwa t'uwa; tooo . . . waaa . . . tooo . . . waa
Dooo—daaa . . . Booo—baaa . . . Shooo—shaaa . . .
Cooo—caaa . . . Looo—laaa . . . Mooo—maaa . . ."

"Pooo—paaa," said Ikem. "Great song!"

"BB, you may be wondering why I am behaving so strangely today. Well, I've come on a mission the like of which I'd never undertaken before . . . I've come to thank you for the greatest present one human being can give another. The gift of insight. That's what you gave me and I want to say thank you."

"Insight? Me? Insight into what?"

"Into the world of women."

I held back a facetious comment trembling on my lip. Ikem's sudden change and extraordinary manner forbade its utterance. I held back and listened to this strange annunciation.

"You told me a couple of years ago, do you remember, that my thoughts were unclear and reactionary on the role of the modern woman in our society. Do you remember?"

"I do."

"I resisted your charge . . ."

"It wasn't a charge."

"It damn well was! But I resisted. Vehemently. But the amazing thing was that the more I read your charge sheet . . ."

"Oh my God!"

". . . the less impressive my plea became. My suspension from the *Gazette* has done wonders for me. I have been able to sit and think things through. I now realize you were right and I was wrong."

"Oh come on, Ikem. You know I detest all born-again people."

"Don't be facetious!"

"I'm sorry. Go ahead. What happened?"

"Nothing happened. It simply dawned on me two mornings ago that a novelist must listen to his characters who after all are created to wear the shoe and point the writer where it pinches."

"Now hold it! Are you suggesting I am a character in your novel?"

"BB, you've got to be serious, or I will leave. I mean it. I'm already losing my train of thought."

"I won't breathe another word. Please go on."

"One of the things you told me was that my attitude to women was too respectful."

"I didn't."

"You bloody well did. And you were damn right. You charged me with assigning to women the role of a fire-brigade after the house has caught fire and been virtually consumed. Your charge has forced me to sit down and contemplate the nature of oppression—how flexible it must learn to be, how many faces it must learn to wear if it is to succeed again and again."

He dug his hand into his shirt pocket and pulled out a folded sheet of paper and carefully unfolded it on his knee. "I wrote this strange love-letter last night. May I read it?" I nodded.

"The original oppression of Woman was based on crude denigration. She caused Man to fall. So she became a scapegoat. No, not a scapegoat which might be blameless but a culprit richly deserving of whatever suffering Man chose thereafter to heap on her. That is Woman in the Book of Genesis. Out here, our ancestors, without the benefit of hearing about the Old Testament, made the very same story differing only in local colour. At first the Sky was very close to the Earth. But every evening Woman cut off a piece of the Sky to put in her soup pot or, as in another version, she repeatedly banged the top end of her pestle carelessly against the Sky whenever she pounded the millet or, as in yet another rendering—so prodigious is Man's inventiveness, she wiped her kitchen hands on the Sky's face. Whatever the detail of Woman's provocation, the Sky finally moved away in anger, and God with it.

"Well, that kind of candid chauvinism might be OK for the rugged taste of the Old Testament. The New Testament required a more enlightened, more refined, more loving even, strategy— ostensibly, that is. So the idea came to Man to turn his spouse into the very Mother of God, to pick her up from right under his foot where she'd been since Creation and carry her reverently to a nice, corner pedestal. Up there, her feet completely off the ground she will be just as irrelevant to the practical decisions of running the world as she was in her bad old days. The only difference is that now Man will suffer no guilt feelings; he can sit back and congratulate himself on his generosity and gentlemanliness.

"Meanwhile our ancestors out here, unaware of the New Testament, were working out independently a parallel subterfuge of their own. *Nneka,* they said. Mother is supreme. Let us keep her in reserve until the ultimate crisis arrives and the waist is broken and hung over the fire, and the palm bears its fruit at the tail of its leaf. Then, as the world crashes around Man's ears, Woman in her supremacy will descend and sweep the shards together.

"Do I make sense?"

"As always. Go on."

"Thank you, BB. I owe that insight to you. I can't tell you what the new role for Woman will be. I don't know. I should never have presumed to know. *You* have to tell us. We never asked you before. And perhaps because you've never been asked you may not have thought about it; you may not have the answer handy. But in that case everybody had better know who is *now* holding up the action."

"That's very kind of you!"

"That was the first part of this love-letter, the part I owe specifically to you. Here's the rest.

"The women are, of course, the biggest single group of oppressed people in the world and, if we are to believe the Book of Genesis, the very oldest. But they are not the only ones. There are others—rural peasants in every land, the urban poor in industrialized countries, Black people everywhere including their own continent, ethnic and religious minorities and castes in all countries. The most obvious practical difficulty is the magnitude and heterogeneity of the problem. There is no universal conglomerate of the oppressed. Free people may be alike everywhere in their freedom but the oppressed inhabit each their own peculiar hell. The present orthodoxies of deliverance are futile to the extent that they fail to recognize this. You know my stand on that. Every genuine artist feels it in his bones. The simplistic remedies touted by all manner of salesmen (including some who call themselves artists) will always fail because of man's stubborn antibody called surprise. Man will surprise by his capacity for nobility as well as for villainy. No system can change that. It is built into the core of man's free spirit.

"The sweeping, majestic visions of people rising victorious like a tidal wave against their oppressors and transforming their world with theories and slogans into a new heaven and a new earth of brotherhood, justice and freedom are at best grand illusions. The rising, conquering tide, yes; but the millennium afterwards, no! New oppressors will have been readying themselves secretly in the undertow long before the tidal wave got really going.

"Experience and intelligence warn us that man's progress in freedom will be piecemeal, slow and undramatic. Revolution may be necessary for taking a society out of an intractable stretch of quagmire but it does not confer freedom, and may indeed hinder it.

"Bloody reformist? That's a term of abuse it would be redundant to remind you I have had more than my fair share of invoking against others across the years. But I ask myself: beyond the pleasant glow that javelin of an epithet certainly brings to the heart of the righteous hurler what serious benefit can it offer to the solution of our problems? And I don't see any.

"Reform may be a dirty word then but it begins to look more and more like the most promising route to success in the real world. I limit myself to *most promising* rather than *only* for the simple reason that all certitude must now be suspect.

"Society is an extension of the individual. The most we can hope to do with a problematic individual psyche is to *re-form* it. No responsible psychoanalyst would aim to do more, for to do more, to overthrow the psyche itself, would be to unleash insanity. No. We can only hope to rearrange some details in the periphery of the human personality. Any disturbance of its core is an irresponsible invitation to disaster. Even a one-day-old baby does not make itself available for your root-and-branch psychological engineering, for it comes trailing clouds of immortality. What immortality? Its baggage of irreducible inheritance of genes. That is immortality.

"It has to be the same with society. You re-form it around what it is, its core of reality; not around an intellectual abstraction.

"None of this is a valid excuse for political inactivity or apathy. Indeed to understand it is an absolute necessity for meaningful action, the knowledge of it being the only protective inoculation we can have against false hopes and virulent epidemics of gullibility.

"In the vocabulary of certain radical theorists contradictions are given the status of some deadly disease to which their opponents alone can succumb. But contradictions are the very stuff of life. If there had been a little dash of contradiction among the Gadarene swine some of them might have been saved from drowning.

"Contradictions if well understood and managed can spark off the fires of invention. Orthodoxy whether of the right or of the left is the graveyard of creativity.

"I didn't owe this insight to you, BB. I drank it in from my mother's breast. All I've ever needed since was confirmation. 'Do I contradict myself?' asked Walt Whitman. 'Very well, I contradict myself,' he sang defiantly. 'I am large, I contain multitudes.' Every artist contains multitudes. Graham Greene is a Roman Catholic, a partisan of Rome, if you like. Why then does he write so compulsively about bad, doubtful and doubting priests? Because a genuine artist, no matter what he says he believes, must feel in his blood the ultimate enmity between art and orthodoxy.

"Those who would see no blot of villainy in the beloved oppressed nor grant the faintest glimmer of humanity to the hated oppressor are partisans, patriots and party-liners. In the grand finale of things there will be a mansion also for them where they will be received and lodged in comfort by the single-minded demigods of their devotion. But it will not be in the complex and paradoxical cavern of Mother Idoto."

He tossed the handwritten paper across to me, saying, "I must go," and beginning to put his shoes back on. I stared at the paper, at the writing—elegant but at the same time, immensely powerful. He got up. I got up too and walked up to him. Impulsively he circled me in his embrace. I looked up at him and he began to kiss me. Everything inside me was dissolving; my knees were giving way under me; I was trembling violently and I seemed to be struggling for air.

"I think you better go," I managed to say. He released me slowly and I sank into a chair.

"Yes, I'd better be going."

And he was gone, not for now as I and perhaps he too thought, but forever. The storm had died down without our having been aware of it. All that was left of it now were tired twitches of intermittent lightning and the occasional, satiated hiccup of distant thunder.

8

Daughters

IDEMILI

THAT WE ARE SURROUNDED by deep mysteries is known to all but the incurably ignorant. But even they must concede the fact, indeed the inevitability, of the judiciously spaced, but nonetheless certain, interruptions in the flow of their high art to interject the word of their sponsor, the divinity that controls remotely but diligently the transactions of the marketplace that is their world.

In the beginning Power rampaged through our world, naked. So the Almighty, looking at his creation through the round undying eye of the Sun, saw and pondered and finally decided to send his daughter, Idemili, to bear witness to the moral nature of authority by wrapping around Power's rude waist a loincloth of peace and modesty.

She came down in the resplendent Pillar of Water, remembered now in legend only, but stumbled upon, some say, by the most fortunate in rare conditions of sunlight rarer even than the eighteen-year cycle of Odunke festivals and their richly arrayed celebrants leading garlanded cattle in procession through village pathways to sacrifice. It rises majestically from the bowl of the dark lake pushing itself upward and erect like the bole of the father of iroko trees its head commanding not the forest below but the very firmament of heaven.

At first that holy lake was the sole shrine to Idemili. But as people multiplied and spread across the world they built little shrines farther and farther away from the lake wherever they found good land and water and settled. Still their numbers continued to increase and outstrip the provisions of every new settlement; and so the search for land and water also continued.

As it happened, good land was more plentiful than good water and before long some hamlets too far from streams and springs were relieving their burning thirst with the juice of banana stems in the worst years of dry weather. Idemili, travelling through the country disguised as a hunter, saw this and on her return sent a stream from her lake to snake through the parched settlements all the way to Orimili, the great river which in generations to come strange foreigners would search out and rename the Niger.

A deity who does as he says never lacks in worshippers. Idemili's devotees increased in all the country between Omambala and Iguedo. But how could they carry to the farthest limits of their dispersal adequate memories of the majesty of the Pillar of Water standing in the dark lake?

Man's best artifice to snare and hold the grandeur of divinity always crumbles in his hands, and the more ardently he strives the more paltry and incongruous the result. So it were better he did not try at all; far better to ritualize that incongruity and by invoking the mystery of metaphor to hint at the most unattainable glory by its very opposite, the most mundane starkness—a mere stream, a tree, a stone, a mound of earth, a little clay bowl containing fingers of chalk.

Thus it came about that the indescribable Pillar of Water fusing earth to heaven at the navel of the black lake became in numberless shrine-houses across the country, a dry stick rising erect from the bare, earth floor.

It is to this emblem that a man who has achieved wealth of crop and livestock and now wishes to pin an eagle's feather on his success by buying admission into the powerful hierarchy of *ozo* must go to present himself and offer sacrifices before he can begin the ceremonies, and again after he has concluded them. His first visit is no more than to inform the Daughter of the Almighty of his ambition. He is accompanied by his daughter or, if he has only sons, by the daughter of a kinsman; but a daughter it must be. This young woman must stand between him and the Daughter of the Almighty before he can be granted a hearing. She holds his hand like a child in front of the holy stick and counts seven. Then she arranges carefully on the floor seven fingers of chalk, fragile symbols of peace, and then gets him to sit on them so lightly that not one single finger may be broken.

If all has gone well thus far he will then return to his compound and commence the elaborate and costly ceremonies of *ozo* with feasting and dancing to the entire satisfaction of his community and their ancient custom. Then he must go back to the Daughter of the Almighty to let her know that he has now taken the high and sacred title of his people.

Neither at the first audience nor at this second does Idemili deign to answer him directly. He must go away and await her sign and pleasure. If she finds him unworthy to carry the authority of *ozo* she simply sends death to smite him and save her sacred hierarchy from contamination and scandal. If, however, she approves of him the only sign she condescends to give—grudgingly and by indirection—is that he will still be about after three years. Such is Idemili's contempt for man's unquenchable thirst to sit in authority on his fellows.

The story goes that in the distant past a certain man handsome beyond compare but in randiness as unbridled as the odorous he-goat from the shrine of Udo planting his plenitude of seeds from a huge pod swinging between hind legs into she-goats tethered for him in front of numerous homesteads; this man, they said, finally desired also the *ozo* title and took the word to Idemili. She said nothing. He went away, performed the rites, took the eagle feather and the titular name Nwakibie, and returned to tell her what he had done. Again she said nothing. Then as a final ritual he took shelter according to custom for twenty-eight days in a bachelor's hut away from his many wives. But though he lived there in the day for all to see he would steal away at dead of night through circuitous moon-swept paths to the hut of a certain widow he had fancied for some time; for as he was wont to ask in his more waggish days: why will a man mounting a widow listen for foot-steps outside her hut when he knows how far her man has travelled?

On his way to resume his hard-lying pretence at cock-crow one morning who should he behold stretched right across his path its head lost in the shrubbery to the left and its tail likewise to the right? None other than Eke-Idemili itself, royal python, messenger of the Daughter of God—the very one who carries not a drop of venom in its mouth and yet is held in greater awe than the deadliest of serpents!

His circuitous way to the bachelor's hut thus barred, his feet obeying a power outside his will took him straight and true as an arrow to the consternation of his compound and his funeral.

BEATRICE NWANYIBUIFE did not know these traditions and legends of her people because they played but little part in her upbringing. She was born as we have seen into a world apart; was baptized and sent to schools which made much about the English and the Jews and the Hindu and practically everybody else but hardly put in a word for her forebears and the divinities with whom they had evolved. So she came to barely knowing who she was. Barely, we say though, because she did carry a vague sense more acute at certain critical moments than others of being two different people. Her father had deplored the soldier-girl who fell out of trees. Chris saw the quiet demure damsel whose still waters nonetheless could conceal deep overpowering eddies of passion that always almost sucked him into fatal depths. Perhaps Ikem alone came close to sensing the village priestess who will prophesy when her divinity rides her abandoning if need be her soup-pot on the fire, but returning again when the god departs to the domesticity of kitchen or the bargaining market-stool behind her little display of peppers and dry fish and green vegetables. He knew it better than Beatrice herself.

But knowing or not knowing does not save us from being known and even recruited and put to work. For, as a newly-minted proverb among her people has it, baptism (translated in their language as Water of God) is no antidote against possession by Agwu the capricious god of diviners and artists.

NWANYIBUIFE

WHEN SHE WAS MARCHED through the ranks of her erstwhile party comrades like a disgraced soldier just cashiered at a court-martial, his epaulette ripped off with his insignia of rank, she was strangely lucid. The soft voice conveying the news of the car waiting below had done it. Her sense of danger had been stabbed into hypersensitivity by the menace of that voice—quiet as before but flashing ever so briefly that glint of metal. Aha! This was the man who, as rumour has it, returned from an intensive course in a Latin American army and invented the simplest of tortures for preliminary interrogations. No messy or cumbersome machinery but a tiny piece of office equipment anyone could pick up in a stationery store and put in his pocket—a paper-stapler in short, preferably the Samsonite brand. Just place the hand where the paper should be—palm up or down doesn't really matter—and bang. The truth jumps out surprisingly fast, even from the hardest of cases.

This extended image flashed through Beatrice's mind in its completeness and in one instant. When she walked through the room behind the major she was likewise able to take in as if by some unseen radar revolving atop her head every detail of the scene. His Excellency was the only party missing from this still life. All the figures, except one, stared at her silently and uninhibitedly from whatever standing or sitting position they were in, the American girl's eyeballs in particular popping out of her head like the eyeballs of a violent idol. One man alone kept his gaze to the carpet on which he sat and seemed to doodle with his finger— Alhaji Mahmoud, Chairman of the Kangan/American Chamber of Commerce. He was the only person at the party just ended with whom Beatrice had not exchanged a single word that evening beyond a lukewarm hello at the introductions.

It was the same car, the same driver, the same escort. The two had jumped out to salute the Major as he brought their passenger down, opened the door of the car for her himself, slammed it shut after her and walked away without a word.

Naturally the journey back was silent. Which suited her perfectly. The sharp prick of physical anxiety caused by that glint of metal hidden inside the Major's velvet voice had passed quickly taking also with it the envelopment of utter desolation which had

preceded it and which it had so effectively punctured. What passed
through her mind and flowed through her senses during the midnight journey could not be assigned a simple name. It was more
complex than the succession of hot and cold flushes of malaria.
Indignation, humiliation, outrage, sorrow, pity, anger, vindictiveness and other less identifiable emotions swept back and forth
through her like successions of waves coming in, hitting shallow
bottom of shoreline, exploding in white froth and flowing back a
little tired, somewhat assuaged.

By rights she should not have slept that night. But she did; and a
deep and plumbless sleep it proved to be. She tumbled into it
without preparation from the brink of wakefulness, in full dress.
And her waking up was just as precipitate. One instant she was
virtually unconscious and the next she was totally awake, her eyes
and head absolutely clear. She was tranquil almost. Why? From
what source? Last night now seemed far away, like something remembered from a long and turbulent dream. Last night? It wasn't
last night. It was the same night, this night. It was still Saturday
night stroke Sunday morning. And it wasn't light yet.

She heard far away the crowing of a cock. Strange. She had not
before heard a cock crow in this Government Reserved Area.
Surely nobody here has been reduced to keeping poultry like common villagers. Perhaps some cook or steward or gardener had
knocked together an illegal structure outside his room in the Boys'
Quarters for a chicken-house. The British when they were here
would not have stood for it. They had totally and completely ruled
out the keeping of domestic animals in their reservation. Except
dogs, of course. That habit, strange to say, has survived but not for
the reasons the British established it. You wouldn't see any of their
black successors walking his dog today but you will find affixed to
the iron grill or barbed wire gate a stern warning: BEWARE OF
DOG, sometimes embellished with the likeness of an Alsatian or
German Shepherd's head with a flaming red tongue. Unfortunately armed robbers of Kangan do not stop at kicking dogs; they
shoot them.

Lying in bed clear-eyed and listening to the sounds of morning
was a new experience for Beatrice. As the faint light of dawn
began timidly to peer through gaps in window blinds and the high
fan-light of her bedroom she heard with a sudden pang of exulta-
tion the song of a bird she had heard so often in the mission

compound of her childhood but not, as far as she could tell, ever since; certainly never before in Bassa. She immediately sat up in her bed.

The bird, her mother had told her, was the chief servant of the king and every morning he asks the guards of the treasury: *Is the king's property correct? . . . Is the king's property correct? . . . The king's property . . . The king's property . . . Is the king's property correct?*

She got up, went into the living-room, picked up the front-door keys from the sideboard and unlocked the grill and the door and went out into her narrow balcony. Standing there among her potted plants she took in deep lungfuls of luxuriously cool, fresh morning air and watched streaks of light brightening slowly in the eastern sky. And then he spoke again, the diligent chamberlain: *Is the king's property correct?* And now she saw him against the light—a little dark-brownish fellow with a creamy belly and the faintest suggestion of a ceremonial plume on the crown of his head. He was perched on the taller of the two pine trees standing guard at the driveway into the block of flats.

Beatrice had never until now shown the slightest interest in birds and beyond vultures and cattle egrets hardly knew any of them by name. Now she was so taken with this conscientious palace official that she decided to find out his name as soon as possible. She knew there was an illustrated book called something like *The Common Birds of West Africa* . . . Again he demanded: *The king's property . . . The king's property . . . Is the king's property correct?*

Strange, but tears loomed suddenly in Beatrice's eyes as she spoke to the bird: "Poor fellow. You have not heard the news? The king's treasury was broken into last night and all his property carried away—his crown, his sceptre and all."

As she scanned the pine trees in the rapidly brightening light she saw that the caretaker of the crown jewels was not alone. There were literally scores of other birds hopping about the twigs preening themselves and making low trilling noises or short, sharp calls of satisfaction. He continued intermittently to make his strong-voiced inquiry until the sun had come up and then, as on a signal, the birds began to fly away in ones and twos and larger groups. Soon the tree was empty.

These birds, she thought, did not just arrive here this morning.

Here, quite clearly, is where they have always slept. Why have I not noticed them before?

Even her poor mother terrorized as she was by her woman's lot could fabricate from immemorial birdsong this tale of an African bird waking up his new world in words of English. A powerful flush of remembering now swept through her mind like a gust of wind and she recalled perfectly every circumstance of the story. Alas, her mother had only told, not invented it. The credit must go to a certain carpenter/comedian who played the accordion at village Christian wakes and performed such tricks as lifting a table between his teeth to chase away sleep from the eyes of mourners and relieve the tedium of hymns and pious testimonies.

Beatrice smiled wryly. So, two whole generations before the likes of me could take a first-class degree in English, there were already barely literate carpenters and artisans of British rule hacking away in the archetypal jungle and subverting the very sounds and legends of daybreak to make straight my way.

And my father—wonders shall never end as he would say—was he then also among these early morning road-makers-into-the-jungle-of-tongues? What an improbable thought! And yet all those resounding maxims he wielded like the hefty strokes of an axeman. *Cleanliness is next to godliness! Punctuality is the soul of business!* (A prelude this, she recalled with a smile now, to the flogging of late-comers to school on rainy mornings.) And then that gem of them all, his real favourite: *Procrastination is a lazy man's apology!* A maxim of mixed mintage, that; half-caste first-fruits of a heady misalliance. Or, as Ikem would have said, missionary mishmash!

She thawed fast and unexpectedly to the memory of this man who was her father and yet a total stranger, like the bird who lived and sang in her tree unknown to her till now.

She was still at the railing of her balcony when Agatha came in to begin her chores. "No breakfast for me Agatha," she called out cheerily to her. "But, make me a nice cup of coffee, please." She drank it at the same spot where she had taken her position at dawn.

A lizard red in head and tail, blue in trunk chased a drab-grey female furiously, as male lizards always seem to do, across the paved driveway. She darted through the hedges as though her life depended on it. Unruffled he took a position of high visibility at the centre of the compound and began to do his endless press-ups no doubt to impress upon the coy female, wherever she might be hiding in the shrubbery, the fact of his physical stamina.

At last she left the balcony and went indoors for a cold shower and then changed into a long, loose dress of blue *adire* embroidered in elaborate white patterns at the neck, chest, sleeves and hem. As she looked at herself in her bedroom mirror and liked what she saw, she thought: We can safely leave grey drabness in female attire to the family of lizards and visiting American journalists.

The case of the lizard is probably quite understandable. With the ferocious sexuality of her man she must need all the drabness she can muster for a shield.

She ate a grapefruit and drank a second cup of coffee while she flipped through the barren pages of the Sunday newspapers much of it full-page portrait obituaries even of grandfathers who had died fifty years ago but apparently still remembered every passing minute by their devoted descendants. And, wedged between memories of the living dead, equally fulsome portraiture of the still living who have "made it" in wealth or title or simply years. And once in a while among these dead-alive celebrities a disclaimer of someone newly disreputable, inserted by his former employer or partner using naturally a photograph of the unflattering quality of a police WANTED poster.

She tossed the papers away irritably wondering why one must keep on buying and trying to read such trash. Except that if you didn't you couldn't avoid the feeling that you might be missing something important, few of us, alas having the strength of will to resist that false feeling. She got up and put Onyeka Onwenu's "One Love" on the stereo and returned to the sofa, threw her head on the back-rest and shut her eyes.

As the morning wore on she seemed to become less and less composed. She looked at her watch frequently. Once, after she had changed a record she picked up the telephone, heard the dialling tone and replaced.

When finally it rang she looked at her watch again. It was eleven exactly. She let the telephone ring five or six times and might have left it longer had Agatha not rushed in from the kitchen to answer it.

It was who she thought it was. Chris.

"So you are back," he joked.

"Yes, I am back," she answered.

"Anything the matter?"

"Like what?"

"Are you all right, BB?"

"Why, of course. Do I sound as if I might not be all right?"

"Yes, you do . . . Are you alone?"

"What do you mean?"

"Look, I'm coming over. See you."

Twenty minutes later his car pulled up outside. Beatrice went not to the front door but to the kitchen door first, opened it and told Agatha that she was expecting someone and did not wish to be disturbed when he came up. Agatha's saucy and suggestive look at this news led Beatrice to lock the kitchen door altogether. Then she went to answer the doorbell.

Chris decided to take the bull by the horn. As soon as he was let in he asked how the party went.

"Party? But that was last night."

"Yes, it was last night. And I am asking how did it go?"

"It went all right."

They were both seated now, she on the sofa, he on a chair across the low centre table standing on a brown circular rug. They sat staring at each other for minutes, if not hours. Chris was completely at a loss. He had never had to cope with BB in such a mood and was quite unprepared. At last he got up, walked a few steps and stopped in front of her.

"Will you be good enough, BB, to tell me in what way I have now offended you."

"Offended me? Who said you offended me?"

"Then why are you behaving so strange."

"I am not behaving strange. You are! Chris, you are behaving very strange indeed. Listen, let me ask you a simple question, Chris. I am the girl you say you want to marry. Right? OK, I am taken away in strange, very strange circumstances last night. I call you beforehand and tell you. You come over here and all you say to me is: 'Don't worry, it's all right.' "

"I never said anything of the sort to you."

"Chris, you asked me, the girl you want to marry, to travel forty miles at night to Abichi . . ."

"To Abichi? You didn't say it was Abichi, did you?"

"That's not the point. You asked the girl you want to marry to go along and keep all options open. Do you remember that? Well, I'm sorry to inform you I did not take your advice."

"You are being . . ."

"Please, don't interrupt. I go off forty miles to this weird party."

"BB, you never told me it was to Abichi."

"Please, let me finish. I am carried off to this strange place and my future husband retires to his bed, sleeps well, wakes up, listens to the BBC at seven, has his bath, eats his breakfast and sits down afterwards to read the papers. Perhaps even take a walk in the garden. It is still only nine o'clock, so perhaps you go to your study and attend to some work you brought home. And then, finally at midday you remember the girl you asked to keep all the options open. You pick up the phone and tell her oh, you're back!"

"I didn't want to call earlier if that's what you are complaining about . . ."

"I am not complaining about anything. You didn't want to call earlier. Exactly. You didn't! You know why you didn't? Because you didn't want to find out if I slept in Abichi with your boss."

"What the hell are you talking about?"

"You didn't want to catch me out. Why? Because you are a very reasonable man, Chris. You are a very considerate man. You wouldn't hurt a fly. Well, I have bad news for you. You are damn too reasonable for this girl. I want a man who cares, not a man . . ."

"BB, you are out of your mind!"

"She wants a man who cares enough to be curious about where his girl sleeps. That's the kind of man this girl wants."

"Well, well!"

"Well, well. Yes, well, well. And about time."

"Listen BB." (He took the remaining steps and made to place a hand on her shoulder.)

"Take your hand off me," she screamed.

"Don't bark at me, BB."

"I'm not barking."

"You are. I don't know what has come over you. Screaming at me like some Cherubim and Seraphim prophetess or something. What's the matter? I don't understand."

He stood there where the hand he had tried to place on her shoulder had been rebuffed, and gazed down at her. She had now folded her arms across her breast and bent her head forward on her chest as if in silent prayer. Neither of them moved again or spoke for a very long time. Then Chris noticed the slightest heaving of her chest and shoulders and went and sat down on the sofa beside her and placed his left arm across her shoulder and with his right hand raised her chin gently and saw she was crying. She did not resist then as he pulled her to him and reverently tasted the salt of her tears.

As their struggle intensified to get inside each other, to melt and lose their separateness on that cramping sofa, she whispered, her breathing coming fast and urgent: "Let's go inside. It's too uncomfortable here." And they fairly scrambled out of the sofa into the bedroom and peeled off their garments and cast them away like things on fire, and fell in together into the wide, open space of her bed and began to roll over and over until she could roll no more and said: "Come in." And as he did she uttered a strangled cry that was not just a cry but also a command or a password into her temple. From there she took charge of him leading him by the hand silently through heaving groves mottled in subdued yellow sunlight, treading dry leaves underfoot till they came to streams of clear blue water. More than once he had slipped on the steep banks and she had pulled him up and back with such power and authority as he had never seen her exercise before. Clearly this was her grove and these her own peculiar rites over which she held absolute power. Priestess or goddess herself? No matter. But would he be found worthy? Would he survive? This unending, excruciating joyfulness in the crossroads of laughter and tears. Yes, I must, oh yes I must, yes, oh yes, yes, oh yes. I must, must, must. Oh holy priestess, hold me now. I am slipping, slipping, slipping. And now he was not just slipping but falling, crumbling into himself.

Just as he was going to plead for mercy she screamed an order: "OK!" and he exploded into stars and floated through fluffy white clouds and began a long and slow and weightless falling and sinking into deep, blue sleep.

When he woke like a child cradled in her arms and breasts her eyes watching anxiously over him, he asked languorously if she slept.

"Priestesses don't sleep."

He kissed her lips and her nipples and closed his eyes again.

"YOU CALLED ME a priestess. No, a prophetess, I think. I mind only the Cherubim and Seraphim part of it. As a matter of fact I do sometimes feel like Chielo in the novel, the priestess and prophetess of the Hills and the Caves."

"It comes and goes, I imagine."

"Yes. It's on now. And I see trouble building up for us. It will get to Ikem first. No joking, Chris. He will be the precursor to make straight the way. But after him it will be you. We are all in it, Ikem, you, me and even Him. The thing is no longer a joke. As my father used to say, it is no longer a dance you can dance carrying your snuff in one cupped hand. You and Ikem must quickly patch up this ridiculous thing between you that nobody has ever been able to explain to me."

"BB, I can't talk to Ikem any more. I am tired. And drained of all stamina."

"No, Chris. You have more stamina than you think."

"Well, I certainly seem to. But only under your management, you know." He smiled mischievously and kissed her.

"You know I am not talking about that, stupid."

She left him in bed, had a quick shower, came back and only then retrieved her dress where she had flung it and put it back on. All the while Chris's eyes were glued on her flawless body and she knew it. She next retrieved Chris's things and stacked them neatly at the foot of the bed. Then she left the room to find out about lunch. Agatha seething with resentment was seated on the kitchen chair, her head on the table, pretending to be asleep. Yes, she had finished lunch she answered while her narrowed, righteous eyes added something like: while you were busy in your sinfulness.

Beatrice prepared a plate of green salad to augment the brown beans with fried plantain and beef stew. Agatha had not bothered to make any dessert no doubt expecting to have the pleasure of hearing her mistress's complaint. Beatrice simply ignored her and quickly put together from cakes and odds and ends in the fridge two little bowls of sherry trifles. Then she went back to the room and woke Chris up.

It would appear from the way she beamed at him when he appeared at the table that Agatha did not include him in her moral censure. Girls at war! thought Beatrice with a private smile which the other apparently noticed and answered with a swift frown. Even Chris noticed the sudden switch.

"What's eating your maid?" he asked as soon as she had returned to the kitchen.

"Nothing. She is all smiles to you."

"Familiarity breeding contempt, then?"

"No, more than that. She is a prophetess of Jehovah."

"And you are of the House of Baal."

"Exactly. Or worse, of the unknown god."

OVER LUNCH she told him about last night at Abichi. Or as much as it was possible to tell. Chris took in the introductory details warily knowing that the gaiety in her voice was hiding something awful. When she finally let it out he was so outraged he involuntarily jumped up from his seat.

"Please sit down and eat your food." He sat down but not to eat. Not another morsel.

"I can't believe that," he kept saying. Beatrice's efforts to get him to resume his lunch failed totally. He had gently pushed his plate away.

"Look, Chris, this salad is not Agatha's. *I* made it specially for *you.*"

He relented somewhat and shovelled two or three spoonfuls of vegetables into his mouth and set the spoon down again. Finally she gave up, saying she should have known better and not shot her stupid mouth till he had eaten. She called Agatha and asked her to put the dessert back in the fridge and bring them coffee things. Without answering, she began instead to clear the table.

"Agatha!"

"Madam!"

"Leave the table alone and get us coffee, please. After that you can clear the table."

"Yes, madam."

"Let's go and sit more comfortably," she said to Chris. "We will have coffee and brandy. I insist on that. I want a little celebration. Don't ask me for what. A celebration, that's all. *Kabisa!*"

SLOWLY, VERY SLOWLY under Beatrice's expert resuscitation his spirits began to rally. She dwelt on the amusing trivia as much as possible and underplayed the shocks. But most masterly of all she got Chris to actively participate in recreating the events.

"Who is that Alhaji fellow, Chairman, I think, of the Kangan/ American Chamber of Commerce?" she asked.

"Oh that one. Alhaji Abdul Mahmoud. Didn't you know him? I thought you did. You see, that's the trouble with being such a recluse. If you came out to even one cocktail party a month you would know what was going on . . . Alhaji Mahmoud is himself a bit of a hermit though. He hardly appears anywhere and when he does, hardly says a word. Rumour has it that he has in the last one year knocked all other Kangan millionaires into a cocked hat. Eight ocean liners, they say, two or three private jets; a private jetty (no pun intended). No customs officials go near his jetty and so, say rumour-mongers, he is the prince of smugglers. What else? Fifty odd companies, including a bank. Monopoly of government fertilizer imports. That's about it. Very quiet, even self-effacing but they say absolutely ruthless. All that may or may not be standard fare for multi-millionaires. What I find worrying and I don't think I can quite believe it yet is that (voice lowered) he may be fronting you know for . . . your host."

"No!"

"Don't quote me. Rumours rumours rumours. I should know though. After all I am the Commissioner for Information, aren't I? But I'm afraid I have very little information myself . . . Incidentally BB, how can you be so wicked? Imagine confronting me with that embarrassing catalogue of my morning's activities including the BBC at seven! Absolutely wicked . . . But I suppose it could have been worse. You might have added, for instance, that while the ministry over which I preside dishes out all that flim-flam to the nation on KBC I sneak away every morning when no one is watching to listen to the Voice of the Enemy."

"That was a good performance of mine, was it?"

"Absolutely flawless. And devastating. I don't know why you still haven't written a play. You would knock Ikem into a cocked hat."

"That would take some doing. But thanks all the same."

Before he finally left her flat a little after six she had made another passionate plea to get him to agree to patch things up with Ikem.

"What I heard and saw last night frightened me. Ikem was being tried there in absentia and convicted. You have to save him, Chris. I know how difficult he is and everything. Believe me, I do. But you simply have to cut through all that. Ikem has no other friend and no sense of danger. Or rather he has but doesn't know how to respond. You've tried everything in the book, I know. But you've just got to try them all over again. That's what friends are for. There is very little time, Chris."

"Little? There may be *no* time at all left . . . I should do something; I agree, but what? You see there is nothing concrete on which Ikem and I quarrel. What divides us is style not substance. And that is absolutely unbridgeable. Strange isn't it?"

"Very strange."

"And yet . . . on reflection . . . not so strange. You see, if you and I have a quarrel over an orange we could settle it by dividing the orange or by letting either of us have it, or by handing it over to a third party or even by throwing it away. But supposing our quarrel is that I happen to love oranges and you happen to hate them, how do you settle that? You will always hate oranges and I will always love them; we can't help it."

"We could decide though, couldn't we, that it was silly and futile to quarrel over our likes and dislikes."

"Yes," he answered eagerly. "As long as we are not fanatical. If either of us is a fanatic then there can be no hope of a settlement. We will disagree as long as we live. The mere prospect of *that* is what leaves me emotionally drained and even paralysed . . . Why am I still in this Cabinet? Ikem calls us a circus show, and he is largely right. We are not a Cabinet. The real Cabinet are some of those clowns you saw last night. Why am I still there then? Honour and all that demands that I turn in my paper of resignation. But can I?"

"Yes, you can."

"Well, I've just told you I have no energy to do it."

"Nonsense!"

"And even if I were to make one hell of an effort and turn in my paper today, what do I do after that? Go into exile and drink a lot of booze in European capitals and sleep with a lot of white girls after delivering revolutionary lectures to admiring audiences seven worlds away from where my problem is. BB, I have seen that option; I have considered it and believe me it's far less attractive than this charade here."

"So?"

"So I will stay put. And do you know something else; it may not be easy to leave even if I wanted. Do you remember what he said during that terrifying debate over his life presidency? I told you, didn't I? For one brief moment he shed his pretended calmness and threatened me: If anyone thinks he can leave the Cabinet on this issue he will be making a sad mistake."

"Anyone walking out of that door will not go home but head straight into detention. Yes I remember that. So?"

"I am not saying that such a ridiculous threat is what is keeping me at my post. I mention it only to show how tricky things can become of a sudden. That's why I have said a hundred million times to Ikem: Lie low for a while and this gathering tornado may rage and pass overhead carrying away roof-tops and perhaps . . . only perhaps . . . leave us battered but alive. But oh no! Ikem is outraged that I should recommend such cowardly and totally unworthy behaviour to him. You yourself have been witness to it again and again. And you are now asking me to go yet again and go on my knees and ask an artist who has the example of Don Quixote and other fictional characters to guide him . . ."

"Oh, that's not fair, Chris. That's most unfair. Ikem is as down to the ground, in his way, as either of us. Perhaps, more so . . . You only have to compare his string of earthy girlfriends to yours truly . . ."

Having said it Beatrice immediately regretted her indulgence. She should have resisted the temptation of a soft diversionary remark. Power escaped through it leaving her passionate purpose suddenly limp . . . They talked on desultorily for a little while longer and then parted without denting the problem. Chris merely restated his position before leaving.

"You are asking a man who has long despaired of fighting to hold back a combatant, fanatical and in full gear. My dear, all he'll ever get for his pains is to be knocked flat on his face."

9

Views of Struggle

IKEM'S DRIVE that hot afternoon was not in answer to Chris's instruction to send a reporter to the Presidential Palace. A reporter was indeed sent and he must have duly reported. Ikem went for reasons of his own, in search of personal enlightenment.

He arrived on the grounds of the Palace just as the party was breaking up. So he could do no more for the present than exchange courtesies with the white-bearded leader of the Abazon delegation and arrange a later meeting with him and his group at the hotel where they were lodged.

Harmoney Hotel is a sleazy establishment in the northern slums of the capital and, judging by the ease with which Ikem's inquiry led him to it, a popular resort in the neighbourhood. It is the kind of place that would boast a certain number of resident prostitutes; a couple of rooms used by three or four young men of irregular hours and unspecified occupation who sleep mostly by day; and a large turnover of small-time traders from up-country visiting Bassa periodically to replenish their stock of retail goods. It is busy and homely in a peculiar kind of way.

Ikem had already discovered at the Presidential Palace that the delegation was not five hundred strong as he had been told but a mere six, and that the large crowd that had accompanied it to the Palace were Abazon indigenes in Bassa: motor mechanics, retail traders, tailors, vulcanizers, taxi- and bus-drivers who had loaned their vehicles, and others doing all kinds of odd jobs or nothing at all in the city. A truly motley crowd! No wonder His Excellency was reported to have received the news of their sudden arrival on his doorstep with considerable apprehension. I would too if I were in his shoes, admitted Ikem mischievously to himself.

They were seated around five or six tables joined together in the open courtyard of the hotel, not five hundred of them now, but perhaps twenty, drinking and discussing excitedly their visit to the Palace.

As soon as they saw Ikem enter from the street through the main iron gate into the roughly cemented courtyard everybody got up including the six visiting elders and received him with something approaching an ovation. He shook hands all round and was looking for a vacant seat when someone, a kind of master of ceremonies, indicated a vacated place of honour for him beside the white-bearded elder. Then he shouted "Service!" very importantly and when a slouching waiter in a dirty blue tunic appeared, ordered six bottles of beer and three more roast chicken. "Quick, quick," he said.

Then he surveyed the assembled group, picked up an empty beer bottle and knocked its bottom on the table for silence:

"Our people say that when a titled man comes into a meeting the talking must have to stop until he has taken his seat. An important somebody has just come in who needs no introduction. Still yet, we have to do things according to what Europeans call protocol. I call upon our distinguished son and Editor of the *National Gazette* to stand up."

Ikem rose to a second tremendous ovation.

"When you hear Ikem Osodi Ikem Osodi everywhere you think his head will be touching the ceiling. But look at him, how simple he is. I am even taller than himself, a dunce like me. Our people say that an animal whose name is famous does not always fill a hunter's basket."

At this point Ikem interjected that he expected more people to beat him up now that his real size was known, and caused much laughter.

But in spite of the drinking and eating and the jolly laughter the speaker was still able to register his disappointment that this most famous son of Abazon had not found it possible to join in their monthly meetings and other social gatherings so as to direct their ignorant fumblings with his wide knowledge. He went on with this failing at such length and relentlessness that the bearded old man finally stopped him by rising to his feet. He was tall, gaunt-looking and with a slight stoop of the shoulders.

The shrillness in the other man's voice was totally absent here but the power of his utterance held everyone captive from his very first words. He began by thanking Abazon people in Bassa for receiving him and the other five leaders from home. He thanked the many young men a few only of whom were now present for turning out in their hundreds to accompany the delegation to the Palace and showing Bassa that Abazon had people. Then he turned sharply to the complaint of the last speaker:

"I have heard what you said about this young man, Osodi, whose doings are known everywhere and fill our hearts with pride. Going to meetings and weddings and naming ceremonies of one's people is good. But don't forget that our wise men have said also that a man who answers every summons by the town-crier will not plant corn in his fields. So my advice to you is this. Go on with your meetings and marriages and naming ceremonies because it is good to do so. But leave this young man alone to do what he is doing for Abazon and for the whole of Kangan; the cock that crows in the morning belongs to one household but his voice is the property of the neighbourhood. You should be proud that this bright cockerel that wakes the whole village comes from your compound."

There was such compelling power and magic in his voice that even the MC who had voiced the complaints was now beginning to nod his head, like everybody else, in agreement.

"If your brother needs to journey far across the Great River to find what sustains his stomach, do not ask him to sit at home with layabouts scratching their bottom and smelling the finger. I never met this young man before this afternoon when he came looking for us at the compound of the Big Chief. I had never met him before; I have never read what they say he writes because I do not know ABC. But I have heard of all the fight he has fought for poor people in this land. I would not like to hear that he has given up that fight because he wants to attend the naming ceremony of Okeke's son and Mgbafo's daughter.

"Let me ask a question. How do we salute our fellows when we come in and see them massed in assembly so huge we cannot hope to greet them one by one, to call each man by his title? Do we not say: To everyone his due? Have you thought what a wise practice our fathers fashioned out of those simple words? To every man his own! To each his chosen title! We can all see how that handful of words can save us from the ache of four hundred handshakes and the headache of remembering a like multitude of praise-names. But it does not end there. It is saying to us: Every man has what is his; do not bypass him to enter his compound . . .

"It is also like this (for what is true comes in different robes) . . . Long before sunrise in the planting or harvesting season; at that time when sleep binds us with a sweetness more than honey itself the bush-fowl will suddenly startle the farmer with her scream: o-o-i! o-o-i! o-o-i! in the stillness and chill of the grassland. I ask you, does the farmer jump up at once with heavy eyes and prepare for the fields or does he scream back to the bush-fowl: *Shut up! Who told you the time? You have never hoed a cassava ridge in your life nor planted one seed of millet.* No! If he is a farmer who means to prosper he will not challenge the bush-fowl; he will not dispute her battle-cry; he will get up and obey.

"Have you thought about that? I tell you it is the way the Almighty has divided the work of the world. Everyone and his own! The bush-fowl, her work; and the farmer, his.

"To some of us the Owner of the World has apportioned the gift to tell their fellows that the time to get up has finally come. To others He gives the eagerness to rise when they hear the call; to rise with racing blood and put on their garbs of war and go to the boundary of their town to engage the invading enemy boldly in battle. And then there are those others whose part is to wait and when the struggle is ended, to take over and recount its story.

"The sounding of the battle-drum is important; the fierce waging of the war itself is important; and the telling of the story afterwards—each is important in its own way. I tell you there is not one of them we could do without. But if you ask me which of them takes the eagle-feather I will say boldly: the story. Do you hear me? Now, when I was younger, if you had asked me the same question I would have replied without a pause: the battle. But age gives to a man some things with the right hand even as it takes away others with the left. The torrent of an old man's water may no longer smash into the bole of the roadside tree a full stride away as it once did but fall around his feet like a woman's; but in return the eye of his mind is given wing to fly away beyond the familiar sights of the homestead . . .

"So why do I say that the story is chief among his fellows? The same reason I think that our people sometimes will give the name Nkolika to their daughters—Recalling-Is-Greatest. Why? Because it is only the story can continue beyond the war and the warrior. It is the story that outlives the sound of war-drums and the exploits of brave fighters. It is the story, not the others, that saves our progeny from blundering like blind beggars into the spikes of the cactus fence. The story is our escort; without it, we are blind. Does the blind man own his escort? No, neither do we the story; rather it is the story that owns us and directs us. It is the thing that makes us different from cattle; it is the mark on the face that sets one people apart from their neighbours."

The footfalls of waiters padding about the cemented courtyard rose to a new prominence in the profound silence.

"So the arrogant fool who sits astride the story as though it were a bowl of foo-foo set before him by his wife understands little about the world. The story will roll him into a ball, dip him in the soup and swallow him first. I tell you he is like the puppy who swings himself around and farts into a blazing fire with the aim to put it out. Can he? No, the story is everlasting . . . Like fire, when it is not blazing it is smouldering under its own ashes or sleeping and resting inside its flint-house.

"When we are young and without experience we all imagine that the story of the land is easy, that every one of us can get up and tell it. But that is not so. True, we all have our little scraps of tale bubbling in us. But what we tell is like the middle of a mighty boa which a foolish forester mistakes for a tree trunk and settles upon to take his snuff . . . Yes, we lay into our little tale with wild eyes and a vigorous tongue. Then, one day Agwu comes along and knocks it out of our mouth and our jaw out of shape for our audacity and hands over the story to a man of his choice . . . Agwu does not call a meeting to choose his seers and diviners and

artists; Agwu, the god of healers; Agwu, brother to Madness! But
though born from the same womb he and Madness were not created by the same *chi*. Agwu is the right hand a man extends to his
fellows; Madness, the forbidden hand. Madness unleashes and
rides his man roughly into the wild savannah. Agwu possesses his
own just as securely but has him corralled to serve the compound.
Agwu picks his disciple, rings his eye with white chalk and dips his
tongue, willing or not, in the brew of prophecy; and right away
the man will speak and put head and tail back to the severed trunk
of our tale. This miracle-man will amaze us because he may be a
fellow of little account, not the bold warrior we all expect nor
even the war-drummer. But in his new-found utterance our struggle will stand reincarnated before us. He is the liar who can sit
under his thatch and see the moon hanging in the sky outside.
Without stirring from his stool he can tell you how commodities
are selling in a distant market-place. His chalked eye will see every
blow in a battle he never fought. So fully is he owned by the
telling that sometimes—especially when he looks around him and
finds no age-mate to challenge the claim—he will turn the marks
left on him by the chicken-pox and yaws he suffered in childhood
into bullet scars . . . yes, scars from that day *our men* pounded
their men like palmfruit in the heavy mortar of iroko!"

*The tense air was broken suddenly by loud laughter. The old man
himself smiled with benign mischief.*

"But the lies of those possessed by Agwu are lies that do no
harm to anyone. They float on the top of story like the white
bubbling at the pot-mouth of new palm-wine. The true juice of the
tree lies coiled up inside, waiting to strike . . .

"I don't know why my tongue is crackling away tonight like a
clay-bowl of *ukwa* seeds toasting over the fire; why I feel like a
man who has been helped to lower a heavy load from off his head;
and he straightens his neck again and shakes the ache from it. Yes,
my children, I feel light-headed like one who has completed all his
tasks and is gay and free to go. But I don't want to leave thinking
that any of you is being pushed away from his proper work, from
the work his creator arranged with him before he set out for the
world . . ."

*He stopped speaking. The silence was so complete that one could hear
him gnashing his teeth. Ikem realized that other people, habitués of the
Harmoney Hotel, drinking their beer at single tables in different parts of*

*the courtyard, had also fallen under this old man's spell and now had
their eyes trained on him.*

"When we were told two years ago that we should vote for the
Big Chief to rule for ever and all kinds of people we had never
seen before came running in and out of our villages asking us to
say yes I told my people: We have Osodi in Bassa. If he comes
home and tells us that we should say yes we will do so because he
is there as our eye and ear. I said: if what these strange people are
telling us is true, Osodi will come or he will write in his paper and
our sons will read it and know that it is true. But he did not come
to tell us and he did not write it in his paper. So we knew that
cunning had entered that talk.

"There was another thing that showed me there was deception
in the talk. The people who were running in and out and telling us
to say yes came one day and told us that the Big Chief himself did
not want to rule for ever but that he was being forced. Who is
forcing him? I asked. The people, they replied. That means us? I
asked, and their eyes shifted from side to side. And I knew finally
that cunning had entered the matter. And I thanked them and they
left. I called my people and said to them: The Big Chief doesn't
want to rule for ever because he is sensible. Even when a man
marries a woman he does not marry her for ever. One day one of
them will die and the marriage will end. So my people and I said
No."

*There was a huge applause, not only from the tables where the Abazon
people sat but from other tables as well.*

"But that was not the end. More shifting-eyes people came and
said: Because you said no to the Big Chief he is very angry and has
ordered all the water bore-holes they are digging in your area to
be closed so that you will know what it means to offend the sun.
You will suffer so much that in your next reincarnation you will
need no one to tell you to say yes whether the matter is clear to
you or not.

"God will not agree," replied many voices.

"So we came to Bassa to say our own yes and perhaps the work
on our bore-holes will start again and we will not all perish from
the anger of the sun. We did not know before but we know now
that yes does not cause trouble. We do not fully understand the
ways of today yet but we are learning. A dancing masquerade in

my town used to say: It is true I do not hear English but when they say *Catch am* nobody tells me to take myself off as fast as I can."

There was loud laughter from all parts of the courtyard, some of the people savouring the joke by repeating it to themselves or to their neighbours and laughing all over again.

"So we are ready to learn new things and mend our old, useless ways. If you cross the Great River to marry a wife you must be ready for the risk of night journey by canoe . . . I don't know whether the people we have come to see will listen to our cry for water or not. Sometime ago we were told that the Big Chief himself was planning to visit our villages and see our suffering. Then we were told again that he was not coming because he had just remembered that we had said no to him two years ago. So we said, if he will not come, let us go and visit him instead in his house. It is proper that a beggar should visit a king. When a rich man is sick a beggar goes to visit him and say sorry. When the beggar is sick, he waits to recover and then goes to tell the rich man that he has been sick. It is the place of the poor man to make a visit to the rich man who holds the yam and the knife."

"That is indeed the world," replied the audience.

"Whether our coming to the Big Chief's compound will do any good or not we cannot say. We did not see him face to face because he was talking to another Big Chief like himself who is visiting from another country. But we can go back to our people and tell them that we have struggled for them with what remaining strength we have . . . Once upon a time the leopard who had been trying for a long time to catch the tortoise finally chanced upon him on a solitary road. *'Aha,'* he said; *'at long last! Prepare to die.'* And the tortoise said: *'Can I ask one favour before you kill me?'* The leopard saw no harm in that and agreed. *'Give me a few moments to prepare my mind,'* the tortoise said. Again the leopard saw no harm in that and granted it. But instead of standing still as the leopard had expected the tortoise went into strange action on the road, scratching with hands and feet and throwing sand furiously in all directions. *'Why are you doing that?'* asked the puzzled leopard. The tortoise replied: *'Because even after I am dead I would want anyone passing by this spot to say, yes, a fellow and his match struggled here.'*

"My people, that is all we are doing now. Struggling. Perhaps to no purpose except that those who come after us will be able to say: *True, our fathers were defeated but they tried.*"

WHEN IKEM GOT to his parked car outside the big iron archway on which HARMONEY HOTEL shone in fluorescent letters he found a huge police motor cycle parked in such a way behind it as, quite clearly, to prevent its moving out. As he looked around in surprise a police constable stepped out of the shadows and asked:

"Na you get this car?"

"Yes, anything the matter?"

"Why you no put parking light?"

Parking light. That was a new one. He had never been asked about parking light in Bassa before. But never mind.

"Well, I didn't see any need. With all this light around."

He waved his hand at the many fluorescent tubes shining from Harmoney Hotel's perimeter walls.

"So when you see electric for somebody's wall it follow say you no go put your parking light? What section of Traffic Law be that one?"

"It's a matter of common sense, I should say."

"Common sense! So me self I no get common sense; na so you talk. OK, Mr. Commonsense, make I see your particulars."

A number of people had come out of the hotel premises to watch the palaver and were joined by a few passers-by on the road. Very soon every Abazon man still around had joined the scene and the Master of Ceremonies stepped forward and asked the policeman if he did not know the Editor of the *National Gazette.*

"I no know am! Na sake of editor he come abuse me when I de do my work. He can be editor for his office not for road."

"He no abuse you. I de here all the time," said one bystander.

"Make you shut your smelling mouth there, Mr. Lawyer. Abi you want come with me for Charge Office to explain? You no hear when he say I no get common sense. That no be abuse for your country? Oga, I want see your particulars. Na you people de make the law na you dey break am."

Without uttering another word Ikem produced his papers and handed over to the policeman.

"Wey your insurance?"

"That's what you are looking at."

He opened a notebook, placed it on the bonnet of the car and began to write, now and again referring to Ikem's documents. The growing crowd of spectators stood in silence in a circle around the car and the chief actors, the policeman playing his role of writing down somebody's fate with the self-important and painful slowness of half-literacy . . . At long last he tore out a sheet of his note-paper and handed it like a death warrant to Ikem.

"Come for Traffic Office for Monday morning, eight o'clock sharp. If you no come or you come late you de go answer for court. *Kabisa.*"

"Can I have my papers back?"

The policeman laughed indulgently at this clever-stupid man.

"That paper wey I give you just now na your cover till Monday. If any police ask you for particular show am that paper. And when you come for Monday make you bring am."

He folded Ikem's documents and put them with his notebook into his breast pocket and buttoned down the flap with the flourish of a judge's gavel.

The Master of Ceremonies was boiling into another protest but Ikem made the sign of silence to him—a straight finger across sealed lips, and then swung the same finger around to hint at the law officer's holster.

"Don't provoke a man doing his duty. The police have something they call accidental discharge."

"No be me go kill you, my friend."

This retort was made frontally to Ikem. With a strange expression of mockery and hatred on his face the policeman mounted his heavy machine and roared away. The Master of Ceremonies asked Ikem:

"Did you get his number?"

"I'm afraid I didn't think of that. Anyway it doesn't matter."

"Here it is."

And he held to him a number written with biro on the palm of his left hand and Ikem took it down on the back of his summons paper.

MONDAY MORNING at the Traffic Police Office. Ikem had decided to do what he rarely did—use his clout. There were more important things to do with his time than engage in fisticuffs with a traffic warden. So he had telephoned the Superintendent of Traffic from his office and made an appointment for nine-thirty.

There was a senior officer waiting for him at the Desk Sergeant's front room who took him straight into the Superintendent's office.

"I never meet you before in person sir," said the Superintendent springing out from behind his massive wooden desk. "Very pleased to meet you sir . . . I was expecting a huge fellow like this," and he made a sign sideways and upwards.

"No, I am quite small. Anyone who feels like it can actually beat me up quite easily."

"Oh no. The pen is mightier than the sword. With one sentence of your sharp pen you can demolish anybody. Ha ha ha ha ha. I respect your pen, sir . . . What can I do for you, sir. I know you are a busy man and I don't want to waste your time."

As Ikem told his story he thought he saw something like relief spreading through the man's face.

"Is that all? You shouldn't have come all this way for that. You should have told me on the phone and I should have asked the stupid fellow to bring your particulars himself to you and to stay there and wash your car before coming back. These boys have no common sense."

"Well, I suppose he was only doing his job."

"What kind of nonsense job is that? To go about contravening important people."

He slapped his open palm on the buzzer with such violence that the orderly who scampered in from the outer office was confusedly straightening his cap, holding his loose belt and attempting a salute all at the same time.

"Go and bring me at once everybody who was on road duty on Saturday night."

"Sorry, it was Friday night," said Ikem.

"Sorry, Friday! Everybody here one time. Except those on beat . . . Again Mr. Osodi, I must apologize to you for this embarrassment."

"No problem, Superintendent." He had thought of putting in another mitigating word for the constable but remembered his utterly atrocious behaviour and held his peace.

At that point eight worried constables were marched in. Ikem spotted his man at once but decided that even engaging his eye would be a mark of friendship. They saluted and stood stock-still, their worried eyes alone swivelling around like things with a life of their own.

The Superintendent gazed at them in turn without saying a word. In his code they were *all* guilty at this stage.

"Do you know this gentlemen?"

They all shook their heads.

"How you go know? Stupid ignoramuses. Who contravened him on Friday night at . . . Mr. Osodi, where did it happen?"

"Outside Harmoney Hotel on Northwest Street."

This announcement was followed by the briefest pause of surprise or even shock which was mercifully overtaken by the constable's owning up.

"Na me, sir."

"Na you! You no know who this man be? But how you go know? When you no de read newspaper. You pass standard six self?"

"Yes sir."

"Na lie! Unless na free primary you pass. This man is Mr. Osodi, the Editor of the *National Gazette*. Everybody in the country knows him except you. So you carry your stupid nonsense and go and contravene a man of such calibre. Tomorrow now if he takes up his pen to lambast the Police you all go begin complain like monkey wey im mother die . . . Go and bring his particulars here one time, stupid yam-head."

The poor fellow scampered out of the room.

"Now all of you listen well. You see this man here, make una look im face well well. If any of you go out tomorrow and begin to fool around his car I go give the person proper *gbali-gbali*. You understand?"

"Yes sir."

"Nonsense police. You think na so we do am come reach superintendent. Tomorrow make you go contravene His Excellency for road and if they ask you you say you no know am before. Scallywags. Fall out!"

BECAUSE OF HIS VISIT to the Police Traffic Department at the other end of town Ikem had had to conduct his daily Editorial Conference two hours late. In making his apologies he naturally recounted his recent brushes with the police the details of which added considerable entertainment to the proceedings of a routine conference. The only person who did not seem to find any of it in the least amusing was Ikem's second-in-command, an earnest but previously obsequious fellow who in the last several months had struck Ikem as becoming suddenly a lot more aloof and inclined to disagree openly with whatever he said.

Back in his room Ikem's officious stenographer gave him two messages, one from John Kent, the Mad Medico, who asked Ikem to call him back and the other from Elewa who said she would call again.

MM picked up the phone at the first ring and went straight into his business. He was wondering whether Ikem would be free to drop by for a quick drink this afternoon to meet a friend of his, a poet and editor from England. Ikem accepted most enthusiastically.

"Sure! I haven't seen you in a long time. What have you been doing with yourself? And as for meeting a live poet and editor I just can't believe the luck. Can I bring my girlfriend?"

"But of course. Which one by the way? Never mind bring whoever you like . . . Fivish. See you then. Cheerio."

It was amazing, Ikem thought, how brief and businesslike MM could be at work. No sign of his madness once he climbed into that chair as the Hospital Administrator. Except the one near-fatal relapse—the Strange Case of the Graffiti, as Ikem called it in a famous editorial.

10

Impetuous Son

Africa tell me Africa
Is this you this back that is bent
This back that breaks under the weight of humiliation
This back trembling with red scars
And saying yes to the whip under the midday sun
But a grave voice answers me
Impetuous son, that tree young and strong
That tree there
In splendid loneliness amidst white and faded flowers
That is Africa your Africa
That grows again patiently obstinately
And its fruit gradually acquire
The bitter taste of liberty

DAVID DIOP, "Africa"

THEY WERE JUST ABOUT LEAVING his flat for MM's place when
the doorbell rang and two strange men smiling from ear to ear

faced him at the landing. Ikem stood his ground at the doorway the apprehension that would certainly have been in order relieved only by those vast smiles.

"Can I help you?"

"We just come salute you."

"Me? Who are you? I don't seem to remember."

"We be taxi-drivers."

"I see."

Elewa had now joined him at the door. The visitors were still smiling bravely in spite of the cold welcome. As soon as Elewa came into view one of the visitors said:

"Ah, madam, you de here."

"Ah, no be you carry me go home from here that night?"

"Na me, madam. You remember me. Very good. I no think say you fit remember."

"So wetin you come do here again? Abi, you just discover I no pay you complete? Or perhaps na counterfeit I give you."

"No madam. We just come salute this oga."

At this point the normal courtesies which the prevalence of armed robberies had virtually banished from Bassa could no longer be denied. Ikem and Elewa moved back into the room and the visitors followed them in.

"Ah, madam I no know say I go find you here, self."

"Why you no go find me here? This man na your sister husband?"

"No madam I no mean am like that."

"Don't worry. Na joke I de joke. Make una sidon. We de go out before but you fit sidon small."

By this time Ikem had realized who one of the visitors was—the taxi driver who had taken Elewa home late one evening about a week ago. But why he should be back now with another man and smiling profusely like an Air Kangan passenger who has achieved a boarding pass, was still a mystery. Elewa put it a little differently.

"When I see you smiling like person wey win raffle I say: who be this again? Then my brain just make *krim* and I remember . . . Who your friend be?"

"My friend de drive taxi like myself and he be member for Central Committee of Taxi Driver Union."

"Welcome."

"Thank you madam. Thank you oga."

"Even na this my friend tell me that day say na oga be Editor of *Gazette*. Wonderful! And me I no know that."

"How you go know? You de read paper?"

"Ah, Madam I de try read small. The thing we this oga de write na waa. We like am plenty."

"Tell me one thing you done read."

"Ah. How I go begin count. The thing oga write too plenty. But na for we small people he de write every time. I no sabi book but I sabi say na for we this oga de fight, not for himself. He na big man. Nobody fit do fuckall to him. So he fit stay for him house, chop him oyibo chop, drink him cold beer, put him air conditioner and forget we. But he no do like that. So we come salute am."

"Thank you very much," said Ikem deeply touched. "Can I offer you a drink of something?"

"Don't worry sir," they said. They knew he was going out and must not delay him too much. It was then the real story of the visit came out. This man was not only the driver who drove Elewa home from here that evening over a week ago. He was by the strangest of coincidences the driver Ikem got into a bizarre contest with for a tiny space of road in a dreadful traffic jam. And now he had come, and brought a friend along, to make an apology!

"Oh my God. You don't owe me any apology. None whatsoever. I should apologize to you, my friend."

Ikem walked up to him to shake his hand but he offered not one but both his hands as a mark of respect. The trade unionist did the same.

Ikem felt awkward, but also in a strange way, somehow elated. It was uncomfortable to be reminded that with his education and all that he could so easily get embroiled in a completely ridiculous fight with a taxi-driver. The elation came perhaps from this rare human contact across station and class with these two who had every cause to feel hatred but came instead with friendship, acting out spontaneously and without self-righteousness what their betters preach so often but so seldom practise.

Apparently it was the trade unionist who was in the car behind the car behind Ikem in the traffic and it was he who recognized Ikem as he turned into the Presidential Palace and promptly told the other; and the two decided on a visit of apology immediately. But it had taken them all this time to track down Ikem's address, only to discover that one of them had been there so recently. Na

God him work, was the way he summed up the string of coincidences.

The trade unionist who had so far played only a supporting role to his friend now spoke up:

"I want answer that question which Madam ask my friend: to call one thing we done read for *Gazette*. Me self I fit call hundred things but time no dey. So I go talk about the one every taxi-driver know well well. Before before, the place where we get Central Taxi Park for Slaughterhouse Road de smell pass nyarsh. Na there every cattle them want kill come pass him last shit, since time dem born my grandfather. Na him this oga take him pen write, write, write sotay City Council wey de sleep come wake up and bring bulldozer and throway every rubbish and clean the place well well. So that if you park your taxi there you no fit get bellyache like before, or cover your nose with cloth. Even the place so clean now that if the akara wey you de chop fall down for road you fit pick am up and throw for mouth. Na this oga we sidon quiet so na him do am. Na him make I follow my friend come salute am. Madam, I beg you, make you de look am well. Na important personality for this country."

"Make you no worry for that," said his friend, "Madam de look am well well. That day I come pick madam from here I think say them make small quarrel . . ."

"Shut your mouth. Who tell you say we de make small quarrel?"

"Madam, I no need for somebody to tell me when man and woman make small quarrel. When you see the woman eye begin de flash like ambulance you go know. But that day when I de vex because oga shine torch for my eye the same madam wey de grumble come tell me not to worry because the oga can talk sharp but na very kind man. No be so you tell me as we drive for night?"

Elewa nodded.

"But why you no tell me at the same time say na Editor of *Gazette?*"

"Why I go tell you? And if I tell you wetin you go do with am? Illiteracy de read paper for your country?"

"Wonderful! You no see say because you no tell me, I come make another big mistake. If I for know na such big oga de for my front for that go-slow how I go come make such wahala for am? I de craze? But the thing wey confuse me properly well be that kind old car wey he come de drive. I never see such! Number one, the car too old; number two, you come again de drive am yourself. Wonderful! So how I fit know na such big man de for my front? I just think this I-go-drive-myself na some jagajaga person wey no fit bring out money to pay driver, and come block road for everybody. To God, na so I think."

"Never mind," said Ikem. "That wahala for road no be such bad thing as he come make us friends now for house."

"That na true, oga. Wonderful!"

As he drove to Mad Medico's place that afternoon Ikem turned over and over in his mind one particular aspect of the visit of the taxi-driver and his friend—how it seemed so important to him to explain his failure to recognize an admired "personality" like Ikem; and how adroitly he had shifted the guilt for this failure round to the very same object of admiration for driving a battered old Datsun instead of a Mercedes and for driving with his own hands instead of sitting in the owner's corner and being driven. So in the midst of all their fulsome and perfectly sincere praise of Ikem those two also managed to sneak in a couple of body-blows.

Ikem could understand well enough the roots of the paradox in which a man's personal choice to live simply without such trimmings as chauffeurs could stamp him not as a modest and exemplary citizen but as a mean-minded miser denying a livelihood to one unemployed driver out of hundreds and thousands roaming the streets—a paradox so perverse in its implications as to justify the call for the total dismantling of the grotesque world in which it grows—and flourishes.

But even in such a world how does one begin to explain the downtrodden drivers' wistful preference for a leader driving not like themselves in a battered and spluttering vehicle but differently, stylishly in a Mercedes and better still with another downtrodden person like themselves for a chauffeur? Perhaps a root-and-branch attack would cure that diseased tolerance too, a tolerance verging on admiration by the trudging-jigger-toed oppressed for the Mercedes-Benz-driving, private-jet-flying, luxury-yacht-cruising oppressor. An insistence by the oppressed that his oppression be performed in style! What half-way measures could hope to cure that? No, it had to be full measure, pressed down and flowing over! Except that in dictatorships of the proletariat where roots have already been dug up and branches hacked away, an atavistic tolerance seems to linger, quite unexpectedly, for the stylishness of dachas and special shops etc. etc., for the revolutionary elite. Therefore what is at issue in all this may not be systems after all but a basic human failing that may only be alleviated by a good spread of general political experience, slow of growth and obstinately patient like the young tree planted by David Diop on the edge of the primeval desert just before the year of wonders in which Africa broke out so spectacularly in a rash of independent nation states!

When finally Ikem's thoughts broke out into words seeking Elewa's view on the matter her response was sharply and decisively on the side of basic nature and the taxi-drivers:

"I no tell you that before say this kind car wey you get de make person shame. To day he no get battery, tomorrow him tyre burst. I done talk say if you no want bring money for buy better car why you no take one good Peugeot from office as others de do and take one driver make he de drive am for you. Your own work different than other people? No be the same government work? Me I no understand am-o."

11

THE SENSE OF EXHILARATION which had descended on Ikem after the taxi-drivers' visit stayed with him all afternoon and into the night, a night in which Elewa, touched by the flame of this novel excitement opened to him new reserves of tenderness exceptional even for her. Back now from driving her home he brewed himself a strong cup of black coffee to ward off physical languor from the precincts of his charged and alert mind and sat back to think. In such situations much of his thinking came in strong, even exaggerated, images.

He saw himself as an explorer who has just cleared a cluster of obstacles in an arduous expedition to earn as a result the conviction, more by intuition perhaps than logic, that although the final goal of his search still lies hidden beyond more adventures and dangers, the puzzles just unravelled point unambiguously to inevitable success.

The drivers' visit was probably not the cause but only the occasion of this sense of thrill and expectancy—a culmination perhaps of several related events beginning with the happenings of last Friday. Or perhaps it merely triggered an awareness going far, far back in his subconscious mind waiting like a dormant seed in the dry season soil for the green-fingered magician, the first rain.

In any event he had always had the necessity in a vague but insistent way, had always felt a yearning without very clear definition, to connect his essence with earth and earth's people. The problem for him had never been whether it should be done but how to do it with integrity.

At some point he had assumed, quite naively, that public affairs so-called might provide the handle he needed. But his participation in these affairs had yielded him nothing but disenchantment and a final realization of the incongruity of the very term "public" as applied to those affairs shrouded as they are in the mist of unreality and floating above and away from the lives and concerns of ninety-nine percent of the population. Public affairs! They are nothing but the closed transactions of soldiers-turned-politicians, with their cohorts in business and the bureaucracy. Ikem could not even guarantee now that his own limited participation had not been fatally flawed. His most poignant editorials such as his condemnation of the human blood sport called public execution; his general dissatisfaction with government policies; his quarrels and arguments with Chris; everything now began to take on the vaporous haze of a mirage.

Of course, he admitted bitterly, we always take the precaution of invoking the people's name in whatever we do. But do we not at the same time make sure of the people's absence, knowing that if they were to appear in person their scarecrow presence confronting our pious invocations would render our words too obscene even for sensibilities as robust as ours?

The prime failure of this government began also to take on a clearer meaning for him. It can't be the massive corruption though its scale and pervasiveness are truly intolerable; it isn't the subservience to foreign manipulation, degrading as it is; it isn't even this second-class, hand-me-down capitalism, ludicrous and doomed; nor is it the damnable shooting of striking railway-workers and demonstrating students and the destruction and banning thereafter of independent unions and cooperatives. It is the failure of our rulers to re-establish vital inner links with the poor and dispossessed of this country, with the bruised heart that throbs painfully at the core of the nation's being.

Naive romantics would have us believe that this heart at the core is in perfect health. How could it be? Sapped by regimes of parasites, ignorant of so many basic things though it does know some others; crippled above all by this perverse kindliness towards oppression conducted with panache! How could it be in perfect health? Impossible! But despite its many flaws this can be said for it that it does possess an artless integrity, a stubborn sense of community which can enable Elewa to establish so spontaneously with the driver a teasing affectionateness beyond the powers of Ikem.

How then, he asked himself, how can he partake of this source of stability and social meaning? Not (again as the romantics would have him do) by pretending to be like the poor; by wearing specially and expensively aged and patched jeans in mockery of their tatters. Why should he add to the insults they already bear? How then?

What about renouncing my own experience, needs and knowledge? But could I? And should I? I could renounce needs perhaps, but experience and knowledge, how? There seems no way I can become like the poor except by faking. What I know, I know for good or ill. So for good or ill I shall remain myself; but with this deliberate readiness now to help, and be helped. Like those complex, multivalent atoms in biochemistry books I have arms that reach out in all directions—a helping hand, a hand signalling for help. With one I shall touch the earth and leave another free to wave to the skies.

Aha! Come to think of it, that might explain the insistence of the oppressed that the oppressor must not be allowed to camouflage his appearance or confuse the poor by stealing and masquerading in their clothes. Perhaps it is the demand of that primitive integrity of the earth . . . Or, who knows, it might also be something less innocent (for the earth does have its streak of peasant cunning)—an insistence that your badge of privilege must never leave your breast, nor your coat of many colours your back . . . so that . . . on the wrathful day of reckoning . . . you will be as conspicuous as a peacock!

HIS EXCELLENCY was pacing agitatedly like a caged tiger in the confined space between his desk and the far wall, his hands held tensely behind him, right fist gripped in left palm. He motioned Chris to sit and continued to pace for what seemed like a full minute more before he spoke:

"At last! But God knows I did not ask for it. It's you, my oldest friends, you and Ikem who swore for reasons best known to you to force a show-down. What more can I say except: So be it . . . While investigations continue into Ikem's link with the Abazon agitators he cannot continue to edit the *National Gazette.* But I must still do things properly and constitutionally no matter the provocation. That's why I have sent for you. I want you as Commissioner for Information to issue a formal letter suspending him with immediate effect."

"Hold it, Your Excellency. I don't understand. What exactly is he supposed to have done?"

"Are you serious? You really don't know?"

"I am afraid no."

"Well, let's not waste time by getting into who knows what, now . . . Intelligence reports have established that he was involved in planning the recent march on this Palace by agitators claiming to come from Abazon. In fact they were found on careful investigation to be mostly motor-park touts, drug pushers and other criminal elements right here in Bassa."

"I am sorry but I can't believe that."

"In this job Chris, beliefs are not my primary concern. I am no bishop. My concern is the security of this state. You should know that; you are Commissioner for Information. Anyhow, let me assure you there is incontrovertible evidence that Ikem was in contact with these fellows in the quadrangle right here and later drove to a hotel in North Bassa to hold a secret meeting with them. How's that? Well, you seem to be in a sceptical mood; what will you say then if I tell you that the security agents shadowing him actually arrested him for a minor traffic offence outside the hotel as he was about to leave? Just to make sure no alibis are invented . . . Good, isn't it, to know that some organs of government still perform effectively in this country."

"Can I speak with him?"

"How do you mean? Have you not been speaking with him? Oh, I think I see what you mean. He isn't in custody or anything of the sort. Not yet. So I certainly think you should see him. But first of all I want him suspended from duty and barred completely from the premises of the *Gazette*. Is that clear?"

"No it is not. I am sorry Your Excellency but I will not write a letter suspending the Editor of the *National Gazette* simply because some zealous security officer has come up with a story . . ."

"I see I have been wasting my breath . . ."

"If they think they have a case against him let them send him a query themselves or suspend him if they have no patience for such bureaucratic niceties as queries. I don't see how I come into it."

"Listen. The way I see it this matter is not likely to end with mere suspension for conspiring with thugs to invade the Presidential Palace. That may be only the merest tip of the iceberg. There is some indication that Ikem might have colluded with these same people to sabotage the presidency referendum two years ago. I don't mind telling you that your own role in that fiasco was never cleared up satisfactorily either and may well come up for further investigation."

"What on earth are you talking about . . . ?"

"So I sincerely hope—and pray—that you will not make your own position . . . you know . . . more difficult at this stage. It would be most unwise I can assure you. If I were in your shoes I would go and issue the letter as instructed and await further developments."

"And if I refuse?"

"I shouldn't if I were you."

"Well, Your Excellency, for once I am turning you down. I will not carry out this instruction and I hereby tender my resignation."

"Resignation! Ha ha ha ha ha. Where do you think you are? Westminster or Washington DC? Come on! This is a military government in a backward West African State called Kangan . . ."

"We wouldn't be so backward if we weren't so bent on remaining so . . ."

"Some day you will have a chance to change all that when you become the boss. Right now this boss here won't accept resignations unless of course he has taken the trouble himself to ask for them. Right? This may sound strange to you I know because up until now this same boss has allowed you and others to call the shots. Not any more, Chris. I will be doing the calling from now on and I intend to call quite a few before I am done. Now is that clear? I want that letter to be in Ikem's hands by close of work today, without fail. You may go now."

Chris left without another word but unshaken in his defiance. He made for his office, intending to begin right away the removal of his private papers and odds and ends to his residence until he could vacate there as well. As soon as he stepped into his office, however, he was handed the telephone by a flustered secretary. His Excellency on the line.

"Yes, Chris. I have reconsidered this matter. You do have a point in not wishing to write the suspension letter yourself. I wanted to do you the honour of appearing to be still in charge of your ministry. But never mind. We will take it from here. Meanwhile the SRC Director will be chatting with you on a number of leads he has developed on the bungling of the referendum and other matters. For God's sake give him maximum cooperation."

HIS EXCELLENCY was living up to his threat to do things constitutionally even in the face of all the provocations. The letter to Ikem which was hand-delivered to his flat by a police despatch-rider that afternoon had been signed by a certain Chairman, Board of Directors of Kangan Newspapers Corporation, publishers of the *National Gazette.* A certain chairman because the board and the corporation in question had been moribund for the past three years or more. Ikem had never met the said Chairman or seen a single letter signed by him since he took up the editorship. Incredible!

He carried the letter like a trophy to Chris's house after he got a message that Chris wanted to see him urgently. Beatrice was already there when he arrived. She had something like a puzzled look on her face when she greeted him. Perhaps she had expected him to come in bristling with combativeness instead of which he seemed so strangely composed, even serene. Was it the look of a prospective martyr who has successfully trained his soul's gaze to look past the blurred inpending ordeal to the sharply focussed crown of glory far beyond. She noted but said nothing about this new person and the effect it seemed already to be having on his host, for it was truly extraordinary the way these two sat down quietly and began to trade details of their separate and related predicaments like a pair of hypochondriacs reminiscing on their sweet injuries.

Without realizing it, Beatrice had responded by striking her characteristic pose of detachment—sitting somewhat stiff and erect, her arms folded firmly across her breasts. But instead of staring fixedly away into median space to complete the attitude she made a concession to her indestructible interest by constantly swivelling her glance from one face to the other as the two men carried on their surprising duet. At last her loaded silence struck Chris.

"BB, you are saying nothing."

"What do you want me to say?"

"BB said all that needed to be said when it might have been useful."

"But we were too busy with our private diversionary war."

"Don't be so hard on us; we were not alone in that. All the wars ever fought in this country were, are, diversionary. So why not the little running battles we staged now and again to keep our sanity. You seem to doubt my claim? All right, you tell me one thing we . . . this government . . . any of us did in the last three years . . . or for that matter in the previous nine years of civilian administration that wasn't altogether diversionary."

"Well the diversion has ended," said Beatrice.

"Has it? I'm not so sure. This letter here and all this new theatre of the absurd that Sam is directing to get rid of me and to intimidate Chris, what's it in aid of? Diversion, pure and simple. Even the danger I see looming ahead when the play gets out of hand, what has any of this to do with the life and the concerns and the reality of ninety-nine percent of the people of Kangan? Nothing whatsoever."

"Well, I still think that if you and Chris had listened to me and stopped your running battles as you call them early enough he would not now be trying to disgrace you."

"Disgrace? I'm surprised at you, BB. I didn't know you could be so incredibly sanguine. Disgrace? The fellow wants to kill us! He is mad, I tell you. His acting has got into his head, finally."

"Well, I think BB is closer to the mark. As usual. I agree the fellow is completely deluded and can therefore be very dangerous. But his interest at this point is limited to making us look small, not murder. What he told me on the telephone this morning was very significant I think. He was giving me a chance, he said, to still appear as the Commissioner for Information."

"Did he say that? And what does that mean?"

"Well, *appearing* is very important to him. *Not appearing* is, of course, the worst kind of disgrace. And all this is tied up in his mind with his failed referendum for life president. The pain still rankles. I don't think I told this to either of you at the time. But after the failure of the referendum he had complained bitterly to Professor Okong that I had not played my part as Commissioner for Information to ensure the success of the exercise and that you had seen fit to abandon your editorial chair at that crucial moment and take your annual leave."

"Professor Okong told you?"

"Yes, but I then confronted him. At first he pretended to make light of it but I wouldn't let go. So in the end he revealed his bitterness. He said that he was deeply wounded that we, his oldest friends, found it possible to abandon him and allow him to be disgraced. Those were his very words."

"Did he really say that?"

"I reminded him that he never really wanted to be Life President. That made him truly, hopping mad. '*I didn't*,' he said, '*and you know I didn't but the moment it was decided upon you had a clear responsibility, you and Ikem, to see it succeed. You chose not to.*' I never before heard so much bitter emotion in his voice."

"And you didn't mention this to Ikem? I don't ask about myself, who am I? But to Ikem, no? You never cease to surprise me, Chris. Nothing in this world can make your heart race!"

"That was more than two years ago. I didn't think then it was all that important. In fact I never thought of it in this light until you used the word *disgrace* just now."

"It doesn't speak too highly of your power of analysis or insight which is what I have always told you."

"Please, Ikem, please, let's not slip back into our routine running battles, yet . . ."

"No no, BB. I am serious. If Chris had reported this to me at the time I should have insisted that we both resign there and then and we would not be in this mess today. You see what I mean?"

"Perhaps. But we lost that chance. What I want to know is what Chris proposes to do now and what he recommends you do."

"Simple. I shall draft my letter of resignation tonight and have it delivered to him tomorrow morning. For Ikem I strongly, most strongly, urge a period of silence until . . ."

"Rubbish, Chris, rubbish! The very worst prescription for a suspended editor is silence. That's what your proprietor wants. Because he makes reams of paper available to you he believes he owns your voice. So when he feels like it he withdraws the paper to show you how silent you can be without his help. You musn't let him win."

"So are you going to set up a new paper of your own then?"

"Don't be ridiculous. If you can't write you can surely get up and talk. You haven't lost your vocal chords."

"Where do you intend to talk? In a corner of Gelegele market?"

"Oh, Chris!"

"Never mind. All I say is *careful! That's all. Or Kabisa.* Though I haven't heard him use that lately."

"Not when it has filtered down to motor mechanics," said Beatrice.

"That's right."

"Ikem, I think Chris is right. You've got to lie low for the next couple of weeks, so we can plan our moves properly. Chris is right about that though I think you are closer to the mark about the danger."

"Well I wasn't exactly going to create Hyde Park Corner in Gelegele in spite of Chris's insinuations. But people are going to ask me questions, and I shall bloody well answer. I'm not going to crawl into a hole . . ."

A taxi-cab seemed to be having some difficulty with the police sentry. Chris who had a view of the gate from where he sat, got up, moved to the entrance door, clapped his hands to attract the sentry's attention and signalled to him to let whoever it was come in. But the taxi-driver had already lost his patience, it appeared, and was heatedly discharging his passenger right there.

The passenger turned out to be Elewa. She paid and collected her change in a state of flutter clearly discernible from where Chris stood and rushed into the house breathless and deeply agitated. Ignoring welcoming greetings from everybody she flung herself at Ikem.

"Wetin I de hear, Ikem? Na true say dem done sack you?"

Ikem nodded his head as he pressed her to himself. She burst into tears and violent crying and in that brief instant exploded the atmosphere in the room. All three were embarrassed by this intrusive emotion, but more especially the men, and each put in a clumsy word or two to console the girl and restore the original calm.

"Oh come on, Elewa. I am only suspended not sacked . . . Who told you anyway?"

That did it. She stopped crying almost as dramatically as she had begun. But her voice, when she spoke, was broken and heavy with grief.

"Everybody de talk am for our yard. Even my mama wey de sick hear am small for six o'clock news from our neighbour him radio. But me I go chemist for buy medicine for am."

"Never mind, my dear. You see I still de alive and well."

"I thank God for that."

"How mama be today?"

"E de better small . . . You say no be sack them sack you na . . . weting you call am?"

"Na suspend they suspend me."

"Weting be suspend? . . . I beg, BB weting be suspend?"

"My sister, make you no worry yourself. As we de alive so, na that one better pass all . . . I no know say your mama no well. Sorry. You done take am go hospital?"

"Hospital? Who get money for hospital? And even if you find money, the wahala wey de there . . . My sister, na chemist we small people de go."

IT WAS ELEWA'S KEEN EARS which picked up the radio news signal from some distant set turned too high probably in someone's Boys' Quarters in the neighbourhood, and her voice which screamed "News!" Chris sprang up and dashed to his television set, switching it on and checking his wristwatch at the same time. Elewa was right. The eight o'clock national news was about to begin. They all sat back in grim-faced silence to watch.

Ikem's suspension was the first headline. Something approaching an amused look crept into his features for the brief duration of his limelight—a straightforward announcement without frills. Then all of a sudden he was stung as if by a scorpion and he screamed and leapt to his feet.

"Oh no!" he shouted. "They can't do that! Chris did you hear that? And you say I should lie low. Lie low and let these cannibals lay their dirty hands on a holy man of the earth. Switch that damn thing off!" He was already making for the television set when

Chris's voice telling him to get a hold of himself told him also that this was not his television set, nor this his house. He went back and sank into his seat, his left thumbnail between his teeth. Then he got up again:

"Elewa, let's go!"

What had caused all this agitation had been a subsidiary item tagged on to Ikem's news because of its relative unimportance and prefaced accordingly with the formula: *In another development . . .*

Yes, in another development, according to this smug newscaster dispensing national anguish in carefully measured milligrammes, six leaders from Abazon who were involved in a recent illegal march on the Presidential Palace without police permit as required by decree had been arrested. And (in the same development) the office of the Director of SRC had informed the Crime Correspondent of KTV that the six men who had made useful statements were being held in BMSP.

12

ON THE TWO previous occasions when Ikem had spoken before
audiences at the University of Bassa he had attracted large crowds,
but nothing quite on the scale of the present event. Every seat in
the two-thousand-capacity Main Auditorium was taken and a large
overspill sat or stood on gangways or peeped in through doors and
windows from the two side-corridors running the length of the
hall. It would appear that his suspension from the *National Gazette*
had pushed his popularity rating, already pretty high, right to the
top of the charts. Even more remarkable than the size of the
crowds was their patience. The lecture took off at least forty minutes behind schedule while sweating Students Union officials
dashed in and out of the hall occasionally shouting, "Testing! Testing! Testing!" into a dead microphone. But such was the good
humour of this audience that when the system finally came alive it
was given a thunderous ovation.

A few last-minute consultations by the organizers and the lecture seemed finally set to begin. But no. First the introductions. A

minor union official took the microphone and introduced the Master of Ceremonies, a tall handsome fellow in a white three-piece suit, who in turn and at some length introduced the President of the Union who delivered a most elaborate introduction of the Chairman for the occasion who—at long last—introduced Mr. Ikem Osodi. It was all so reminiscent of the style of campaign meetings in the good old Byzantine days of politicians who, should they rise now from the bowels of their rat-holes and station themselves cautiously just below the surface, would be watching shiny-eyed, twitching their whiskers in happy remembrance.

Ikem called his lecture "The Tortoise and the Leopard—a political meditation on the imperative of struggle." This announcement was greeted with tumultuous approval. No doubt it had the right revolutionary ring to it and Ikem smiled inwardly at the impending *coup d'état* he would stage against this audience and its stereotype notions of struggle, as indeed of everything else.

"Mr. Chairman, sir . . ." he said, bowing mock-deferentially to the Professor who had just been eulogized by the Students' Union President as a popular academic admired by all and sundry for his clarity and Marxist orientation who, as the youngest professor in Kangan, had ably redirected Political Science from bourgeois tendencies under Professor Reginald Okong to new heights of scientific materialism . . .

"May I crave your indulgence and begin this meditation—not lecture by the way, I never can muster enough audacity to lecture —I meditate. May I begin with a little story."

And he told, to remarkable dramatic and emotional effect, the story of the Tortoise who was about to die.

"That story was told me by an old man. As I stand before you now that old man who told me that incredible story is being held in solitary confinement at the Bassa Maximum Security Prison."

No! Why! Opposed! Impossible! and other sounds of shock and anger flew like sparks and filled the air of the auditorium.

"Why? I hear you ask. Very well . . . This is why . . . Because storytellers are a threat. They threaten all champions of control, they frighten usurpers of the right-to-freedom of the human spirit—in state, in church or mosque, in party congress, in the university or wherever. That's why."

It was a brief presentation, twenty to twenty-five minutes long, that was all; but it was so well crafted and so powerfully spoken it took on the nature and scope of an epic prose-poem. It was serious but not solemn; sometimes witty without falling into the familiarity of banter.

The audience sat or stood silently entranced. Its sudden end was like a blow and it jolted them into shouts of protest. Calls of *Fire! Fire! More! More!* and even *Opposed!* soon turned into a rhythmic chant when Ikem sat down.

The Chairman turned to him and said, "They want some more!"

"Yes! More! More! More!"

"I thank you, my friends, for the compliment. But as someone once said: There is nothing left in the pipeline!"

"No! No! Opposed!"

"In any case you have listened to me patiently. Now I want to hear you. Dialogues are infinitely more interesting than monologues. So fire your questions and comments and let's exchange a few blows. You've been at the receiving end. But, as the Bible says, it is better to give than to receive. So let's have a few punches from your end. That's what I've come here for."

And true enough, it was during question-time that he finally achieved the close hand-to-hand struggle he so relished. By nature he is never on the same side as his audience. Whatever his audience is, he must try not to be. If they fancy themselves radical, he fancies himself conservative; if they propound right-wing tenets he unleashes revolution! It is not that he has ever sat down to reason it out and plan it; it just seems to happen that way. But he is aware of it—after the event, so to say, and can even offer some kind of explanation if asked to do so: namely that whatever you are is never enough; you must find a way to accept something however small from the other to make you whole and save you from the mortal sin of righteousness and extremism.

A couple of months ago he had been persuaded against his normal inclination to speak at the Bassa Rotary Club weekly luncheon. On that particular occasion the club had more cause than usual to be happy with itself for it had just bought and donated a water-tanker to a dispensary in one of the poorest districts of North Bassa, an area that has never had electricity nor pipe-borne water. In the after-dinner haze of good works, cigar smoke and liqueur his hosts sat back to hear what their distinguished guest had to tell them . . . Well, as usual, he left what he should have told them and launched into something quite unexpected. Charity, he thundered is the opium of the privileged; from the good citizen who habitually drops ten kobo from his loose change and from a safe height above the bowl of the leper outside the supermarket; to the group of good citizens like yourselves who donate water so that some Lazarus in the slums can have a syringe boiled clean as a whistle for his jab and his sores dressed more hygienically than the rest of him; to the Band Aid stars that lit up so dramatically the dark Christmas skies of Ethiopia. While we do our good works let us not forget that the real solution lies in a world in which charity will have become unnecessary.

The rotund geniality of his hosts was instantly shattered and distorted into sharp-pointed shapes of aggressiveness.

That world of yours will be in heaven, sneered one gentleman. Even in heaven, said another, there is seniority. Archangels are senior to common angels.

As early as possible Ikem was escorted out of the room by two club officials—a normal practice indeed but which on this occasion was performed with such icy civility that it took on the appearance of showing an ungracious dinner guest to the door straight from the table he has insulted.

But this was no Rotary Club and dealing with it would be easier in some ways, but in others probably more difficult.

The first questioner was apparently a young member of faculty rather than a student. His question was prefaced with a little lecture of his own on the manifest failure of bourgeois reformism to address the fundamental problems of the Third World in general and Kangan in particular. Did Mr. Osodi not consider, in view of the above, the necessity of putting the nation now under the democratic dictatorship of the proletariat?

"No, I don't. I wouldn't put myself under the democratic dictatorship even of angels and archangels. As for the proletariat I don't think I know who they are in the case of Kangan."

"Workers and peasants," said the Chairman, helpfully.

"Workers and peasants," Ikem repeated into the microphone, "I have just been told."

"And students," a voice from the audience called, causing much laughter.

"Fair enough," said Ikem. "Charity begins at home." More

laughter. "Any other suggestions. We have peasants, workers and students . . . Excellent! Will peasants in this hall please stand."

There was now hilarious laughter from all corners of the auditorium, especially when another three-piece-suited gentleman got up and offered himself.

"No, you are not a peasant my good friend. Sit down. I want a proper peasant . . . Well, ladies and gentlemen it does appear we have no peasants here tonight. Perhaps they don't even know we are having this meeting . . . I am told, by the way, by those who attend shareholders' annual general meetings that there is something called a proxy form which you send nominating somebody else to stand in for you when you cannot yourself be present. Is there anybody here carrying such a document on behalf of peasants? Mr. Chairman, was any proxy form delivered to you?"

The learned professor in spite of the heavy burden of his earnestness felt obliged now to join in some of this rather awkward fun. So he shook his head, not too vigorously but well enough to win the applause of the ticklishly humorous crowd.

"Very well. I think we should leave peasants out of the discussion. They are not here and have sent no one to speak on their behalf . . . That leaves us with workers and students . . ."

"And market women," chipped in a high female voice from the audience, to a renewed burst of merriment.

"Market women, my dear girl, are in the same category as peasants. They are not here either . . . I will let you into a secret I have told nobody else. My prospective mother-in-law is a market woman." Laughter!

"A cash madam," offered someone.

"No, not a cash madam. A simple market woman . . . This is not a joke now. I am really serious. My prospective mother-in-law sells tie-die cloth in Gelegele market. She is not a cash madam as I have said; she can carry all her worldly wares in one head-load. So she qualifies along with peasants for a seat among the proletariat. But she has not given me, her future son-in-law, any authority to be her proxy at this shareholders' meeting . . . So let's move on and deal with those we are competent to speak for, namely ourselves. Workers and students. Let's take workers first. Who are they? The same workers who go on strike when outdated and outrageous colonial privileges like motor vehicle advances and allowances are threatened; whose leaders cannot give satisfactory

account of millions they collect every month from the compulsory
workers' check-off scheme; who never in their congresses attack
absenteeism, ghost workers, scandalously low national productiv-
ity. Above all, workers whose national president at last year's All-
Africa Congress refused to leave his hotel room until an official
Peugeot 504 assigned to him was replaced with a Mercedes. His
reason you remember: that workers' leaders are not, in his very
words, *ordinary riff-raffs.* You find that funny? Well I don't. I find it
tragic and true. Workers' leaders are indeed *extraordinary riff-raffs.*
There has been, for a few years now, a running battle between me
and the Civil Service Union. You know that, don't you?" *Yes,*
roared the audience, laughing. "The reason for our little disagreement is because I have not attempted to hide my opinion of them
as plain parasites." More laughter. "Those of you who follow our
battles may remember that it all came to a head last year when I
wrote a stinging editorial on the eve of their Annual Congress."
There was smiling recognition on some faces, some nodding of the
head and scattered remnants of laughter. "In their communiqué at
the end of the Congress they referred to certain bourgeois, elitist
hack writers who are no more and no less than running dogs of
imperialism!" Loud laughter. "You probably didn't know who
they were alluding to but it was their way of replying to my editorial. Their way is indeed peculiar. Our proverb says that the earth-
worm is not dancing, it is only its manner of walking." Laughter.

"The charge of elitism never fails to amaze me because the same
people who make it will also criticize you for not prescribing their
brand of revolution to the masses. A writer wants to ask questions.
These damn fellows want him to give answers. Now tell me, can
anything be more elitist, more *offensively* elitist, than someone
presuming to answer questions that have not even been raised, for
Christ's sake? Give us the answer! Give us the answer! You know
it was the same old cry heard by Jesus Christ from his lazy-minded,
soft-brained, bread-hungry hangers-on in Galilee or Gadarene or
wherever it was." Tremendous outburst of cheers. "Give us a miracle! Give us a miracle and we will believe in you. Cut out the
parables and get to the point. Time is short! We want results!
Now, now!" Renewed laughter and more cheers greeted this unexpected and quixotic exploitation of the Holy Writ. "No I cannot
give you the answer you are clamouring for. Go home and think! I
cannot decree your pet, text-book revolution. I want instead to

excite general enlightenment by forcing all the people to examine the condition of their lives because, as the saying goes, the unexamined life is not worth living . . . As a writer I aspire only to widen the scope of that self-examination. I don't want to foreclose it with a catchy, half-baked orthodoxy. My critics say: There is no time for your beautiful educational programme; the masses are ready and will be enlightened in the course of the struggle. And they quote Fanon on the sin of betraying the revolution. They do not realize that revolutions are betrayed just as much by stupidity, incompetence, impatience and precipitate action as by doing nothing at all." Mixed, cautious applause. He paused as if to consider his next move.

"I think I should take the advantage of this forum to propound the new radicalism which I believe we should embrace." Applause of expectation. "First and foremost, this radicalism must be clear-eyed enough to see beyond the present claptrap that will heap all our problems on the doorstep of capitalism and imperialism . . . Please don't get me wrong. I do not deny that external factors are still at the root of many of our problems. But I maintain that even if external factors were to be at the root of *all* our problems we still must be ready to distinguish for practical purposes between remote and immediate causes, as our history teachers used to say." Smiles of recognition. "May I remind you that our ancestors—by the way you must never underrate those guys; some of you seem too ready to do so, I'm afraid. Well, our ancestors made a fantastic proverb on remote and immediate causes. If you want to get at the root of murder, they said, you have to look for the blacksmith who made the matchet." Loud laughter. "Wonderful proverb, isn't it? But it was only intended to enlarge the scope of our thinking not to guide policemen investigating an actual crime." Laughter.

"When your fat civil servants and urban employees of public corporations march on May Day wearing ridiculously undersize T-shirts and school-boy caps"—Laughter—"Yes, and spouting clichés from other people's histories and struggles, hardly do they realize that in the real context of Africa today they are not the party of the oppressed but of the oppressor." Applause. "For they are the very comrades who preside over the sabotage of the nation by their unproductivity and fraud, and that way ensure that the benefits of modern life will ever remain outside the dreams of the real victims of exploitation in rural villages." Mixed noises.

"I hear some of you cry *Opposed!* I like that! Let me substantiate. I never make charges without substantiating." A few cries of *Fire!*

"Indeed I will fire! Let's take the Electricity Corporation of Kangan as one example out of many. What do we see? Chaotic billing procedures deliberately done to cover their massive fraud; illegal connections carried out or condoned by their own staff; theft of meters and a host of other petty and serious crimes including, if you please, the readiness at the end of the day to burn down the entire Accounts and Audit Departments if an inquiry should ever be mooted . . ." Loud laughter. "This is not funny you know . . ." *Don't mind them!* said a loud-voiced young man on the front row, frowning severely at his ticklish neighbours. "To blame all these things on imperialism and international capitalism as our modish radicals want us to do is, in my view, sheer cant and humbug . . . It is like going out to arrest the village blacksmith every time a man hacks his fellow to death." Loud laughter and applause, catching even the severe young man off his guard. "Shall I go on? No! I will say simply that these people are not workers by any stretch of the imagination. They are parasites, I tell you. And I will not agree to hand over my affairs to a democratic dictatorship of parasites. Never! . . . Now what about students? I should really be very careful here as I am quite anxious to get home safely tonight." Explosion of laughter. "However, truth will out! I regret to say that students are in my humble opinion the cream of parasites." Redoubled laughter. "The other day, did not students on National Service raze to the ground a new maternity block built by peasants? Why? They were protesting against their posting to a remote rural station without electricity and running water. Did you not read about it?" The laughter had died all of a sudden. "Perhaps someone can show me one single issue in this country in which students as a class have risen above the low, very low, national level. Tribalism? Religious extremism? Even electoral merchandising. Do you not buy and sell votes, intimidate and kidnap your opponents just as the politicians used to do?" The applause was beginning to revive now, albeit far less robustly. "Are you, as you should be, more competent than those of our countrymen and women not nearly as lucky as yourselves on whom we have squandered our meagre educational resources? It took an hour to start this lecture because a microphone could not be found . . . I walked up to this dais exploding groundnut shells under my feet all the way. So what are we talking about? Do you not form tribal pressure groups to secure lower admission requirements instead of striving to equal or excel any student from anywhere? Yes, you prefer academic tariff walls behind which you can potter around in mediocrity. And you are asking me to agree to hand over my life to a democratic dictatorship of mediocrity? No way! . . . Now, don't misunderstand me. I have no desire to belittle your role in putting this nation finally on the road to self-redemption. But you cannot do that unless you first set about to purge yourselves, to clean up your act. You must learn for a start to hold your own student leaders to responsible performance; only after you have done that can you have the moral authority to lecture the national leadership. You must develop the habit of scepticism, not swallow every piece of superstition you are told by witch doctors and professors. I see too much parroting, too much regurgitating of half-digested radical rhetoric . . . When you have rid yourselves of these things your potentiality for assisting and directing this nation will be quadrupled." Tremendous applause. Surprisingly?

The questions kept coming hard and fast. In the end the chairman simply had to get up and say: Enough! It was then close to midnight. He thanked Mr. Ikem Osodi for a most stimulating lecture and equally stimulating answers to audience questions. He praised the lecturer's contributions to the nation's cultural and political growth in the fields of journalism and literature and hoped that whatever misunderstanding had been responsible for his suspension from duty would soon be resolved. Applause. But there were two issues which he would like to touch upon however briefly. Mild restive protests from the floor. He promised to be brief. He was raising these issues as a sociologist of literature in the context of a writer's ideological development and clarity. First he must confess that he found Mr. Osodi's concept of struggle too individualistic and adventuristic. Some applause. Secondly, on a general note he must state once again his well-known contention that writers in the Third World context must not stop at the stage of documenting social problems but move to the higher responsibility of proffering prescriptions. Applause.

"Writers don't give prescriptions," shouted Ikem. "They give headaches!"

Uproarious laughter.

"Well, on that note we say thank you to Mr. Osodi for a most entertaining evening."

13

ONE OF THE MANY questions Ikem had had to field in the course of his lecture, some briefly and others at some length, concerned a fairly persistent rumour that the Central Bank of Kangan was completing plans to put the President's image on the nation's currency. Was it true and if so what did the honourable lecturer think about such an eventuality?

"Yes I heard of it like everybody else. Whether there is such a plan or not I don't know. All I can say is I hope the rumour is unfounded. My position is quite straightforward especially now that I don't have to worry about being Editor of the *Gazette*. My view is that any serving President foolish enough to lay his head on a coin should know he is inciting people to take it off; the head I mean."

The statement which was roundly applauded in the auditorium was to reverberate louder still throughout the country from the very next morning when the *National Gazette* came out brandishing in the heaviest possible type the headline: EX-EDITOR ADVOCATES REGICIDE!

One of the ifs of recent Kangan history is what the fate of Ikem might have been had he backed out of that speaking engagement at the university. Those who hold that the lecture was decisive are probably underrating the sheer indefatigability of Major Johnson (Samsonite) Ossai, Director of SRC. For he was moving and closing in relentlessly on a number of alternative fronts the most menacing coming from the direction of the controversial expatriate Director of Administration at the Bassa General Hospital, Mr. John Kent, popularly called the Mad Medico. For over a year now the perspicacious Major had had the foresight to keep Mr. Kent under very close but discreet surveillance. And what accrued to the Major from this particular exercise was of such crucial importance that it might have sufficed by itself even if the lecture had not happened. This is not by any means to underrate the new opening offered by the lecture for it did make a dramatic pincer movement and quick kill easy and inevitable.

Mr. Kent was hauled in quietly for interrogation, held secretly and incommunicado for four days at the BMSP, released under tight security and deported within forty-eight hours. A terse radio and television announcement of his deportation for activities prejudicial to state security issued by the Directorate of State Research Council when Mr. Kent was already airborne was the first and last official intimation Kangan had of this unexpected event. Few at first could have linked it clearly with the suspension of the Editor of the *National Gazette* announced earlier although the two announcements coming so close to each other left in many minds the impression that the uneasy calm of the past twelve months might at last be speeding to a close.

And then a few hours later there was yet another special announcement. This time it was issued by the Army Council (a body that no one could recall announcing anything in years), and it told the nation simply that, in an extraordinary meeting of the Army Council, Major Johnson Ossai, Director of the State Research Council, was promoted to the rank of full colonel. End of special announcement.

He is certainly sticking to his promise to do things constitutionally, thought Chris when he heard this latest bulletin.

It was all very well for Beatrice to make fun of his morning routine of informational alienation but no one had yet suggested to him a better way for getting to know what was going on, not in the outside world—that had always known how to wait—but right here in Kangan. So instead of the BBC at seven as usual he got up earlier the next morning and tuned in to its six o'clock news. And true enough Mr. Kent's deportation from the West African state of Kangan, although extremely scanty in detail, had made world news!

With one ear glued to the little transistor radio he dialled Ikem's number. He had failed to reach him last night when the news about MM first broke. The houseboy who answered the phone said he had gone out in the afternoon with dat gal . . . And now the telephone was ringing away and nobody was picking it up. Ikem was notorious as a late riser and positively hated to be disturbed early in the morning, but Chris thought that in present circumstances he might at least pick up his phone . . . No. Very well.

He tried Beatrice next. She answered sleepily at first but on hearing who and what became instantly and intensely alert.

"Try and get the BBC. They are likely to have a fuller story in the African news after the world bulletin."

"But how does one get the BBC? You know I have never yet been able to find them. All I get is that infuriating thing in special English from the Voice of America. I think my radio must be made by CIA . . ."

A little later she called back, her voice utterly dejected, to report failure yet again.

"Never mind, dear. Come right over. I managed to record MM off transmission. Meanwhile I am trying to reach Ikem. His ability to sleep through storms is beginning to irritate me . . . See you."

By the time Beatrice went over at about seven-forty-five, Chris had been alerted and was making frantic calls all over Bassa without any success. As soon as her car drove in he rushed out. "Ikem's not in his flat though he went to bed there last night . . ."

"He may have gone out early."

"His car is in the garage and . . . let's go and see for ourselves. Can you drive us?"

"Sure." She noticed he was trembling.

The front door was locked so they went round to the back and through the kitchen door to which the houseboy held a spare key. The flat was in a shambles. Books and papers and clothes were strewn everywhere in the living-room and in the master and spare bedrooms. An alarm clock lay among shards of its broken glass beside the bed.

The houseboy was repeating what he had already told Chris on the telephone a short while ago when there was a tap on the door and a woman came in uncertainly, and then a man. They were Ikem's neighbours in the adjacent flat. The man, a civil servant, recognized the Commissioner for Information at once.

"Good morning, sir," he said. Finding the Commissioner there seemed to have lifted his morale and removed some of the gloomy timidity with which he had come in. "Agnes, this is the Commissioner for Information, Mr. Oriko. Sir, this is my wife."

"Good morning sir," said Agnes the wife also brightening up considerably.

"Thank you. Have you seen anything of your neighbour? Since last night?"

The man looked at Beatrice questioningly and then around the room and the open doors.

"There is nobody else here. You know who I am. This is Beatrice Okoh, Senior Assistant Secretary, Finance. We are not police or security, just friends of Mr. Osodi. Did you see anything?"

"Pleased to meet you madam . . . I was fast asleep when Agnes woke me up and said there were two jeeps outside . . ."

"Army jeeps?"

"So I went to the window to look and she was right. There were two jeeps standing in the yard and by that time the people were banging on our neighbour's front door. Then after some time we could hear the door open."

"Did they identify themselves? Did they say who they were?"

"I think they said they were from State Research Council."

"Yes, that's what they said. And we heard him say that he was coming before he opened the door."

"Yes?"

"We were not sure that they were soldiers. You know how armed robbers can sometimes say they are soldiers. So we were afraid to go out."

"That's understandable. When exactly did this happen?"

"They were here exactly one-fifteen or so. And they left at around two-thirty. That was when they came out with our neighbour."

"How many were they?"

"They plenty-o. Some came inside and some stayed outside. My husband said they must be up to ten but I didn't count."

"Did you get any vehicle numbers?"

"I tried to but they parked under the umbrella tree, so the security light could not shine there for me to see the number well."

"Was he rough-handled? Listen, you can speak without fear."

"Unless inside the house. But outside they did everything quiet."

"So there was no struggling or pushing or something like that . . . outside?"

"No. I didn't see anything like that."

"But our neighbour's hand was inside hand-cuff," said the wife, "and his face . . ."

"We couldn't see very well sir. As I told you it was dark . . ."

"His face?" asked Chris turning fully to the wife.

"We couldn't see very well whether his face was swell up. It was too dark. So we don't know whether it was because of the dark or that his face was swell up."

"Thank you very much. You have given us the first solid information. You need not worry. We shall not mention you in any way."

"Thank you sir, thank you madam. This our country na waa. Na only God go save person."

WHEN CHRIS FIRST HEARD through a friend's telephone call of MM's deportation at six p.m. the day before, he had tried to speak to Ikem but he had apparently gone out with Elewa. So the last time they talked together was the morning of the regicide story. Containing his irritation as much as possible he had wanted to know exactly what Ikem had said at the lecture. He fully expected an explosion from the other end in answer to his query but to his delight Ikem seemed quite upset that whatever he said had been so atrociously distorted and he was then drafting a stiff letter to the editor and even mentioned possible court action.

Standing there now ineffectual, in the ruins of his flat, Chris's mind, locked out as it were on a barren corridor of inactivity, fluttered, panic-stricken, from one closed door to the next.

"I wonder if he did send the letter."

"What letter?"

"To the Editor of the *Gazette.* It is important that they print his denial."

"You think they will. With that odious fellow licking his lips. Anyway phone him and ask him why the letter has not appeared. He used to be a poodle of yours . . ."

"We must reach Elewa. Who knows there may have been hints of this earlier in the day."

"How?"

"I don't know really. But she was here till six."

"The people came at one in the morning. Still I agree that Elewa ought to be told, anyway. Do you happen to know where she lives. No? Nor do I. The houseboy might know."

"That's an idea."

The houseboy didn't know where she lived nor where she worked.

"Let's see, I believe she told me she was a sales-girl in an Indian or was it Lebanese shop. Textiles I think. But which particular shop . . . I suppose we could try all the ones in the Yellow Pages . . . But Elewa who? We don't know that either, do we? Oh well I am sure she will hear one way or another and come back here."

They left the flat so that Beatrice could go to work. Chris advised her not to make enquiries on the matter from her office but to leave everything to him.

He spent the entire morning on the telephone. The mental immobility which the devastation in Ikem's flat had induced in him had now lifted completely. His mind got clearer on what he had to do as he went along doing it. Major Ossai was not available to speak to him and nobody else in the Directorate could help with the information he required.

The President's Principal Secretary would not put him through but promised to call him back as soon as the President was free to talk to him. What was the subject of his discussion? Oh, but that is not a matter for the President. You want to speak to the Director of SRC.

Then he called the Attorney-General who said he didn't know about it.

"But aren't you supposed to know?"

"Well, yes and no. If it is purely a matter of state security it could be tricky . . . I will know ultimately of course, you know . . ."

Professor Okong hadn't heard; and the Chief Secretary to the Government had just this minute been told by the Attorney-General.

Oh, well! No point continuing to search for the living among the dead! So he changed tack. It was clear that Major Samsonite Ossai and his boss were adopting a quiet line. Therefore he must embark on a massive publicizing of the abduction. He knew he could count on some of the representatives in Bassa of foreign news agencies, their press and radio. On the home front there was no comparable resource to lean on but there was the enormous potential of that great network nicknamed VOR, the Voice of Rumour, the despair of tyrants and shady dealers in high places. Before evening both systems, foreign and local seemed set to start buzzing in the interest of the abducted man.

Then at six o'clock yet another Special Announcement from the Directorate of State Research Council was on the air:

In the discharge of its duty in safeguarding the freedom and security of the State and of every law-abiding citizen of Kangan the State Research Council has uncovered a plot by unpatriotic elements in Kangan working in concert with certain foreign adventurers to destabilize the lawful government of this country.

This dastardly plot was master-minded by Mr. Ikem Osodi until recently Editor of the government-owned *National Gazette.*

Investigations by top security officers, of SRC have revealed Mr. Osodi's involvement in three separate aspects of the plot:

(1) He was the key link between the plotters in Kangan and their foreign collaborators.

(2) He was the lynchpin between the plotters in Bassa and a group of disgruntled and unpatriotic chiefs in the Province of Abazon.

(3) Under the guise of a public lecture at the University of Bassa on 26 September, Mr. Osodi furthered the aim of the plotters by inciting the students of the University to disaffection and rebellion against the government and the life of His Excellency the President and the peace and security of the State.

In the early hours of this morning a team of security officers effected the arrest of Mr. Osodi in his official flat at 202 Kingsway Road in the Government Reservation Area and were taking him in a military vehicle for questioning at the SRC Headquarters when he seized a gun from one of his escorts. In the scuffle that ensued between Mr. Osodi and his guards in the moving vehicle Mr. Osodi was fatally wounded by gunshot.

His Excellency has already appointed a high-level inquiry into the accident to be headed by the Chief of Staff, Major-General Ahmed Lango, with the directive to commence investigations immediately and to report within fourteen days.

Meanwhile investigations are proceeding with a view to uncover all aspects of the plot and to bring to book any other person or persons, no matter how highly placed, involved in this treasonable conspiracy to divert our great and beloved country from its chosen path of orderly progress into renewed bloodshed and anarchy. Long live His Excellency the President! Long live the Republic of Kangan.

Signed Colonel Johnson Ossai,
Director of the State Research Council.

That is the end of this Special Announcement. There will be a repeat of the announcement at seven o'clock.

Chris threw a few things into his travelling bag while he waited nervously for Beatrice to arrive. As soon as she drove in he went out with the bag, locked the front door and left his house, as it turned out, for good.

The decision to leave had little at first to do with fear for his own safety although that factor was to loom larger with every passing day. But right now in his mind the overwhelming issue which had been crystallizing even as the announcement was issuing from the box was how to counter the hideous lie. Not tomorrow, it could be too late, but now!

As soon as he got to his first hideout he picked up the telephone and summoned two foreign correspondents to meet with him at eight o'clock that night. Then he went to the back room where a camp-bed and writing-table had been set up for him and began to draft his statement. His mind was strangely efficient and lucid; no detail seemed to escape him. A few minutes after he began working he re-emerged in the living-room where his host and Beatrice were making phone calls and told them to make sure that people understood that Ikem was not just wounded but dead. He was convinced that the drafters of the government statement had deliberately chosen a phrase which was popularly misunderstood in order to diffuse the shock of the news by revealing its full extent only in stages. Beatrice thought the theory a little ingenious but didn't argue the point.

When she got home that night a little after eleven she found Elewa whom she had failed to locate all day, distraught, waiting in her flat. And, just as Chris had said, she had totally misunderstood the announcement! For a brief while she toyed with the idea of leaving her in her ignorance till morning. But she immediately realized that if she did it would not be necessarily out of consideration for Elewa but more likely from the cowardly fear of having to handle such a terrible task all by herself. And that decided her. The future she saw unfolding so relentlessly before them would demand brutal courage, not squeamishness, from the likes of Elewa and herself, from now on.

And strange are the ways of deep emotion, Elewa proved the tougher of the two! One piercing cry that continued to reverberate in Beatrice's brain like a rifle-shot in salute to a fallen comrade and Elewa sat down, still and silent. It was Beatrice herself who then gave way to emollient tears she had reserved all evening making frenetic phone calls in Chris's secret command post.

By late afternoon of the next day it was obvious that the State Research Council had begun to look for Chris. One of the foresighted steps he had taken was asking Beatrice to return to her flat and to go to work as usual in the morning and not try to make physical contact until further notice. Just before close of work her secretary asked her to take a call from the Director of SRC. She picked up the phone with deliberate slowness which gave her time to compose her voice and attitude. When she spoke she was cold and indifferent but not hostile.

"Colonel Johnson Ossai speaking."

"I see. Anything I can do for you, Colonel?"

"Well, yes . . . You see I have this very important message for Commissioner Oriko from His Excellency . . . I have tried him at the Ministry of Information several times but he is not on seat. I have tried his house but no answer. I wonder . . . erm . . . if you know his . . . erm . . . whereabouts. It is . . . ."

"No I don't."

"I see. I am sorry . . . ."

"Not at all, Colonel. Goodbye."

Meanwhile Chris had, in addition to the foreign correspondents, made very useful contact with other opinion-makers. He was particularly encouraged by his meeting with the President of the University of Bassa Students Union. For security reasons they had met not in his hideout but in a rendezvous in another area of the Government Reservation. But as it turned out this precaution proved quite unnecessary. The Students Union had been so incensed by the crude regicide story of the *National Gazette* that copies of the newspaper were now regularly seized by students from newsvendors on campus and publicly burnt in the middle of Freedom Square. The Union had also written a long, angry letter to the Editor demanding an apology for the insult to students and their guest lecturer.

Chris handed him a copy of the statement he had prepared and watched him as he read it. The paper soon began to tremble in his hands. When he returned it he drew the back of one hand across his eyes. He tried to speak but the words were at first blocked by a violent movement of his Adam's apple.

"I need a copy of this," he managed finally. "Can I copy it and return?"

"That's your copy," said Chris, giving it back to him, "if you need it."

"Thank you, sir. We will run off two thousand copies tonight so that every student will have it first thing tomorrow morning. This government has now committed suicide."

"Well, young man," said Chris getting up and offering his hand as a signal for parting. "I hope you are right. I certainly hope so. But we must not count too much on wickedness obliging us so readily . . . I am glad we've had this chance to talk."

"Thank you sir. You can count on us."

"This country counts on you. Take care now."

CHRIS'S LAST VISITORS for the night were the two taxi-drivers. It had taken Elewa the whole morning and half the afternoon to locate one of them and arrange for them to meet with Chris at the same rendezvous.

By the third morning the BBC which had already broadcast news of Ikem's death carried an interview between their Bassa correspondent and Chris who was described as a key member of the Kangan government and friend of the highly admired and talented poet, Ikem Osodi, whose reported death while in police custody had plunged the Military Government of this troubled West African State into deep crisis. In a voice full of emotion but steady and without shrillness Chris had described the official account of Ikem's death as "patently false." How could he be sure of that? Because Ikem was taken from his flat in handcuffs and so could not have wrenched a gun from his captors. So you are saying in effect that he was murdered? I am saying that there is no shred of doubt that Ikem Osodi was brutally murdered in cold blood by the security officers of this government.

The correspondent was deported the next day. But by that time the Students Union had taken up the story and were demanding a judicial inquiry and the immediate dismissal of Colonel Ossai and his prosecution for murder.

Two jeeploads of mobile police sent to apprehend the President and Secretary of the Union bungled the arrest; the young men gave them the slip. As if that was not dangerous enough other students began to taunt them as brainless morons. Now teasing the Kangan Mobile Police is worse than challenging a hungry Alsatian. They went berserk. But somehow, for reasons no one had been able to explain, they did not whip out their guns. Perhaps the bloody outcome of a similar invasion two years ago did after all leave its mark . . . Perhaps in the thousand ages of divine-like patience even this rock of mindlessness will be dented by the regular dripping of roof water! With *koboko* and truncheons they fell upon their fleeing victims chasing them into classrooms, the library, the chapel and into dormitories. In the Women's Hostel, which some of the attackers had originally gained in the blind accident of hot pursuit they all finally congregated and settled into a fearful orgy of revenge, compounding an ancient sex-feud with today's war of the classes.

As ambulances screamed in later to collect the wounded and move them to hospital an announcement was made on the radio closing the university indefinitely and ordering all students out of the campus by six o'clock that very evening.

THE BRITISH HIGH COMMISSIONER in Bassa went to the Ministry of Foreign Affairs to protest about the deportation of two British nationals but instead was given a preview of a letter the security services were said to have intercepted and advised to return to his chancery and await a summons to the Ministry.

The letter, a blue aerogramme, was addressed to Mr. John Kent and signed Dick. A section of it highlighted by a red line running down the margin read:

Delighted particularly to have met that poet fellow who I believe edits the government daily. Splendid chap. Quite astonishing in view of the image one had of African dictatorships to have had a chance of sitting around and hearing treason spoken so casually and the local dictator dismissed as a comic fool! And by such a prominent member of his own government. The editors of *The Times* and the *Guardian* could use a holiday in Bassa! I'm doing a short piece for the *Telegraph*.

Chris could no longer move freely from one hideout to another because of a large number of army and police roadblocks springing up all over the city. Beatrice driving past his deserted official residence on recce saw a jeep stationed in the front yard and some riot policemen standing around. She drove on to the city centre, left her car in the parking lot opposite the Roman Catholic Cathedral, walked back across the street and made a call from a public telephone.

She went to bed early that night but sleep came to her only in short, fitful spells. The third or fourth time she had woken up she thought she heard sounds coming from the direction of the spare bedroom. She got up and tiptoed there and could see at once from the doorway in the faint illumination filtering in from the security lights outside that she was sitting on the bed.

"Elewa!" she said switching on the ceiling light at the same time. "You no fit carry on like this-o."

Beatrice had decided to look after her for a few days and had pushed her writing-desk against the wall and set up a bed for her. She had talked to her at length this evening, given her five milligrams of Valium and left her sleeping before retiring herself. And now here she was sitting on the bed her face a mirror of devastation. Her distracted look actually scared Beatrice. It was not mere grief. It was more. Something of the frightened child was showing strongly now—bewilderment, alarm, panic.

"You no fit carry on like this at all. If you no want save yourself then make you save the pickin inside your belle. You hear me? I done tell you this no be time for cry. The one wey done go done go. The only thing we fit do now is to be strong so that when the fight come we fit fight am proper. Wipe your eye. No worry. God dey."

Elewa exploded into loud crying now. Beatrice went and sat beside her and brought her head against her breast with one hand and began to tap her shoulder rhythmically with the other. When she had quietened her down she slowly disengaged her embrace and laid her gently on the pillow. She went to the wall and switched off the lights and returned to sit on the bed.

"Make you lie down," said Elewa in a voice washed clear by tears. Beatrice complied and lay down on her back beside her in silence. After a while she slowly turned on her side and raised Elewa's head and ensconced it tenderly in the crook of her arm and began to tap a steady rhythm again on her shoulder. The door of memory was unlocked and she saw herself as a child tapping the only doll she ever had, a wooden thing with undeveloped hands, a rigid, erect trunk and the stylized face of the masked maiden spirit. Elewa's chest, richly proportioned, heaved spasmodically like a child's in the aftermath of crying. In the end Beatrice could tell from her deep breathing that she had at last floated into sleep broken now and again by sudden violent starts of nightmare which mercifully did not wake her up. She needed the sleep, poor child. Soon she herself was dozing off.

The car lights first, sensed in the vague indeterminacy of unformed dreams, and then the harsh crunch of tyres on the pebbled driveway. She sprang to her feet. Out of the glass louvres she could see three jeeps unmistakable in the night from the sinister, narrow, closely-set eyes of headlamps. Her heart thumping she rushed to her bedroom, snatched a tough pair of jeans from her wardrobe, leapt into them, zipped up and belted. Then she searched and pulled out another pair. Elewa was standing beside her.

"Put this on quick!"

Then she pulled out two dressing gowns . . .

A number of heavy knocks on her door . . .

"Miss Okoh. This is State Security. Open up at once!"

She put on her dressing gown, helped Elewa into hers and ordered her back into the spare bedroom with hand-and-head gestures.

"Miss Okoh. This is the last warning. Open the door now. State Security."

"I am coming."

"Well, hurry up!"

She took the bunch of keys from the sideboard and began to unchain the iron grills. Her hands were shaking so violently she couldn't get the key into the keyhole. Elewa snatched the bunch from her, turned the padlock and unchained the heavy grill. Then Beatrice shocked into calmness by this action snatched back the keys and, whispering "Go inside!" to Elewa who ignored the command, turned the lock in the steel and glass crittall door. It was wrenched out of her grip and swung outwards. Then a huge soldier rushed in pushing the two women aside so powerfully to his right and left in a dry breast-stroke movement that sent Elewa, slight as a reed, down on the floor on her bottom.

"Easy, Sergeant!" This from an officer who followed less dramatically. Three others came in after the officer while the rest stayed at the door.

"Miss Okoh?"

"Yes."

"I am sorry to disturb you at this hour. But I have instructions to search your flat. May I proceed?"

"Anything in particular you are looking for?"

"What kind nonsense question be dat."

"OK, Sergeant. I will do the talking. So keep quiet! Well, yes, Miss Okoh, there are certain things we are looking for but it is not our practice to discuss them first. Incidentally I advise that anybody in the flat should come out right away. All the exits are guarded and anyone trying to escape will be shot. Is that clear? Now we will proceed." He deployed his men to different locations in the flat with the silent gestures of a field commander. Thereafter he went from one sector to another supervising the operations. Beatrice followed him at a discreet distance.

The red-eyed sergeant who was given charge of Beatrice's bedroom was executing it with a vengeance. He had pulled out the bedsheets off the bed and thrown them on the floor where he walked all over them as he frenziedly darted from one object to another. It was fortunate that Beatrice never learnt to lock suitcases and things. So the sergeant's fury had nothing to wrench open. He merely spilt clothes everywhere. The officer came in and asked him again to go easy and picked up the bedsheets himself and threw them back on the bed. As the captain turned his back Beatrice caught in the eye of the sergeant a flash from the utmost depths of contempt and hatred.

"Miss Okoh, excuse my asking. Who is this young lady?"

"She is Elewa . . . my girlfriend."

"Your *girl*friend? Interesting. What does she do?"

"What do you mean?"

"I mean does she have a job?"

"Yes. She is a sales-girl in a Lebanese shop."

"Does she live with you normally?"

"No, she is just visiting."

"I see."

Elewa's eyes darted from one to the other as they discussed her like the seller and prospective buyer of some dumb animal brought to the market. Her grief had temporarily been displaced by these strange events now going on around her. In her oversize jeans and dressing gown she looked almost comical. She was not walking around with Beatrice and the officer but had taken her position on a dining-chair in the living-room annexe.

Beatrice, worried about her fall, asked as many times as she came through the living-room how she felt. No trouble, she would answer. Perhaps it was the Valium making her unusually calm.

In Elewa's room the soldier detailed there was looking through papers and books on the table when Beatrice trailing the officer came in again.

"Are you looking for books too?"

"Everything," replied the officer on behalf of the soldier. "My people have a saying which my father used often. A man whose horse is missing will look everywhere even in the roof."

He searched everywhere for his missing horse for about an hour, apologized for disturbing Beatrice's sleep, saluted and left. What kind of enigma was this? Could there really be even one decent young man in the Security Services or indeed the entire Kangan Army and Police. Or was this the ultimate evil—the smiling face of Mephistopheles in the beguiling habit of a monk? Safer by far to believe the worst.

14

As SHE WAS drowsily getting dressed for work the bedside telephone rang. Startled, she grabbed it on the second ring. A voice
said: "Miss Okoh?"

"Yes. Who is that?" Her heart was thumping and the telephone
in her unsteady hand bobbed up and down against her ear. Silence
at the other end. Was he gone? Then:

"Never mind who. I know where the horse is. But I don't want
to find him. Get him moved. Before tonight." He rang off.

Or was he cut off? She stood transfixed, the handset in her hand
vibrating still against her ear. Hoping the voice would return?
Had they been intercepted? Slowly she replaced and sank with
leaden weariness into her unmade bed.

Move him? Was it a trap? To lure him into the soldier-infested
streets? Who exactly was this fellow? Could he be genuine? Who
in God's name could one ask? Tears of loneliness began to form in
her eyes. She got up, wiped them and blew her nose and then
tiptoed to Elewa's room. She was sleeping beautifully, childlike,

beguiled perhaps by a dream in which the bad news had not yet been heard, where what happened here had not yet happened. She tiptoed out again leaving her to snatch what strength she could from the short reprieve of her dreams. She picked up her handbag and went alone in search of a safe telephone.

Later in the office she had a restless day wondering whether any of the score of accidents that could happen to the move had happened, and which. Only one was needed. Just as they say of bullets . . . The worst thing was sitting there so inactive signing daft letters, and not knowing what was going on. Should she risk a quick phone call from another office just to know, even without saying a word, whether his host, already gone to work when she had transmitted the message, had been reached to come back to arrange the move. And again that officer, was he genuine? Could anyone be genuine in these shark-infested waters? What then could his game be? Oh God! But why couldn't she just slip into one of the offices down the corridor, dial the number and see who picks up the phone? But Chris would be mad; he had been so insistent that she must not . . . And if she simply dialled the number and didn't speak, that could cause panic at the other end and might lead to a false step . . . Oh my God!

She left her office like a bird released from its cage, on the dot of three-thirty. (Chris had also insisted that she must not leave before closing time on his account because her movements would then attract attention. Damn his efficiency!) She did not head straight for home but went ostensibly shopping. From the crowded parking-lot, however, she went elsewhere than the shops.

There was a sprightliness in her walk as she returned to the parking-lot that told all her news. She decided to treat herself to a phial of Blue Grass and went into the shops. Instead of one bottle she bought two; one for Elewa. Then she picked up a loaf of bread and a few other groceries and set out jauntily for home. At the car-park she deposited her bag of purchases on the bonnet of her car and unzipped her handbag for the key. She searched one compartment and then the other. Her ill-used heart began to palpitate again. She told herself to keep calm, take a deep breath, and search the bag more thoroughly. She did, and even emptied the contents on the bonnet. But the little bunch was not there. She half-ran all the hundred or so yards to the public telephone. A man was making a call. She knocked on the glass door and tried to slide it open. The man interrupted his conversation to protest.

"I am sorry. I'm looking for my car key."

"There is no car key here," said the man angrily as he wrenched the door from her hand, shut it firmly and resumed his conversation, after a hissing sound longer than men generally could manage. She returned dejectedly to the car after she had retraced her steps with mounting hopelessness through the various stops she had made inside the shop and the different cashiers' stations where she had brought out her wallet from her handbag and made payments. Everyone, especially the perfumery girls, remembered her, but not her bunch of keys.

She was tired; hugely tired. The sun's routine oppression had changed all at once into a special act of vindictiveness against her in reprisal perhaps for the nervous energy she had just displayed instead of the languor decreed from above. All around her in the parking-lot she saw vaguely in slow motion hundreds, more wise than she, who obeyed and prospered.

She turned around for no apparent reason and took a look inside the car, and saw the keys dangling from the key-hole. Transports of joy! Now she could go home and even if she failed to locate her spares—which had become a major fear since she had begun considering strategies—she could bring a mechanic, even a car-thief, and force the door-lock or do something with the glass, and move the car.

Smiling, she went in search of a taxi. Was it happiness about the keys or something deeper, a response called up by the crisis in which she and her friends were enmeshed? Whatever it was, she struck up a conversation with the taxi-driver and very soon she was learning things she didn't know, about the death of Ikem, about the missing Commissioner for Information and about the planned meeting tomorrow of the Taxi Drivers Union "to put their mouth into this nonsense story" of Ikem's death.

"If you get somewhere to go make you go today. Tomorrow no taxi go run."

By the time they got to her flat the rapport between Beatrice and the driver was such that although she took a little time finding her spare keys he did not mind in the least. The beer she offered him to make the time pass more pleasantly he put away under his dashboard until his break-time. He promised to bring the empty bottle back tomorrow on his way to the meeting.

"Don't worry about the bottle," said Beatrice.

"Why I no go worry? I be monkey wey dem say to give im water no hard but to get your tumbler back?"

Beatrice burst into laughter as she climbed back into the car for the return journey to the parking-lot. Even the joker had to laugh then at his own joke.

CHRIS'S LAST HIDEOUT had been raided as promised at midnight. Beatrice had got ready quite early but had had to wait until there was adequate traffic on the roads before venturing out to put a call through to the house. The conversation was brief and undetailed, without proper names.

"Any visitors?"

"Yes they came at twelve."

"Any problems?"

"None so far."

"So far?"

"Well, none really. Nothing at all."

"Thank God."

Click!

She went into her flat as she sometimes did, quietly by the kitchen entrance. Elewa was at the table dipping dry bread in a mug of Ovaltine while Agatha watched her leaning on the doorway between the kitchen and the dining-annexe.

"What are you watching her for? And what sort of breakfast is this? No eggs . . . no margarine . . ."

"But she no ask me for egg or margarine."

"She no ask you?"

"Make you no worry, BB. This one done do."

"Agatha, you are a very stupid girl and a very wicked girl . . . Get out of my way!"

She pushed past her back into the kitchen, broke and whisked three eggs for an omelette. While it simmered she brought breakfast things out of the refrigerator to the table—margarine, marmalade, honey, orange juice, milk. Then she sat down and insisted that Elewa eat the egg and drink the fresh orange juice. She literally waited on her not just because her grief entitled her to it but she wanted her solicitude to be a ringing rebuke to Agatha who had made no attempt to conceal her resentment at having to serve someone she clearly felt, judging from the contempt in her eyes and the way she curled her lips, was no better than a servant herself.

After the first surge of anger Beatrice found herself feeling for the first time for this poor, twisted, desiccated, sanctimonious girl something she had never before thought of extending to her—pity. Yes, she thought, her Agatha deserved to be pitied; this girl who danced and raved about salvation from dawn to dusk every Saturday, who distributed free leaflets (she had once even sneaked up to Chris when Beatrice stepped out of the room and given him one). Yes, this Agatha who was so free with leaflets dripping with the saving blood of Jesus and yet had no single drop of charity in her own anaemic blood.

As she drank her coffee and nibbled at the bread and omelette she was having just to keep Elewa company and make sure she had a little something nourishing and needful for her condition she wondered why Agatha should want to be so beastly to the girl.

Of course being a servant could not be fun. Beatrice knew that. She had never belittled the problem or consciously looked down on anyone because she was a servant, so help her God. For she was sensitive enough and intelligent enough to understand, and her literary education could not but have sharpened her perception of the evidence before her eyes: that in the absurd raffle-draw that apportioned the destinies of post-colonial African societies two people starting off even as identical twins in the morning might quite easily find themselves in the evening one as President shitting on the heads of the people and the other a nightman carrying the people's shit in buckets on his head. So how could a girl like Beatrice, intelligent, compassionate, knowing that fact of our situation look down on another less lucky and see more to it than just that—blind luck?

But there was more to it. There had to be. Look at Elewa. Was she not as unlucky as Agatha in the grand capricious raffle? A half-literate salesgirl in a shop owned by an Indian; living in one room with a petty-trader mother deep in the slums of Bassa. Why had she not gone sour? Why did she radiate this warmth and attraction and self-respect and confidence? Why did it seem so natural to install her in the spare bedroom and not, like Agatha, in the servant's quarters? She was Ikem's girl, true. But was that all? And how come Ikem singled her out in the first place to be his girl from the millions just as unlucky as herself? There was something in her that even her luckless draw could not remove. That thing that drew Ikem to her, and for which she must be given credit.

Ikem! Oh yes, Ikem. Provocative, infuriating, endearing Ikem! He was, had to be, at the root of these unusual musings! She recalled the last visit he had paid her in this flat. Though she was to see him a couple of times again subsequently, the last time only the other day at Chris's place when they had all watched the news of his suspension together, that last visit here at her flat had risen with his death to dominate her consciousness of him and driven earlier and even later memories firmly into the background.

It was perhaps the strong, spiritual light of that emergent consciousness that gave Elewa, carrying as it turned out a living speck of him within her, this new luminosity she seemed to radiate which was not merely a reflection of common grief which you could find anywhere any hour in Kangan, but a touch, distinct, almost godlike, able to transform a half-literate, albeit good-natured and very attractive, girl into an object of veneration.

But even more remarkable was the way this consciousness was now, at the ebb-tide of her anger impinging on despised Agatha, who had wilfully placed herself until now beyond the reach of Beatrice's sympathy by her dry-as-dust, sanctimonious, born-again ways; yes, impinging on her of all people and projecting on to the screen of the mind a new image of her; and in the background the narrator's voice coming through and declaiming: *It is now up to you women to tell us what has to be done. And Agatha is surely one of you.*

And do you know what? Perhaps it might even be said that by being so clearly, so unpleasantly, so pig-headedly unhappy in her lot Agatha by her adamant refusal to be placated may be rendering a service to the cause more valuable than Elewa's acceptance; valuable for keeping the memory of oppression intact, constantly burnished and ready. How about that?

It was Agatha's habit to cry for hours whenever Beatrice said as much as boo to her; and Beatrice's practice to completely ignore her. But today, after she had deposited the used plates in the sink, Beatrice turned to where Agatha sat with her face buried in her hands on the kitchen-table and placed her hand on her heaving shoulder. She immediately raised her head and stared at her mistress in unbelief.

"I am sorry Agatha."

The unbelief turned first to shock and then, through the mist of her tears, a sunrise of smiles.

THE VOICE had become expansive, even self-indulgent. Two calls in one day! In the morning it was to give her full marks for moving the horse; but, if the horse was still in Bassa, to impress upon her that the city was not a safe environment for him. So she had better be thinking quite soon of a cross-country gallop.

"It's not me you should worry about; I can promise never to find a horse. It's the others who are more efficient than myself in the matter of finding horses."

Completely bemused at the end of this strange mixture of whimsy and deadliness Beatrice found herself saying the words: "Are you genuine?" which rang almost as strangely in her ear as the communication that had given rise to it. He gave no answer. Perhaps he was already half-way to replacing his telephone and didn't hear the question. Or perhaps he heard but did not wish to put himself in the vulnerable position of being questioned. If so, fair enough. One should not look a gift-horse in the mouth. The fellow wasn't hired by her as her private detective, so he was within his rights to lay down conditions for his freely volunteered assistance.

Assistance, did she say? So she was already assuming he was on her side, already taking him for granted. So early in the day. Careful now, Beatrice, careful. How did her people say it? Don't disparage the day that still has an hour of light in its hand.

That evening he called again to answer the question.

"You asked was I genuine? If by that you mean do I ride horses or do I play polo the answer is an emphatic no. But if you mean do I like horses, yes. I am a horse-fancier." Click!

So he did hear it. Only he needed the time, a whole day, to work out a clever answer. Oh, well. She couldn't really complain . . . though she must admit to being a little troubled by the tone of sportiveness creeping into his manner. But again, why not? Why should this unconventional benefactor be judged by her own sedate sense of seriousness. Was she forgetting that kind though he might have been to her on one occasion he was still a practising hangman? And what could be more natural than for a man in his profession to have a somewhat unorthodox sense of humour—gallows humour, in fact!

Two other things that happened that day compounded Beatrice's anxiety. The *National Gazette* had come out in the morning with a strange story: The Commissioner for Information, Mr. Christopher Oriko, who had not been seen in his office or his residence for the past one week had according to unconfirmed reports left the country in a foreign airliner bound for London disguised as a Reverend Father and wearing a false beard.

What were they up to now? Was this a smoke-screen behind which they hoped to eliminate their second victim less messily than the first?

Then at six o'clock came a police statement declaring Mr. Christopher Oriko, Commissioner for Information wanted by security officers in connection with the recent coup plot and calling on anyone who had information concerning his whereabouts to contact the nearest police station and warned citizens that concealing information about a coup plotter was as serious as failing to report a coup plot or taking part in a coup plot; and the penalty for each was death.

This announcement had not come as a complete surprise to Beatrice. Still to hear those idiotic accusations made against the backdrop of that unflattering full-face picture of Chris dug up from God knows where staring out at you from the screen injected a chill into one's circulation, even without the ominous death sting at the end.

She and Elewa sat in reflective silence after the announcement. Agatha who seemed to have heard it from the kitchen and moved up to the door was leaning on the doorway, silently. Then the telephone rang as though on cue shattering the dramatic silence. Elewa sat up, her head held high like a deer that sniffs danger, its erect ears waiting for a confirming rustle. But no stealthy sound came and no flashing movement, and she sat back again. Beatrice's change of countenance, the tone and words of her half of the conversation had dispelled the air of dread which had lately attended telephone calls. The conversation was indeed about the announcement but whoever Beatrice was talking to seemed merely to be expressing friendly concern. When she dropped the telephone Elewa and Agatha had been having a quiet discussion of their own on the matter.

"Madam, make you no worry at all," said Agatha. "Whether they look from here to Jericho, they no go find am. By God's power."

"Amin," replied Elewa. "Na so we talk."

15

CHRIS MEANWHILE had been weaving a nest of heady activity in the circumscribed quarters of his retreat. If only Beatrice had had more direct access to him in those few days of his rapid metamorphosis into the new career of prized quarry she might have learnt to be less surprised by the strange behaviour of his hunter; for even in his harried run Chris had still left himself scope for heightening the drama of the chase. This apparent luxury made his tight corners not only more enjoyable to him but on occasion went so far as to offer him the illusion that he had turned hunter from hunted; that he had become the very spider manning a complicated webwork of toils and not the doomed fly circling in orbits of seeming freedom that nevertheless narrowed imperceptibly to a fatal impingement. Was this a necessary part of the psychology of hot pursuit that it will deceive even its own purpose, not to talk of the predicament of its victim, into liberal-looking sportiveness and fairplay?

Chris's new network was fastened on the support of friends who harboured him in spare rooms and Boys' Quarters and even, on one dramatic occasion, pitched him through a loose board into the steamy darkness of the ceiling. This hide-and-seek gave everyone concerned a nice conspiratorial feeling of being part of an undertaking admittedly risky but still far short of menacing. However, after the police announcement spelling out the death penalty for everything including this kind of game, Chris and his current host had a serious talk together and decided that they could not rule out the chances that one or two people who had played a role in the affair so far might be frightened by this turn of events into quietly informing against him to buy their own peace. So the need for him to move out of Bassa entirely became suddenly urgent. But it was going to be tricky and there was no way it could be accomplished in one step in the short time he had. So it was arranged that he and his aide-de-camp, Emmanuel, should make a preliminary move out of the Government Reservation Area to the northern slums under the care of the taxi-driver, Braimoh.

Emmanuel Obete was the President of the Students Union who after a couple of visits had brought his bag along one afternoon and simply stayed on.

"Why have you come to me?" Chris asked him, not on the first day nor the second but as they ate a hurried breakfast of fried plantains and corn pap with his host on the third morning.

"For protection," said Emmanuel who was revealing a new side of himself as a clown of sorts. Chris and his host looked at each other and laughed.

"Do your people have a proverb about a man looking for something inside the bag of a man looking for something?"

Emmanuel laughed in his turn and said no they didn't . . . but wait . . . they did have something that resembled it: about digging a new hole to get sand to fill an old one.

"He is something else," said Chris to his friend. And he did not trouble the young man again about his reasons.

Emmanuel was also a fugitive wanted by the police. But being of only middling importance in police estimation he was not given the VIP treatment of having his wait-and-take picture on television. A troublesome Students Union official was nothing new to the Kangan Police, and they were not about to make a song and dance about him.

"Now I want to tell you the real reason I came to you," said Emmanuel later in the day.

"I see," said Chris. "Actually the one you gave in the morning was good enough for me. What is it this time?"

"Well, this time it is because the security people are so daft they will look for me everywhere except where you are."

"There you go again underrating the state security. Very dangerous, you know. Better to overrate your enemy than to underrate him. OK, look at this matter of the fatal gunshot. Anyone who can come up with that kind of thing can't be a complete fool."

"I don't believe they came up with it, sir. Pure accident, that's all."

Emmanuel's low opinion of the army and police was matched only by his dismal estimate of Kangan journalists. Between the two he would give a slight edge in fact to the security officers. And fortunately for him the incredible ease with which he had planted the story of Chris's escape to London in the *National Gazette* came in handy as indisputable proof. He, Chris and their host had such a laugh when the news appeared; and Chris had to admit, shame-facedly as a former Editor of the *Gazette,* that the affair put the journalistic profession in Kangan in a very poor light indeed.

"Of course it would not have happened under your editorship or Ikem's," said Emmanuel in a tone that was not entirely free of certain impish ambiguity.

"Thank you, Emmanuel. Such gallantry."

"No, I mean every word, sir." And it seemed, this time, he did.

But Chris had some difficulty getting the matter off his mind. Long after the merriment over Emmanuel's brilliant success had subsided he kept repeating to himself: "One telephone call! From a senior Customs Officer who for obvious reasons would rather not reveal his identity! Unbelievable!"

Chris's disguise for his first hop was nothing as fanciful as Emmanuel's priest's cassock. He wore Braimoh's everyday clothes and cap to match, and a few smudges of pot-black on his face and neck and arms to tone down a complexion too radiant for his new clothes or pretended calling as a retail dealer in small motor-car parts. The one-week growth of beard he had nurtured just in case, was discarded as not too great a success, especially when his host suggested, half-seriously, that the Reverend Father's beard in Emmanuel's rather more successful fiction might have the result of drawing police attention instinctively to people's chins for some days to come.

Braimoh had two passengers in the back seat of his old cab when he arrived to pick up Chris for the critical journey to the north of the city. His estimate was eight or nine odd security road-blocks to cross. Chris said good afternoon to the two strangers behind and took the front seat beside the driver. Before driving away Braimoh reached into the untidy junk in his glove-box and brought out three kolanuts and offered them to Chris.

"Make you de chew am for road. Anybody wey see you de knack am so go think say you never chop breakfast."

The two men behind laughed rather a lot at this and Chris not being sure whether they were people who laughed much ordinarily or hid malice behind laughter cast a questioning glance at Braimoh, even as he reached for the gift.

"Dem two na my people. No worry."

Chris took the proffered kolanuts, and thanked Braimoh. Then he gave one to the two men behind as though in appeasement and put the others in his pocket. Seeing where they had been fished out of he would need to wash them before eating.

Emmanuel darted out for a quick goodbye and vanished again behind the main house into the Boys' Quarters. It had been agreed that he would travel separately to rejoin Chris later.

They passed the first three check-points without trouble. The soldiers and police looked tired and waved cars through rather inattentively. Chris was almost certain that Emmanuel's *Gazette* story must be more than marginally responsible for thus putting the law off their guard. He was something else, that boy Emmanuel. Why did we not cultivate such young men before now? Why, we did not even know they existed if the truth must be told! We? Who are we? The trinity who thought they owned Kangan as BB once unkindly said? Three green bottles. One has accidentally fallen; one is tilting. Going, going, bang! Then we becomes I, becomes imperial We.

The traffic was beginning to slow down at the big bend in the road just before the Three Cowrie Bridge. Another check-point, no doubt. Stupid fellows the police; they would choose the approaches to a bridge to disrupt traffic! At long last Braimoh cleared the corner, and ran full tilt into it! This was no ordinary check-point but a major combined army and police operation.

There were two military jeeps by the roadside and three police patrol-cars flashing their roof-lamps. Ahead, passengers were being ordered out of vehicles.

Braimoh panicked and made the first move of a hasty U-turn, which was a serious error considering the flashing patrol-cars waiting to give chase! The man behind Chris shouted to Braimoh to get back into line, and he promptly complied. But it would seem his ill-considered move had already been noticed.

"Oga come out quick! Make we use leg."

Chris was out of the car like a shot and so was the man who had spoken. They were on the kerb side of the road, fortunately.

"Quick, make we de go!"

As they walked smartly away from their car towards the bridge the soldier who seemed to have noticed Braimoh's suspicious move was coming briskly towards them. Chris was watching him through the corner of his eye until they drew level. The soldier stopped.

"Hey, stop there!" he shouted. Chris and his companion halted on the sidewalk and turned to him, standing on the road. His face was scarred by three heavy marks on either side. He had accompanied his order with the unslinging of his automatic weapon. The width of a car separated him from Chris and his companion.

"Where you de go?"

"We de go Three Cowrie Market."

"Wetin de inside that bag? Bring am here."

Chris's companion walked down the kerb between two cars and opened his dirty shopping bag for the soldier to inspect.

"You there, come down here. Wetin be your name?"

"Sebastian," replied Chris, using the name of his steward from instant inspiration.

"Sebastian who?"

He didn't know. But luckily he realized quickly enough that it didn't much matter.

"Sebastian Ojo."

"What work you de do?"

"He de sell motor part."

"Na you I ask? Or na you be him mouth?"

"I de sell motor parts," said Chris.

"How you de sell motor part and then come de march for leg?"

"Him car knock engine."

"Shurrup! Big mouth. I no ask you!"

But he had already diverted the scorching fire away from Chris and given him a little respite just when he was beginning to wilt and quiver a bit at the knees. His right hand, heavy and idle beside him, stirred into life and went to his trouser pocket where it found one of the kolanuts and brought it out. The soldier's eye caught it and lit up. Chris split the nut and gave the bigger half to him and put the other into his own mouth. The soldier took the offering eagerly and crunched it with noisy greed.

"Thank you brother," he said, fixing his gaze on him and squinting in what might be an effort of memory. "Na only poor man de sabi say him brother never chop since morning. The big oga wey put poor man for sun no de remember. Because why? Him own belle done full up with cornflake and milik and omlate." He resumed his squint at Chris and then tapped his forehead. "I think say I done see you before before."

"Sometime you buy small something for repair your machine for him shop?" said Chris's companion.

"Which machine? I tell you say I get machine?"

"Make you no mind. No condition is permnent. You go get. Meself as I de talk so, you think say I get machine? Even common bicycle I no get. But my mind strong that one day I go jump bicycle, jump machine and land inside motor car! And somebody go come open door for me and say *yes sir!* And I go carry my belle like woman we de begin to pregnant small and come sitdon for owner-corner, take cigarette put for mouth, no more kolanut, and say to driver *comon move!* I get strong mind for dat. Make you get strong mind too, everything go allright."

The soldier now wore a wistful smile which sat strangely on his savaged face.

Across the bridge they walked leisurely, waiting for Braimoh and his lone passenger to get through their own ordeal. Chris's spirits had returned to such a degree that a certain jauntiness was discernible in his walk. He even suggested to his companion that walking through check-points would seem to be their best bet from now on.

"You think you no go forget your job again?" his companion asked teasingly. "When you no fit talk again that time, fear come catch me proper and I begin pray make this man no go introduce himself as Commissioner of Information!"

"Me Commissioner? At all. Na small small motor part na him I de sell. Original and Taiwan."

"Ehe! Talkam like that. No shaky-shaky mouth again. But oga you see now, to be big man no hard but to be poor man no be small thing. Na proper wahala. No be so?"

"Na so I see-o. I no know before today say to pass for small man you need to go special college."

His companion liked that and laughed long and loud. "Na true you talk, oga. Special College. Poor Man Elementary Cerftikate!"

They walked along merrily discussing in confidential tones their recent success. Chris wondered why the soldier had stopped them in the first place. Had he noticed them get down from the taxi?

"At all!" Said his companion. "Make I tell you why he stop us? Na because of how you de walk as to say you fear to kill ant for road. And then you come again take corner-corner eye de look the man at the same time. Nex time make you march for ground with bold face as if to say your father na him get main road."

"Thank you," said Chris. "I must remember that . . . To succeed as small man no be small thing."

16

THE JOURNEY to the North began five days later. The choice of Abazon as sanctuary came quite naturally. At the purely sentimental level it was Ikem's native province which, although he had rarely spent much time there in recent years, still remained in a curious paradoxical way the distant sustainer of all his best inspirations, so that going there now in his death became for Chris and Emmanuel something of a pilgrimage.

Then it was a province of unspecified and generalized disaffection to the regime. One could indeed call it natural guerrilla country; not of course in the literal sense of suggesting planned armed struggle which would be extravagantly far-fetched as yet, but in the limited but important meaning of a place where, to borrow the watchword of a civil service poster, you could count on having your secrets kept secret.

And lastly, Braimoh's wife, Aina was, as it turned out, a native of southern Abazon and Braimoh had volunteered to personally escort the distinguished refugee and hand him over to his in-laws up there for safe-keeping.

All these attractions of Abazon had of course to be set against the one considerable disadvantage of being a place where the regime might be sleeping with one eye open especially since the death of Ikem and the ugly eruption of a new crisis over the government's refusal to turn over his body to his people for burial under the provocative pretext that investigations were still proceeding into the circumstances of his death!

The night before the journey had been quite extraordinary. Beatrice, at her own insistence, had been brought by Braimoh in a friend's taxi through devious routes to say farewell to Chris. She wore for the occasion long-discarded clothes fished out of a big, red canvas bag in which she threw odds and ends awaiting the visit of the Salvation Army collector. With her came Elewa. It was to have been a brief visit after which the two young women would take another taxi to Elewa's mother's place a couple of kilometres away and spend the night there to avoid a late journey back to her flat at the GRA which might attract undue attention.

But the strain and the confusing events of recent days and nights which Beatrice had borne all on her own with such intrepidity seemed all of a sudden to assume an unbearable heaviness on her shoulders at this tantalizing reunion. Why should she accept this role of a star-crossed lover in a cheap, sentimental movie waving frantically from the window of an express train at her young man at his window in another train hurtling away on opposite tracks into a different dark tunnel? And so she rebelled with a desperate resolve grounded on a powerful premonition that Chris and she had tonight come to a crossroads beyond which a new day would break, unpredictable, without precedent; a day whose market wares piled into the long basket on her head as she approached the gates of dawn would remain concealed to the very last moment.

And so, timidly for once, Beatrice chose to hang by a thread to the days she had known, to spin out to infinite lengths the silken hours and minutes of this last familiar night.

"I shall stay here till morning," she pronounced from that rock-like resolve just as Braimoh peeped through the door a second time for instructions about a taxi. Glances were exchanged all round but no one dared to demur. Rather, new arrangements were quickly taken in hand, debated and concluded around Beatrice's now-aloof stance while she, immobile as a goddess in her shrine, her arms across her breasts, stared away fixedly into the middle distance.

She heard the debate and the conclusions remotely: Elewa would take Emmanuel to her mother's place in the taxi; Braimoh would pack the five children off to sleep in a neighbour's house . . .

"Oh no no no!" said Chris suddenly out of a reverie, stamping his foot firmly on the linoleum-covered floor. All eyes turned to him but he merely went on shaking his head for a while longer before saying quite decisively that the children must not be moved. The thinking which had produced this sharp reaction had gone somewhat as follows: I arrived here and failed to prevent Braimoh and Aina his wife from abandoning their matrimonial bed to me and going out every night to sleep God-knows-where. I'll be damned if their five children will now be ejected from their floor because of Beatrice.

He leaned over and explained these thoughts to her in excited whispers. Her response was instantaneous. Her mind and all her thoughts had been so totally focussed on Chris's metamorphosis from disembodied voice back into flesh and blood that she had left herself no room whatever to consider such things as beds and floors and at what and whose cost. Now she spoke as firmly as Chris in favour of the children. She went further to say, in sincere atonement, that as far as she was concerned the chair on which she sat was all she needed for the night.

Later, she had to be summoned several times by Chris before she left that chair and, stepping over the sleeping children, hung her head-tie on a nail driven into the wall and went over to the bed. She was still suffering a sense of shame for her thoughtlessness. But how was she to have known that by simply obeying an impulse to stay close to Chris this one night before a journey into the unknown she was selfishly putting out a poor family? Why did no one tell her? Or was she, as her people say, just to sniff her finger and know? Then who was to tell her? Braimoh? Look, Miss, my wife and I go out to pass the night on a neighbour's floor while our five children sleep here on this floor; so you can't stay here. Or Chris? Yes, Chris the Information man should have informed, not *after* but *before.* But how was even he to know the impulse bubbling inside her and erupting in her pronouncement? The fault is then hers. Although she had not consciously thought about it she must have made the assumption in some inattentive zone of her mind that one or two of all those doors that gave into the long odoriferous corridor running through the belly of this airless block-house must lead into other rooms used by Braimoh and his family. Why did she make that assumption? Surely everyone had heard that large families of the urban poor lived in single window-less rooms. Did she imagine then that for her that piece of infor-mation would stay in the domain of hearsay, that it would never fall to her luck to encounter it in a living family and even share its meagre resources for a single night?

Chris called out again to her from the bed screened by two large curtains of cheap cotton print hung on a rope that stretched from one wall to the other with a sag in the middle that made one want to get up and pull the rope tighter around the nail on which it was fastened.

She picked her steps carefully through the confusion of young sleeping bodies on straw mats on the floor and gained the bed. She had brought pyjamas in her picnic bag but had left the bag un-opened beside her chair. Sitting now on the edge of the bed she took off her blouse and hung it on the sagging curtain-rope. She then loosed her *lappa* from her waist and retied it above the breast and lay down beside Chris.

Their love-making that night was cramped by distractions. At least two of the children lying on the floor beyond the cotton screen—a boy and a girl—could easily possess enough street-lore to know if something was going on and what. Then there was the multiple-pitched squealing of the bed ,at the slightest change of position.

There was one door to the room; it led into the long central corridor and was bolted from inside. There was also a tiny plain-board window which gave directly on to the bed and opened out to a huge, choked and stagnant drain. So it had to be kept shut at all times to keep down the smell and the mosquitoes.

But enough of both still got in. As soon as the lone lightbulb in the room was turned off the mosquitoes began to sing to the ear which was always worse than their bite and, some would say, even worse than the bite of bedbugs which soon followed the mos-quitoes in a night-long assault on these smooth-skinned intruders from the GRA. No wonder Chris looked so haggard and worn-out, thought Beatrice.

But although these specific distractions surely must have worked their own havoc on the rites of this closing night to a long drama that had drawn together more than these two survivors in enactments of love and friendship, betrayal and death, there was something deeper than the harassment of heat and bugs laying a restraining hand on the shoulder of the chief celebrant.

Chris had noticed it from the very moment she had walked in that evening that she carried with her a strong aura of that other Beatrice whom he always described in fearful jest as goddessy. And then lying in bed and summoning her to join him and watching her as she finally rose from her chair in the thin darkness of the room she struck him by her stately stylized movement like the Maiden Spirit Mask coming in to the arena, erect, disdainful, high-coiffured, unravished yet by her dance.

She did not rebuff him. But neither did she offer more than the obligatory demands of her ritual. He understood perfectly and soon afterwards led in an effort to divert their minds to childhood fable. The mosquito, which Chris repeatedly but unsuccessfully tried to swat with an old shirt he had brought to bed for the purpose, was taunting the ear in revenge for the insult with which his suit had once been rejected.

"What's the bedbug's excuse," asked Beatrice "for biting without bothering to sing first?"

"Her story is that man once tried to destroy her and her new-hatched brood by pouring a kettle of hot water on them. Her little ones were about to give up the struggle but she said to them: Don't give up, whatever is hot will become cold."

"And so they survived to bite us tonight."

"Exactly."

"I wonder what she will tell them after a good spray of aerosol insecticide?" Which led her to ask Chris why he had not thought of buying himself a can of Flit since getting here.

"I thought of it actually the first night but then decided against it in the morning."

"What?"

"You see, Emmanuel made the point that since aerosol was a remedy our host could not himself afford it was perhaps better not to insult him by introducing it into his household. I was stunned by that argument, and he handed back to me the money I had given him to buy a canister at the petrol station."

Beatrice was silent for a while. Then she said "What a fellow, that Emmanuel of yours! Still I am glad I won't be spending five nights here."

Their low-toned conversation was abruptly interrupted by a major disturbance on the floor. One child, it appeared, had urinated on his brother. The remonstrance, sleepy at first, quickly sharpened into clear-eyed accusations and a general commotion in which someone soon began to cry, calling on his mother. Click! went the switch and the single naked bulb hanging down the centre of the ceiling flooded the room with light. Chris and Beatrice remained still and silent like a couple of mice interrupted far from their hole and sheltering behind utensils in a crowded room.

"Shush!" It must have been either the biggest of the three boys or the bigger of the two girls taking command. Nothing more was heard after that. They were probably speaking by signs and with their eyes, no doubt pointing to the bed and its distinguished occupants. The switch went click again and darkness returned, broken for a while by discreet whispers; and then silence.

THE DECISION by Chris and his two companions to travel to the North by bus instead of Braimoh's taxi was well taken because a bus was bound to attract less attention to itself than a taxi even when it was as old as Braimoh's.

The bus they chose was one of a new generation of transports known, even to the illiterate, as *Luxurious,* so called because they were factory-built and fitted out with upholstered seats. Chris had never been inside a *Luxurious* before. Indeed his last experience in Kangan buses was years and years ago before he had left to study in Britain. In those days buses were still the crude handiwork of bold and ingenious panel-beaters and welders who knocked any sheet-metal that came to hand into a container on wheels, and got a sign-writer to paint BUS in florid letters all over it.

Before embarking on *Luxurious*, Chris walked round it sizing it up like a prospective buyer. He felt a curious pride in its transformation which had not entirely abandoned its origins. The florid lettering had remained virtually unchanged by prosperity. Perhaps the same sign-writers of his younger days were still working or, more likely, had influenced generations of apprentices in their peculiar calligraphy. And to think of it, that imaginative roadside welder who created the first crude buses might be the managing director of the transport company that now had a fleet of *Luxuri-ouses!* If there had been no progress in the nation's affairs at the top there had clearly been some near the bottom, albeit undirected and therefore only half-realized.

The sign-writers had long expanded their assignment from merely copying down the short word BUS into more elaborate messages rather in the tradition of that unknown monk working away soberly by candle-light copying out the Lord's Prayer as he must have done scores of times before and then, seized by a sudden and unprecedented impulse of adoration, proceeded to end the prayer on a new fantastic flourish of his own: *For thine is the kingdom, the power and the glory, for ever and ever, Amen!*

The sign-writers of Kangan did not work in dark and holy seclusions of monasteries but in free-for-all market-places under the fiery eye of the sun. And yet in ways not unlike the monk's they sought in their work to capture the past as well as invent a future. *Luxurious* had inscribed on its blue body in reds, yellows and whites three different legends—one at the back, another at the sides and the third, and perhaps most important, at the masthead, on top of the front windscreen.

Chris, now fully reconciled to his new condition as a wide-eyed newcomer to the ways of Kangan made a mental note of these inscriptions.

The one at the back of the bus, written in the indigenous language of Bassa, concise in the extreme and, for that reason, hard if not impossible to translate said simply: *Ife onye metalu*—What a man commits. At the sides the inscriptions switched to words of English: *All Saints Bus;* and in front, also in English, they announced finally (or perhaps initially!) *Angel of Mercy.*

Chris took a window seat in the middle section of the bus; Braimoh had already secured a place for himself in front just behind the driver; while Emmanuel on an aisle seat at the rear was chatting up a most attractive girl whose striking features had earlier at the ticketing office made not a fleeting impression on Chris himself.

Those three legends now began to tease and exercise his mind; perhaps they came handy as an antidote to anxiety. After the near disaster at the Three Cowrie Bridge he had become persuaded that in moments of stress his face was perhaps too candid a mirror to his mind, and he had set about cultivating what he hoped in future would pass for a relaxed countenance and serve him more prudently.

But practising deep-breathing exercises and other forms of relaxation therapy in front of a mirror was one thing, and being able to actually look relaxed if a team of vicious security men should for example board the bus now, quite another. To paraphrase a recent wise admonition, how was he to give the impression to the world in such an emergency that this unaccustomed bus in which he now sat nervously was actually his father's property?

Paradoxically Braimoh who owned nothing to speak of could pass, by the way he sat up there, as the true son of the proprietor of *Angel of Mercy,* alias *All Saints,* alias *Ife onye metalu.*

Glancing back to the rear of the bus Chris saw Emmanuel who didn't own anything either, at least not for the moment, also pretty much at ease; not to the degree of Braimoh of course, but more so by far than Yours Sincerely who, don't forget, is one of the troika of proprietors who own Kangan itself! He smiled, bitterly. That Beatrice girl of yours must be closely watched!

If he had a book he could perhaps bury his thoughts in it and escape the betrayal of a tell-tale face. But a man reading a book in a Kangan bus in order to evade notice would have to be out of his mind. So the only reading material he had in his bag were a few unsigned and innocuous poems he had salvaged from scattered papers in Ikem's house.

So those body decorations and beauty marks on *Luxurious* rose to occupy his mind. The Christian and quasi-Christian calligraphy posed no problem and held no terror. But not so that other one: *Ife onye metalu,* a statement unclear and menacing in its very inconclusiveness. What a man commits . . . Follows him? Comes back to take its toll? Was that all? No, that was only part of it, thought Chris, the most innocuous part in fact. The real burden of that cryptic scripture seemed to turn the matter right around. Whatever we see following a man, whatever fate comes to take revenge on him, can only be what that man in some way or another, in a previous life if not in this, has committed. That was it! So those three words wrapped in an archaic tongue and tucked away at the tail of the bus turn out to be the opening segment of a full-blooded heathen antiphony offering a primitive and quite deadly exposition of suffering. The guilty suffers; the sufferer is guilty. As for the righteous, those whose arms are straight (including no doubt the owner of *Luxurious*), *they* will always prosper!

After a mental pause Chris began to smile again not at the outrageous theology he had unmasked but at the hard-headed prudence of the owner of *Luxurious* who had the presence of mind to ring his valued property around with a protective insurance from every faith he knew so that if one should fail to ignite the next might be triggered off. He went one better than the pessimist holding up his trousers with a belt as well as a pair of braces; he added a girdle studded liberally with leather-covered little amulets!

17

The Great North Road

THE KIND OF PEOPLE—local bourgeoisie and foreign diplomats —who sidle up to you at cocktail parties to inform you that Bassa was not Kangan are the very ones who go on behaving as though it was. Why? Because, like the rest of the best people, they have never travelled by bus out of Bassa on the Great North Road. If they had, even once, they would have believed and stopped prating! But they always proffer the excuse that it is too dangerous, too sweaty and, above all, too long a journey for busy people.

Now, as the overwhelming force of this simple, always-taken-in-vain reality impinged on each of Chris's five, or was it six, senses even as hordes of flying insects after the first rain bombard street lamps, the ensuing knowledge seeped through every pore in his skin into the core of his being continuing the transformation, already in process, of the man he was.

What would happen now, he wondered, if the wheels of fortune should turn again and return him to the very haunts of his previous life, to the same cocktail circuits, those hollow rituals which in fairness to him, he always loathed for their sheer vapidity and perhaps even more for the physical pain they caused him? For being somewhat weak of hearing he was forced by the cumulative drone of a hundred or more conversations into an aural blockade in which he could do no better than wander aimlessly from one set of moving lips to another, hearing absolutely nothing, smiling idiotically. What would he do if—but make God no 'gree—he should find himself again in that torture chamber? He would pray for courage to tell each pair of lips and set of teeth before moving on to the next: "Yes, but do you know that although you say so, it is actually true?" And for his courage he may perhaps be rewarded with the rare pleasure of seeing, since he could not hear, one vacuous idiot after another shut his trap for a few peaceful seconds in total mystification, because his piston lips may only have asked: *"How the go de go?"* Beatrice was of course absolutely right about never going to cocktail parties, but then Beatrice never had the misfortune to be Commissioner for Information. No, Bassa was certainly not Kangan. From this authoritative windowseat in *Luxurious* Chris could now vouch for that!

The impenetrable rain forests of the South through which even a great highway snaked like a mere game track began to yield ground most grudgingly at first but in time a little more willingly to less prodigious growths; and a couple of hundred kilometres further north, unbelievably, to open parklands of grass and stunted trees. The traveller's spirits rose in step with this diminution of forests which gave the eye a heady facility to roam freely and take in wide panoramas of space stretching to a horizon where tiny trees on distant hills and against clear skies formed miniature Japanese gardens.

Even the asphalt on which *Luxurious* sped towards the North told its own story of two countries. Thickly-laid and cushiony at first it steadily deteriorated into thin black paint applied with niggardly strokes of a brush over the laterite beginning to break up and reveal, as the journey progressed, more and more of the brown underlay, forcing the elegant and beautiful *Luxurious* to lurch from side to side in order to avoid the deepest ruts and potholes. But Chris welcomed this disappointment of comfort for the blessing it had in tow, for it curtailed the recklessness of *Luxurious* which had been conducting herself like a termagant of the highway treating her passengers' safety cavalierly and bullying every smaller vehicle she encountered clean out of the way as though traffic rights were merely a matter of size. Broken roads and bumpy rides had their uses, thought Chris.

The lifting of his spirits which had enabled him to indulge himself in every kind of visual and intellectual conceit was due to one great and happy fact. Once *Luxurious* had left the metropolis of Bassa and headed into the forest tunnels that eventually led into the open country the security checks took a dramatic change for the better. For a while they continued to occur at about the same intervals of distance and were manned by about the same kind of strength. But their purpose had changed. They took hardly any notice of the passengers but concentrated on demanding and receiving gratification from the bus operators. Even when on one occasion a particularly fierce-looking policeman ordered all passengers to disembark it turned out to be no more than a clever ruse for extracting a bigger toll from the driver, and the few passengers including Braimoh who had actually disembarked were smilingly asked to resume their seats. So it was not only the magic of the countryside, though it did play its part, which enabled Chris's mind, so cramped lately, to float away over this wide expanse of grass-covered landscape with its plains and valleys and hills dotted around with small picture-book trees of every imaginable tree-shape and every shade of green. This flight from danger was taking on the colours and contours of a picnic!

The towns and villages on the Great North Road responded in appropriate ways to the general scaling-down in the size of structures as one pushed out of the rain country slowly towards the land of droughts. The massive buildings of the new-rich down the coast gave way to less imposing but still iron-roofed and cement-walled houses, in much the same way as the giant forests of iroko and mahogany and other great hardwoods had given way to flowering trees like flames-of-the-forest.

As the bus lurched from one side of the road to the other trying to avoid the sharp edges of washed-out bitumen Chris noticed that the same iron roofs were now borne more and more on the shoulders of mud walls plastered over with cement. But in due course this pretence was dropped and the walls owned up frankly to being of reddish earth. The march-past of dwellings in descending hierarchies continued until the modest militias of round thatched huts began to pass slowly across Chris's reviewing stand.

Police and army checkpoints came and went fairly regularly and had dropped *their* pretence of looking inside the bus from the forward door. Now they took their money openly from the operators with seeming good humour on both sides. But the driver and his mate never failed to grumble and curse the fellows soon afterwards.

"Make your mother hair catch fire," prayed the driver on one occasion as soon as he had pulled away from a policeman with whom he seemed to have had a few initial problems.

The bus had been travelling for a little over five hours when it pulled up in the famous dusty and bustling market-town of Agbata, rather large and active for that part of the country. It was the main watering-place of the Great North Road beloved of seasoned travellers on this route. The passengers were glad to escape from the stagnant, cooped-up heat inside the bus into the dry hot waves of the open air. As they disembarked they kicked the cramps out of their leg-joints and sought out what privacy they could find in that unsheltered, sandy terrain to ease themselves. Proprietors of eating-houses and other shacks had regular running battles with every batch of freshly disembarked passengers especially the women eyeing their backyards in spite of many bold scrawls: DON'T URINATE HERE. Most of the men emboldened by tradition and regular travel did not wander around to the same extent like a hen looking for a place to drop her egg but simply picked a big parked truck, moved up close enough and relieved themselves against one of the tyres.

The next concern, food, was more readily available. Scores of little huts with grand names competed for the travellers' custom with colourful signboards backed up with verbal appeals: *Goat meat here! Egusi soup here! Bushmeat here! Come here for Rice! Fine Fine Pounded Yam!*

The word *decent,* variously spelt, occurred on most of the signboards. Chris and his companions settled for Very Desent Restorant for no better reason than its fairly clean, yellow doorblind. In the bus the three had prudently behaved like total strangers. But the last hundred and fifty or so kilometres had shown that they did not need that level of caution. And so now they sat boldly at one table and ordered their food; rice for Chris, fried yam and goatmeat stew for Emmanuel and *garri* and bushmeat stew for Braimoh.

They still did not talk much among themselves and could quite easily have passed for three travellers who perhaps knew each other slightly or even struck up acquaintance in the course of the journey.

The waitress brought them a plastic bowl of water to wash their hands and a saucer with caked soap-powder. It was clear the water had not been changed for quite a while and a greasy line of palm-oil circled the bowl just above the murky water.

Chris to whom the water was first offered looked instinctively first at his palm and then at the water and shook his head. Emmanuel also declined. Braimoh, boldest of the group, asked the young lady to change the water, which immediately brought in the smiling-eyed proprietress who had been presiding from a distance.

"Change the water?" she laughed. "You people from the South! Do you know how much we pay for a tin now? One manilla fifty."

"And the tankers have not come today," chipped in the waitress still holding her bowl of dirty water.

"No," said her mistress. "The tankers have not come. Those people you see over there are selling yesterday's water at two manilla." She pointed through the window to a man carrying across his shoulder like a see-saw a stout pole at each end of which was tied a four-gallon tin. There were two or three others like him manoeuvring their heavy and tricky burden expertly through the crowd.

A FEW KILOMETRES north of Agbata there was a fairly long bridge over a completely dry river-bed and beyond it a huge sign-board saying: WELCOME TO SOUTH ABAZON. It was amazing, thought Chris, how provincial boundaries drawn by all accounts quite arbitrarily by the British fifty years ago and more sometimes coincided so completely with reality. Beyond that dried up river there was hardly a yard of transition; you drove straight into scrub-land which two years without rain had virtually turned to desert.

The air current blowing into the bus seemed to be fanned from a furnace. The only green things around now were the formidably spiked cactus serving as shelter around desolate clusters of huts and, once in a while in the dusty fields, a fat-bottomed baobab tree so strange in appearance that one could easily believe the story that elephants looking for water when they still roamed these parts would pierce the crusty bark of the baobab with their tusk and suck the juices stored in the years of rain by the tree inside its monumental bole.

At the provincial boundary Chris suffered a recurrence of sharp anxiety at the sudden sight of a vast deployment of police and troops larger than any they had encountered since leaving Bassa. But they took no interest whatsoever in the passengers, neither did they delay the driver who went down and across the road to see one of them. As he returned to resume his driving-seat he waved to them in what seemed to Chris like a very friendly good-bye. But no sooner had he driven clear of their road bar than he broke into loud and unrestrained complaints about their greed and finally called down the curse of fire to scorch their mothers' bushes.

Security forces! Who or what were they securing? Perhaps they were posted there to prevent the hungry desert from taking its begging bowl inside the secure borders of the South.

As the bus plunged deeper into the burning desolation Chris reached into his bag and pulled out Ikem's unsigned "Pillar of Fire: A hymn to the Sun," and began to read it slowly with fresh eyes, lipping the words like an amazed learner in a literacy campaign class. Perhaps it was seeing the anthills in the scorched landscape that set him off revealing in details he had not before experienced how the searing accuracy of the poet's eye was primed not on fancy but fact. And to think that this was not the real Abazon yet; that the real heart of the disaster must be at least another day's journey ahead! The dust had turned ashen. A man on a donkey was overtaken by the bus, his face a perfect picture of a corpse that died in the harmattan.

. . . And now the times had come round again out of storyland. Perhaps not as bad as the first times, yet. But they could easily end worse. Why? Because today no one can rise and march south by starlight abandoning crippled kindred in the wild savannah and arrive stealthily at a tiny village and fall upon its inhabitants and slay them and take their land and say: I did it because death stared through my eye.

So they send instead a deputation of elders to the government who hold the yam today and hold the knife, to seek help of them.

After Agbata there were numerous empty seats in the bus. Braimoh moved down and sat directly in front of Chris who had been joined by Emmanuel since the girl had deserted him to sit with a fellow student-nurse.

"Young men are not what they used to be," said Chris. "You mean you let a girl like that slip through your fingers on a bus excursion?"

"I did my best but she wouldn't bite. And do you blame her seeing these rags I'm reduced to?" He made a mock gesture of contempt with his left hand taking in his entire person decked out in ill-fitting second-hand clothes. "Such a tramp! And on top of it all you should have heard the kind of pidgin I had to speak."

"Poor fellow," said Chris with a gleam in his eyes. "I am truly sorry for all this inconvenience."

"I must confess I became so frustrated at one point I began asking her if she had ever heard of a certain President of the Students Union on the run."

"You didn't!"

"No. But I nearly did. It is not easy to lose a girl like that."

"And under false pretences!"

"Imagine!"

"Sorry-o."

"Actually she is the shyest thing I have ever met in all my life. I don't think it was my clothes alone."

"I shouldn't have thought so either. Your sterling quality would shine through any rags."

"Thanks! The real trouble was getting her to open her mouth. She spoke at the rate of one word per hour. And it was either *yes* or *no.*"

"How did you find out she was a student-nurse?"

"Na proper tug-of-war."

"What's she called?"

"Adamma. Her father is a Customs Officer in the far north."

"A lot of information to piece together from yes and no."

They laughed and fell into silence as if on some signal. They had each independently come to the same conclusion that though everything had gone reasonably well so far they must not push their luck by talking and laughing too much. It was in the ensuing reverie that Chris, gazing out into the empty landscape, had become aware of the anthills.

When he had read the prose-poem through and read the last

paragraph or two over again he said quietly to Emmanuel: "You must read this," and passed the paper to him.

It was Braimoh who first drew their attention to a large crowd on the road half-a-kilometre or so ahead. Almost simultaneously everybody in the bus seemed to have become aware of the spectacle so unusual and so visible in that flat, treeless country. Many of the passengers had lifted themselves to half-standing positions at their seats the better to see this strange sight. What could it be? A check-point? The driver slowed down to a wary pace. As the scene came closer, a few uniforms began to emerge out of the dusty haze. There were a few cars and trucks parked this side of the crowd and a bus that was heading South and perhaps other vehicles as well slowly became visible beyond.

The uniforms were greatly outnumbered by people in regular outfits, presumably passengers whose journey had been interrupted, and even by ragged peasants attracted from the arid lives of a few scattered hamlets of round huts dotting the landscape.

The bus continued its progress to this mystery but at a mere cautious crawl. A road accident? No! There was something discernible in the prancing about which did not suggest sorrow or anger but a strange kind of merry-making. And now there was no longer any doubt. Beer bottles could be seen in nearly all hands and the dancing—for no other name seemed better for this activity —was constantly accompanied by the throwing of the head backwards and the emptying of bottles direct into gullets without touching the lips.

The bus pulled up to the side. Some of the crowd were rushing towards it like a tipsy welcoming-party. But the pulling up of the bus and the sudden explosion inside it, like a hand-grenade thrown from the crowd, of the word COUP! came on top of each other. The bus was evacuated like a vessel on fire. The driver, unlike a good and honourable captain, shoved people aside to get to the ground first.

Chris plunged into the crowd looking for someone who might have coherent information. Ultimately he sighted the police sergeant and pulled him aside rather brusquely in his breathless eagerness. The fellow was pleased to oblige, a bottle in his right and a Mark IV rifle in his left.

"Na radio there talk am," was how he began. *There* was an unsightly shack of cardboard and metal thrown together to provide occasional relief to the check-point crew from the sun's on-slaught and perhaps also a little privacy for negotiating difficult bribes from motorists. A radio set in there had apparently given the news.

"So at the same time we hear the news this lorry wey dem load beer full up come de pass. So we say na God send am. The driver talk say the beer no be him own, na government get am. So we say: very good. As Government done fall now, na who go drink the beer? So we self we de stand for sun here, no water to drink; na him God send us small beer to make our own cocktail party."

His laughter was actually quite infectious and the little crowd that had quickly gathered around their story-teller nodding assent and swilling the beer at intervals, joined in the laughter. Even Chris had to laugh, but really as a bribe for getting more information, not from genuine amusement.

"Where is the radio?" he asked, thinking they must be putting out other announcements in the midst of martial music.

"They done thief-am. As we dey for road de drink a thief-man go inside carry the radio commot. This country na so so thief-man full am. But na me and them. They no know me? Before any vehicle can move out from here today I go search am well well and the stupid arm-robber wey hold my radio na him soul go rest in peace, with the President."

"Did they say anything about the President?"

The sergeant looked at him suspiciously. "Why you de make all this cross-examination? Wetin concern poor man like you and President, eh? I say wetin concern vulture and barber?" He was clearly enjoying the attention. "Anyways, the President done disappear. They no fit find am again. They say unknown persons enter Palace and kidnap am. So make everybody de watch proper for this check-point." He burst out into another peal of laughter taking his willing hearers. "This our country na waa! I never hear the likeness before. A whole President de miss; like old woman de waka for village talk say him goat de miss! This Africa na waa!"

"No be you tell whiteman make he commot?" asked somebody from the crowd. "Ehe, white man done go now, and hand over to President. Now that one done loss for inside bush. Wetin we go do again?"

"We go make another President. That one no hard," said a third person.

"He no hard, eh? Next tomorrow they go tell you say your new President climb palm-tree and no fit come down again," said the second man to a tremendous outburst of laughter. He was obviously a wit to reckon with, and knew it.

"So wetin we go do now?"

"Make every man, woman and child and even those them never born, make everybody collect twenty manilla each and bring to me and I go take am go England and negotiate with IMF to bring white man back to Kangan."

Chris had detached himself from this bizarre group to look for Emmanuel.

"Can you make any sense of this?" he asked when he found him.

"Not yet, sir. Except it appears His Excellency was kidnapped last night and the Chief of Staff has sworn to find him but has meanwhile taken over the reins of government."

"We must head back to Bassa. Right away. Where is Braimoh? Get our things out of the bus." His obsessed seriousness was a rebuke to Emmanuel's faint-hearted sarcasm and he went away to his assignment somewhat chastened.

Chris plunged into another section of the crowd which was fast degenerating into drunken mayhem. Bottles were smashed on the road after they were emptied and sometimes before, and more than a few unshod feet were already bleeding. Any promising informant he approached was too drunk and, what was more, critical of him for asking sober questions amounting almost to mental harassment of his victims.

"Go and have a drink," one of them said to him, like a man who, before his present state, had been used to exercising authority.

"I have had a drink. Several drinks," said Chris, sounding superior without perhaps intending to.

"If you have drunk . . . As I have drunk . . . why are you standing straight like that? Or is it my eyes." The fellow's head was going from side to side like an albino, though he was shiny-black like ebony.

"I am not standing straight," said Chris, unaccountably mesmerized by this highly articulate drunk.

"No, it is not my eyes . . . You are not standing . . . I mean to say, you *are* standing as straight as a flag-pole. You get me? My difficulty then is: if as you say you drank as much beer as myself, why are you standing straight? Or put it another way. If two of us ate the same palm-oil chop, how come one of us, i.e. yourself, is passing black shit? That is what I want to know, mister. Two people ate palm-oil soup . . ."

"OK, we will talk about that later."

"Later? Why? Procrastination is a lazy man's apology." Hiccup! "As my headmaster used to say." Hiccup! "He loved big words; and something else he loved, I can tell you . . . His cane . . ."

"Thanks! See you," said Chris wrenching himself away.

The girl's desperate shriek rose high over the dense sprawling noises of the road party. The police sergeant was dragging her in the direction of a small cluster of round huts not far from the road and surrounded as was common in these parts by a fence of hideously-spiked cactus. He was pulling her by the wrists, his gun slung from the shoulder. A few of the passengers, mostly other women, were pleading and protesting timorously. But most of the men found it very funny indeed.

She threw herself down on her buttocks in desperation. But the sergeant would not let up. He dragged her along on the seat of her once neat blue dress through clumps of scorched tares and dangers of broken glass.

Chris bounded forward and held the man's hand and ordered him to release the girl at once. As if that was not enough he said, "I will make a report about this to the Inspector-General of Police."

"You go report me for where? You de craze! No be you de ask about President just now? If you no commot for my front now I go blow your head to Jericho, craze-man."

"Na you de craze," said Chris. "A police officer stealing a lorry-load of beer and then abducting a school girl! You are a disgrace to the force."

The other said nothing more. He unslung his gun, cocked it, narrowed his eyes while confused voices went up all around some asking Chris to run, others the policeman to put the gun away. Chris stood his ground looking straight into the man's face, daring him to shoot. And he did, point-blank into the chest presented to him.

"My friend, do you realize you have just shot the Commissioner for Information?'' asked a man unsteady on his feet and shaking his head from side to side like an albino in bright sunshine.

Emmanuel and Braimoh, carrying the bags they had retrieved from the bus, arrived on the scene as Chris sank first to his knees in a grotesque supplicatory posture and then keeled over sideways before settling flat on his back. Emmanuel went down and knelt beside him and the girl knelt on the other side fumbling with the wounded man's shirt-front to stop a big hole through which blood escaped in copious spasms.

''Please, sir, don't go!'' cried Emmanuel, tears pouring down his face. Chris shook his head and then seemed to gather all his strength to expel the agony on his twisted face and set a twilight smile on it. Through the smile he murmured words that sounded like *The Last Grin* . . . A violent cough throttled the rest. He shivered with his whole body and lay still.

The sergeant had dropped his gun and fled into the wild scrubland. Braimoh had raced after him past the clusters of huts and, a hundred yards or so beyond, had wrestled him to the ground. They rolled over and over sending up whirls of dust. But Braimoh was no match for him in size, strength or desperation. The crowd on the road saw him get up again and continue his run, unattended this time, into a red sunset.

18

BEATRICE HAD DECIDED on a sudden inspiration to hold a naming ceremony in her flat for Elewa's baby-girl. She did not intend a traditional ceremony. Indeed except in name only she did not intend ceremony of any kind. It seemed to her unlikely from the look of things that she could face anything remotely resembling a ceremony for a long, long time.

But a baby had to have a name, and there seemed nothing particularly wrong in giving it one in the company of a few friends, or doing it on the seventh market as tradition prescribed. Every other detail, however, would fall into abeyance, for this was a baby born into deprivation—like most, of course; but unlike most it was not even blessed with an incurably optimistic sponsor ready to hold it up on its naming day and call it *The-one-who-walks-into-abundance* or *The-one-who-comes-to-eat* or suchlike and then blithely hand it back to its mother to begin a wretched trudge through life, a parody of its own name. No, this baby would not lie in cushioned safety from the daily stings of the little ants of the earth floor. Indeed it was already having to manage without one necessity even the poorest may take for granted—a father (even a scarecrow father would have sufficed) to hold it in his hands and pronounce its name on this twenty-eighth day of its life.

Beatrice had asked the same handful of friends who had kept together around her like stragglers from a massacred army. That she even managed this residual relationship was a measure of the change she had begun to undergo even before the violent events of the recent past; that she did it in virtual silence an eloquent tribute to the potency of lost causes.

In earlier times she would have responded to Chris's death by retreating completely into herself, selecting as wild beasts often do before they die a dark, lonely corner of the forest, distrustful of the solace of their fellows. But the weeks of ill omen presaging the bloody events of November had already thrown her into a defensive pact with a small band of near-strangers that was to prove stronger than kindred or mere friendship. Like old kinships this one was pledged also on blood. It was not, however, blood flowing safe and inviolate in its veins but blood casually spilt and profaned.

In spite of her toughness Beatrice actually fared worse than Elewa in the first shock of bereavement. For weeks she sprawled in total devastation. Then one morning she rose up, as it were, and distanced herself from her thoughts. It was the morning of Elewa's threatened miscarriage. From that day she had addressed herself to the well-being of the young woman through the remaining weeks to her confinement. When she first attempted during those weeks to resume contact with the desolation inside her heart she was surprised to find that she already felt stronger on her feet and clearer in the head.

She could now return less and less timidly to relive aspects of the nightmare and even begin to reassess her reflexes, feelings and thoughts. Was she right, for instance, to turn down the new Head of State's special invitation to the state funeral he ordered for Chris? Did she hurt her duty to his memory more by keeping away than she honoured it by showing her mistrust of his enemies? Twenty-four hours after the *coup d'état*, before the news of Chris got to her, she had watched with utter revulsion a lachrymose Major-General Ahmed Lango suddenly surface and make his "pledge to the nation to bring the perpetrators of this heinous crime quickly to book." Even the gullible people of Kangan, famous for dancing in the streets at every change of government, were asking where this loyal officer was hiding in the first twenty-four hours after his Commander was kidnapped from the Palace by "unknown persons," tortured, shot in the head and buried under one foot of soil in the bush. But by the time Kangan was asking these questions Beatrice had heard the news of Chris's murder and lost contact with everything else.

The news was brought to her by Captain Abdul Medani. He was in mufti and came in a taxi. But his face had become so deeply etched in Beatrice's mind during the weeks he played the mystery voice that in spite of his dress and the dark glasses she had immediately recognized the officer who had led the search of her flat. And she had read his countenance and deciphered the disaster before he opened his mouth. He said he just wanted to be sure she did not hear it on the air, and left immediately. An hour later it was broadcast on the national radio. Later that evening Emmanuel and Braimoh arrived back.

In the weeks and months that followed, her flat became virtually the home of Emmanuel and Braimoh and the girl Adamma. The Captain also came quite frequently. Sometimes, especially at weekends, they would all be there together and discuss the deepening crisis in the country. At first Beatrice heard the voices and the arguments around her as though they came from an adjoining room behind a closed door. But slowly she began to pick out the words out of the muffled sounds, then snatches of sentences and finally even the occasional joke forcing a faint smile like a twitch on her slow-thawing face.

The door had slowly opened and the words and snatches of sentences coalesced into spirited conversations and even debates mostly between Emmanuel and Abdul. But although Beatrice did seem to hear what was said she still did not take part in the exchanges. She still steered her own thoughts as carefully as she could around them. But there were collisions nonetheless which could not but alter now and again, however slightly, the speed and drift of her own silent activity.

". . . And what I want to know from you is how this latest blood-letting has helped Kangan in its historical march as you call it. The blood of His Former Excellency and the blood of his victims—if indeed they were his victims . . ."

If indeed they were *his* victims, repeated Beatrice in her mind. The very thought that had already visited her dressed, albeit, differently! The explanation of the tragedy of Chris and Ikem in terms of petty human calculation or personal accident had begun to give way in her throbbing mind to an altogether more terrifying but more plausible theory of premeditation. The image of Chris as just another stranger who chanced upon death on the Great North Road or Ikem as an early victim of a waxing police state was no longer satisfactory. Were they not in fact trailed travellers whose journeys from start to finish had been carefully programmed in advance by an alienated history? If so, how many more doomed voyagers were already in transit or just setting out, faces fresh with illusions of duty-free travel and happy landings ahead of them?

That was the day she broke her long silence and asked the two young men: "What must a people do to appease an embittered history?"

The smiles that lit up the faces in the room, especially of the two indefatigable debaters stopped in their tracks, were not addressed to that grave question and its train of echoes from a bottomless pit of sadness. It was rather the ending of an exile that the faces acknowledged, the return of utterance to the sceptical priest struck dumb for a season by the Almighty for presuming to set limits to his omnipotence.

It was not that Beatrice had spoken no words at all before that day. She said hello and even, on occasion, offered hospitality. Certainly she had resumed work in her office one week after Chris's burial; and at home she conducted her domestic life in the company of Elewa and Agatha. But in all this she had only used words that did not threaten to invade her thoughts and drag them into the profanity of the open air. She became more accessible only in slow stages, egged on usually by one little crisis or another in her small community.

Abdul had confided to her that he had been assigned (or had assigned himself—it wasn't too clear which) to watch her and her friends. She had smiled and said, "Good luck!" Weeks later she had decided in fairness to inform Emmanuel. He was outraged.

"The fellow is an *agent provocateur.* How can we be so naive?"

"We? You are such a gentleman, Emmanuel. The weeks with Chris, cooped up together and conspiring, I see, have left their mark. But, no; I'm not naive. The fellow is quite genuine."

"How?"

"Woman's intuition, if you like."

"Since when?"

"What do you mean since when? Are you asking me since when have I become a woman? . . . And I have just called you a gentleman."

For a while after that Emmanuel had shown his resentment by ostentatiously keeping sealed lips whenever Abdul was around. Beatrice watched the two without further intervention. In the end it was curiosity which killed the cat of Emmanuel's silence. It all happened over the rumour about Colonel Johnson Ossai.

"Is it really true that he is missing?" Emmanuel had asked in spite of himself. Abdul had simply nodded without deigning to open *his* mouth. He had become aware of Emmanuel's suspicion and had adopted what Beatrice considered a most sophisticated response—simply ignored it and him.

"But how can a whole boss of State Security just disappear? Like that!"

"I believe you had already left Bassa when the boss of the State itself went missing." Then he positioned himself as if he was talking to Beatrice and the others. "I can give a few facts that have emerged so far. Colonel Ossai was last seen going in to see the Head of State and has not been sighted ever since. You remember Idi Amin? Well, according to unconfirmed reports he used to strangle and behead his rivals for women and put their head in the fridge as a kind of trophy. So perhaps Colonel Ossai is in the cooler, somewhere."

"You don't sound too concerned about your boss," said Beatrice. "That's awful, you know."

"If I told you half of what I know about Ossai you wouldn't be too concerned either."

"What a life!" said Emmanuel.

"Anyway, soldiering is not a sentimental profession. The first thing we learn is: Soja come, soja gwo."

But all that was weeks and months behind them—weeks and months of slow preparation for today's ritual outing.

When Elewa moved up to Beatrice and whispered into her ear what she had just come to suspect as the probable reason for her mother not being there yet Beatrice decided to perform the naming herself and to do it right away. She called the little assembly to order and proceeded to improvise a ritual.

She picked up the tiny bundle from its cot and, turning to Elewa, said: "Name this child."

"Na you go name am."

"OK. You just saved a false step, anyway. Thanks. I will start afresh . . . There was an Old Testament prophet who named his son *The-remnant-shall-return*. They must have lived in times like this. We have a different metaphor, though; we have our own version of hope that springs eternal. We shall call this child AMAECHINA: *May-the-path-never-close*. Ama for short."

"But that's a boy's name."

"No matter."

"Girl fit answer am also."

"It's a beautiful name. The Path of Ikem."

"That's right. May it never close, never overgrow."

"Das right!"

"May it always shine! The Shining Path of Ikem."

"Dat na wonderful name."

"Na fine name so."

"In our traditional society," resumed Beatrice, "the father named the child. But the man who should have done it today is absent . . . Stop that sniffling, Elewa! The man is not here although I know he is floating around us now, watching with that small-boy smile of his. I am used to teasing him and I will tease him now. What does a man know about a child anyway that he should presume to give it a name . . ."

"Nothing except that his wife told him he is the father," said Abdul, causing much laughter.

"Na true my brother," said Braimoh. "Na woman de come tell man say na him born the child. Then the man begin make *inyanga* and begin answer father. Na *yéyé* father we be."

"Exactly. So I think our tradition is faulty there. It is really safest to ask the mother what her child is or means or should be called. So Elewa should really be holding Ama and telling us what she is. What it was like to be loved by that beautiful man Ikem. But Elewa is too shy. Look at her!"

"I no shy at all," she replied, her eyes smiling and holding back tears at the same time like bright sunshine through a thin drizzle. "I no shy but I no sabi book."

"Dis no be book matter, my sister."

"You no sabi book but you sabi plenty thing wey pass book, my dear girl."

"Say that again," said Emmanuel.

"I concur," said Captain Medani.

"Dat na true word," said Braimoh.

"I tell you!" said Aina.

"All of we," continued Beatrice, "done see *baad* time; but na you one, Elewa, come produce something wonderful like this to show your sufferhead. Something alive and kicking."

"That's true. Very true," said the Captain.

"But living ideas . . ." Emmanuel began haltingly.

"Ideas cannot live outside people," said Beatrice rather peremptorily stopping him in mid-stride. He obeyed for a second, scratched his head and came right back blurting defiantly:

"I don't accept that. The ideas in one lecture by Ikem changed my entire life from a parrot to a man."

"Really?"

"Yes, really. And the lives of some of my friends. It wasn't Ikem the man who changed me. I hardly knew him. It was his ideas set down on paper. One idea in particular: that we may accept a limitation on our actions but never, under no circumstances, must we accept restriction on our thinking."

"OK," said Beatrice bowing to this superior, unstoppable passion. "I have also felt what you are saying, though I knew him too as a man. You win! People and Ideas, then. We shall drink to both of them."

As Agatha brought in a tray of drinks and burst into one of the songs of her sect—something with which she had never before graced this house—Emmanuel took the tray from her and placed it on the centre table. Adamma fetched the glasses and they began to serve. Agatha's hands freed meanwhile found more fitting occupation clapping her own accompaniment, and her waist swayed in slow dance.

> Jehova is not a person anyone can deceive
> Jehova is so great who is it can confuse him?
> If Jehova wants to bless who will dare to raise a curse?
> Jehova-jireh let us raise his name!

Aina raised herself from her seat, untied and re-tied her outer
lappa and joined Agatha in her holy seductive dance.

"Abi Aina no be Moslem?" Beatrice asked Elewa in a whisper.

"Na proper grade one Moslem," she replied wondering by way
of a puzzled look what the point of the question was. Then she
seemed all of a sudden to discern the questioner's difficulty. "Dem
talk say make Moslem no dance when Christian de sing?" she
asked in return.

"No I didn't mean *that*," replied Beatrice rather emphatically.
But to herself she said, "Well, if a daughter of Allah could join his
rival's daughter in a holy dance, what is to stop the priestess of the
unknown god from shaking a leg?" She smiled to herself. She was
already swaying her head from side to side in lieu of hands which
were still attempting to rock Ama to sleep.

After five or six repeats of the same words of the catchy little
song Braimoh shouted: "Heep! Heep! Heep!" and the ecumenical
fraternization was neatly terminated with a lusty "Hooray!" and
laughter.

It was at this point that a taxi pulled up outside and discharged
Elewa's mother and uncle. Beatrice and Elewa turned spontane-
ously to each other, one saying, "You were right," and the other,
"I no tell you!", at the same time.

Beatrice knew Elewa's uncle by an unsavoury reputation which
he now seemed quite determined to live up to. Before he fairly sat
down his eyes had become glued to the tray of drinks and his
Adam's apple danced restlessly like the trapped bubble in a brick-
layer's spirit-level.

"Elewa, won't you offer a drink to Mama and your uncle?"

Mama accepted a bottle of mineral water but the uncle declined
the beer which was offered him demanding "Snaps" instead.
When he was told there was no schnapps in the house he merely
said, "Ah?"—a compressed but eloquent way of saying: A naming
ceremony indeed, without schnapps.

Beatrice got up, put the baby down in her cot, went to the
sideboard and soon returned with a bottle of White Horse whisky.
Elewa's uncle accepted the substitute quite readily and proceeded
to swill two thimblefuls in quick succession throwing his head
slightly back for the operation and working his cheeks like a pair
of little bellows before swallowing. He put the little glass down
and then asked for a bottle of beer.

Looking sideways at her late husband's half-brother Elewa's mother said: "It is better that we begin the work we came to do. I don't want anyone dropping my grandchild."

"Nobody is going to drop anybody," replied the uncle lifting his glass of beer to his lips with a lightly quivering hand . . . "Drink does not loosen a man's grip. It makes it stronger," he added after gulping down half of the glass . . . "But since my wife here is troubled, let us agree with her and do as she says. A wise man agrees with his wife and eats lumps of smoked fish in his soup. A fool contradicts his wife and eats lumps of cocoyam."

Abdul's head was tilted towards Emmanuel who was translating the old people for him. Now all eyes turned to Beatrice. She had picked up the baby again, but instead of handing her to the old man who had set down his glass once more to receive it she said:

"This baby has already received its name. She is called Amaechina."

The old people were visibly stunned. The man recovered first and asked: "Who gave her the name?"

"All of us here," said Beatrice.

"All of you here," repeated the old man. "All of you are her father?"

"Yes, and mother."

His explosion into laughter took everybody by surprise and then dragged them all into his bombshell of gaiety. Except Elewa's mother.

"You young people," said the old man. "What you will bring this world to is pregnant and nursing a baby at the same time . . . Give me a little more of that hot drink."

Elewa rushed the whisky bottle and the little glass back to him.

"A jolly old fellow," said Abdul.

"You no know am. So make you wait small."

Elewa's poor mother was left high and dry carrying the anger of outraged custom and usage made none the lighter for having no one to focus it on. In the end she turned and heaped it on the opportunistic old man, a medicine-man hired to chase evil spirits whom evil spirits were now chasing.

"You will return my bottle of Snaps and the fowl," she said to him, to everyone's surprise. His face clouded over for a very brief instant and quickly cleared up again.

"As to that," he said, "what is brought out before a masquerade cannot be taken indoors again. Food goes one way—downwards. If you see it going up you know the man is in trouble."

"You will return my Snaps and the fowl," she repeated obstinately.

"Listen to me my wife and let me give you advice. You are annoyed and I cannot say that I blame you. But what is the use of bending your neck at me like the chicken to the pot when its real enemy is not the pot in which it cooks nor even the fire which cooks it but the knife. Your quarrel is with these young people. Hold your daughter and her friends to refund to you your bottle of Snaps and your fowl. But as for the tribute placed in front of a masquerade, that one is gone with the masquerade into its anthole." He went into another paroxysm of laughter scraping his sides which he now held like a loosening bundle between his palms. Everybody joined him once more, except Elewa's mother. He stopped abruptly and turned to the rest:

"Let me tell you people something. When my wife here came to me and said: Our daughter has a child and I want you to come and give her a name, I said to myself: Something is amiss. We did not hear *kpom* to tell us that the palm branch has been cut before we heard *waa* when it crashed through the bush. I did not hear of bride-price and you are telling me about naming a child. But I did not contradict my wife because I want fish in my soup . . . Do you know why I am laughing like this? I am laughing because in you young people our world has met its match. Yes! You have put the world where it should sit . . . My wife here was breaking her head looking for kolanuts, for alligator pepper, for honey and for bitter-leaf . . ."

"And Snaps and agriculture chicken."

"True. Those as well. And while she is cracking her head you people gather in this whiteman house and give the girl a boy's name . . . That is how to handle this world . . . If anybody thinks that I will start a fight because somebody has done the work I should do that person does not know me. I only fight when somebody else eats what I should eat. So I will not fight. Rather I will say thank you. I will say whoever ate the foofoo let him mop up the soup as well. A child has been named. What else is one looking for at the bottom of the soup-bowl if not fish? Wherever the child sleeps let it wake up in the morning, is my prayer . . . My wife, where is that kolanut? I shall break it after all."

Everybody applauded this strange man's sudden decision, sparked off perhaps by the utterance of the word prayer. Elewa's mother could not keep up against the powerful current in favour of the old man. She opened her bag and handed a kolanut to him.

"Elewa, go and wash this and put it into a plate and bring me water to wash my hands."

Elewa and Agatha went into the kitchen to do as the old man had commanded. After he had washed his hands and wiped them importantly with a sparkling napkin that contrasted so harshly with his own dirt-and-sweat-tarnished jumper that used to be of white lace he assumed a sacramental posture, picked up the kolanut in his right hand and held it between four fingers and thumb, palm up, to the Almighty.

"Owner of the world! Man of countless names! The church people call you three-in-one. It is a good name. But it carries miserly and insufficient praise. Four-hundred-in-one would seem more fitting in our eyes. But we have no quarrel with church people; we have no quarrel with mosque people. Their intentions are good, their mind on the right road. Only the hand fails to throw as straight as the eye sees. We praise a man when he slaughters a fowl so that if his hand becomes stronger tomorrow he will slaughter a goat . . .

"What brings us here is the child you sent us. May her path be straight . . ."

"*Isê!*" replied all the company.

"May she have life and may her mother have life."

"*Isê!*"

"What happened to her father, may it not happen again."

"*Isê!*"

"When I asked who named her they told me All of Us. May this child be the daughter of all of us."

"*Isê!*"

"May all of us have life!"

"*Isê!*"

"May these young people here when they make the plans for their world not forget her. And all other children."

"*Isê!*"

"May they also remember useless old people like myself and Elewa's mother when they are making their plans."

"*Isê!*"

"We have seen too much trouble in Kangan since the white man left because those who make plans make plans for themselves only and their families."

Abdul was nodding energetically, his head bent gently towards his simultaneous translator, Emmanuel.

"I say, there is too much fighting in Kangan, too much killing. But fighting will not begin unless there is first a thrusting of fingers into eyes. Anybody who wants to outlaw fights must first outlaw the provocation of fingers thrust into eyes."

"Isé! Isé!!"

Abdul, a relative stranger to the kolanut ritual, was carried away beyond the accustomed limits of choral support right into exuberant hand-clapping.

"I have never entered a house like this before. May this not be my last time."

"Isé!"

"You are welcome any time," added Beatrice following Abdul's breaking of ritual bounds.

"If something pursues us we shall escape but if we pursue something we shall catch it."

"Isé!"

"As long as what we pursue does not belong to somebody else."

"Isé!"

"Everybody's life!"

"Isé!"

"The life of Bassa!"

"Isé!"

"The life of Kangan."

"Isé!"

AFTER ELEWA'S MOTHER AND UNCLE had left with Aina and Braimoh in the old taxi, the party continued in the quiet and relaxed afterglow of the day's ritual intensity. But it proved a day extraordinary in stamina and before long a new surge of passion was building up secretly below its placid expansiveness.

It began in ripples of simple reminiscence. Emmanuel, it was plain to see, was rather pleased with himself and so chose to congratulate someone else, Beatrice, on the evolution, as he called it, of the two-headed toast to people and ideas. She, on her part, was a captain whose leadership was sharpened more and more by sensitivity to the peculiar needs of her company.

"I must say I liked your spirited stand for ideas."

"Mutual Admiration Club forming up again," sang Abdul.

"And jealousy will get us nowhere," sang Beatrice.

"But looking back on it," continued Emmanuel passing up the bait of banter, "I think you taught me something very important by holding out for people. Do you remember the day you told me that Chris had taught me to be a gentleman?"

"It was only a joke."

"Jokes are serious," said Abdul impishly.

"Yes they are . . . That day and again today you were making me aware of my debt to Chris. I don't know why I never thought of it before but the greatest thing he taught me was seeing the way he died."

The jesting mood died instantly in the air, folded its wings and fell like a stone; the tributary conversations dried up.

"I was kneeling on the road at his side weeping uselessly. She," he nodded his head in Adamma's direction, "was trying to do something. Then I said something idiotic like *Don't go, don't leave us please.* And, I can't describe it, that effort—you could touch it almost—to dismiss pain from his face and summon a smile and then crack a joke. He called it The Last Grin."

Beatrice started in her seat.

"Yes I remember," said silent Adamma. "The last green. But he did not finish it."

Beatrice rushed away into her bedroom. Elewa followed after her. While they were away nothing more was said. After a few minutes Elewa came back.

"Is she all right?" asked Abdul a little ahead of other inquirers.

"No trouble. To cry small no be bad thing. BB no be like me wey de cry every day like baby wey him mother die."

"Madam too strong," said Agatha. "To strong too much no de good for woman."

"E no good for anybody whether na man-o or na woman-o, na the same thing," said Elewa. "E good make person cry small . . . I been try to stop am, I try sotay then I come say no, make you lef am."

"WHY ARE YOU all sitting in darkness?" she said turning the lights on as she walked back into the room almost half an hour after she had left it. She spoke with great calmness in her voice. She had made up her face, and even tried on a smile as she resumed her seat. Then she said:

"I am very sorry."

"Well, I am sorry to have raised that matter today. I didn't . . ."

"No no no, Emmanuel. I am happy you raised it. In fact you can't know how grateful I feel. I can tell you I am happier now, much happier than I have been since that day." She said no more. Perhaps in spite of this composure she could not continue.

To fill the aching void, or perhaps he was already powerless in the grip of a gathering underflow, Emmanuel began again:

"You see I have been present only at two deaths . . ."

"Make you put that your useless story for inside your pocket," ordered Elewa. "Why you de look for trouble so? Abi the one you done cause no belleful you?"

"Leave the young man alone. Emmanuel, please continue."

"The first death I witnessed was my father and then Chris. Without Chris I could not have known that it was possible to die with dignity."

"Your father didn't die with dignity?" asked Abdul quizzically.

"No, he didn't. Though he was an old man compared to Chris, he had not learnt how to die. He snapped at people; he even cried. He was frightened, scared to death. He ran from one doctor to another and when he had run through them all he took up prayer-houses. He had cancer of the prostate. Every day some vulture would descend on us from nowhere with the story of a prophet or prophetess in some outlandish village and my father would drag my poor mother there the next morning. It was a terrible relief when he died, I am ashamed to admit . . . But look at Chris, a young man with all his life still in front of him and yet he was able to look death in the eyes and smile and make a joke. It was too wonderful . . ."

"You don't know why I went in to cry . . . That joke was a coded message to me, to us," said Beatrice, to everyone's surprise. "By the way, Adamma heard it better. What he was trying to say was *The last green*. It was a private joke of ours. The last green bottle. It was a terrible, bitter joke. He was laughing at himself.

That was the great thing, by the way, about those two, Chris and Ikem. They could laugh at themselves and often did. Not so the pompous asses that have taken over."

"Say that again!" said Emmanuel.

"You know why I cried? Chris was only just beginning to understand the lesson of that bitter joke. The bottles are up there on the wall hanging by a hair's breadth, yet looking down pompously on the world. Chris was sending us a message to beware. This world belongs to the people of the world not to any little caucus, no matter how talented . . ."

"And particularly absurd when it is not even talented," said Abdul.

"It was the same message Elewa's uncle was drumming out this afternoon, wasn't it? On his own crazy drum of course. Chris, in spite of his brilliance, was just beginning to be vaguely aware of people like that old man. Remember his prayer? He had never been inside a whiteman house like this before, may it not be his last."

"And we said *Isé!*" said Abdul.

"We did. It was a pledge. It had better be better than some pledges we have heard lately."

"Isé!!"

At last the prodigious passions of that extraordinary day seemed at an end. Silence descended as completely on the party indoors as had darkness outside. Ama whom Beatrice nicknamed Greedymouth having drunk both from the bottle and from Elewa's breast, pendant like a gorgeous ripe papaya on the tree, was sleeping quietly in her cot.

No one spoke or stirred. No one sought another's eyes. Beatrice sat erect, her arms folded across her chest . . .

Then at last, like one just returned from a distant journey of the mind bearing a treasure in her eyes she murmured, to a welcoming party? merely to herself? *Beautiful!* And she said it a second time even more softly: *Beautiful!*

The rest had now turned their faces on her. She alone gazed still at something remote—a third party invisible to the rest, a presence to whom she had spoken her quiet apostrophe?

The change in her when it came was sudden. A deep breath audible through the room and a melting down of the statuesque told of her return . . .

"I can't thank you enough, Emmanuel, for being there and bringing back the message. And you too, of course, Adamma." She looked at each in turn with a strained smile on her countenance. "Truth is beauty, isn't it? It must be you know to make someone dying in that pain, to make him . . . smile. He sees it and it is . . . How can I say it? . . . it is unbearably, yes *unbearably* beautiful. That's it! Like Kunene's Emperor Shaka, the spears of his assailants raining down on him. But he realized the truth at that moment, we're told, and died smiling . . . Oh my Chris!"

Two lines of tears coursed down under her eyes but she did not bother to wipe them . . .

"BB, weting be dis now?" Elewa remonstrated, showing her two palms of innocence to the powers above. "Even *my*self I no de cry like dat! What kind trouble you wan begin cause now? I beg-o. Hmm!"